Praise for the author

EXCLUSIVE

Eden Bradley

"Eden Bradley is going somewhere fast."　　　　　*—Fallen Angel Reviews*

"Ms. Bradley's voice carries a lush sensuality that resonates throughout her work . . . a beautifully rendered love story, filled with incredible passion."　　　　　*—Romance Divas*

"To write love scenes that really draw the reader in is a skill Ms. Bradley has accomplished with ease."　　　　　*—Love Romances & More*

"It's easy to get lost in this swift-moving and scorching love story. Ms. Bradley has woven a delicious tale."　　　　　*—Literary Nymphs*

"[A] quick, erotic, hot summertime read that keeps you turning the pages for more."　　　　　*—Coffee Time Romance*

"A thoroughly enjoyable story for its well-written content and superb sensuality!"　　　　　*—Romance Junkies*

continued . . .

Jaci Burton

"Burton writes with vivid attention to detail, smooth pacing and an exquisite emotional edge."   —*Romantic Times*

"A fabulous read. [Ms. Burton] delivers, in every way possible."
                                                    —*A Romance Review*

"Sizzling hot sex that will have you panting. I highly recommend this story to anyone looking for a hot read."   —*The Romance Studio*

"The sexual tension is high and sure to keep the reader turning the pages."   —*Romance Junkies*

"One hot novel that I could not put down until the last word. This story has it all: mind-boggling sex, unique and unforgettable characters and a wonderful plot that will grip your heart . . . raw, dynamic, explosive. Wow!"   —*Just Erotic Romance Reviews*

Lisa Renee Jones

"Jones scorches the pages with this riveting blend of dark suspense, erotic sex and tender romance. The result is seductive and volatile."
                                                    —*Romantic Times*

"Lisa Renee Jones is an automatic read for me."   —*JoyfullyReviewed.com*

"The love scenes tantalize and titillate readers with a typhoon of sensuality. Lisa Renee Jones has made a name for herself as a talented author."
                                                    —*Romance Junkies*

"Jones does a beautiful job writing characters that you can relate to in situations that will leave you wanting to read more long after the end of the story!"   —*Euro-Reviews*

ECLUSIVE

EDEN BRADLEY

JACI BURTON

LISA RENEE JONES

HEAT | NEW YORK

THE BERKLEY PUBLISHING GROUP
Published by the Penguin Group
Penguin Group (USA) Inc.
375 Hudson Street, New York, New York 10014, USA
Penguin Group (Canada), 90 Eglinton Avenue East, Suite 700, Toronto, Ontario M4P 2Y3,
Canada (a division of Pearson Penguin Canada Inc.)
Penguin Books Ltd., 80 Strand, London WC2R 0RL, England
Penguin Group Ireland, 25 St. Stephen's Green, Dublin 2, Ireland (a division of Penguin
Books Ltd.)
Penguin Group (Australia), 250 Camberwell Road, Camberwell, Victoria 3124, Australia
(a division of Pearson Australia Group Pty. Ltd.)
Penguin Books India Pvt. Ltd., 11 Community Centre, Panchsheel Park, New Delhi—110 017,
India
Penguin Group (NZ), 67 Apollo Drive, Rosedale, North Shore 0745, Auckland, New Zealand
(a division of Pearson New Zealand Ltd.)
Penguin Books (South Africa) (Pty.) Ltd., 24 Sturdee Avenue, Rosebank, Johannesburg 2196,
South Africa

Penguin Books Ltd., Registered Offices: 80 Strand, London WC2R 0RL, England

This is an original publication of The Berkley Publishing Group.

These are works of fiction. Names, characters, places, and incidents either are the product of the
authors' imaginations or are used fictitiously, and any resemblance to actual persons, living or
dead, business establishments, events, or locales is entirely coincidental. The publisher does not
have any control over and does not assume any responsibility for author or third-party websites
or their content.

EXCLUSIVE

First edition: September 2007

Heat trade paperback ISBN: 978-0-425-21707-8

An application to register this book for cataloging has been submitted to the Library of Congress.

PRINTED IN THE UNITED STATES OF AMERICA

10 9 8 7 6 5 4 3 2 1

Contents

SANCTUARY

EDEN BRADLEY

To my friend Carol, for sharing with me some of the moments that make up parts of this story, and for always keeping my deep, dark secrets.

ACKNOWLEDGMENTS

I have to thank my friend and fellow author Jax Crane AKA Jax Cassidy, for her endless hours of brainstorming this story with me. And also, a big thank-you to my Diva girls, for their support and friendship. To my cp's, authors Gemma Halliday and Jennifer Colgan, for their careful eyes and willingness to read every single word I write. To my wonderful agent, Roberta Brown, for all that she's done—and continues to do—for me. And always, to B, for his endless enthusiasm, and for allowing me to spend my days in my pajamas in front of the computer, listening to the voices in my head as they tell me the stories that end up on the page.

ONE

Lights pulsed, music pounded and Devin's heart hammered faster than it ever had in her life. How had she let Kimmie talk her into coming here, to the Ring, on fetish night? She'd never seen anything like it. She'd never imagined she would love it. But she did.

Hundreds of club-goers pressed against the sturdy metal railing that surrounded the Ring, the loft section of Club X, one of the hottest dance clubs in San Francisco, where unusual and wicked things went on. She had to get closer.

Devin followed Kimmie's sleek, dark head as she pushed her way through the crowd with her small, pointed elbows. All around them multicolored lights flashed against dark red walls, into the shadowed alcoves set here and there where club-goers rested on velvet-covered couches, where couples locked in erotic embraces, oblivious to the crowd and the noise.

They were almost up to the front. All around her people writhed and bounced to the beat that reverberated through the club, making the floors tremble so that Devin could feel it in the pit of her stomach.

When they reached the railing, Kimmie pulled on Devin's arm and shoved Devin in front of her. The metal rail pressed into Devin's stomach as the crowd surged forward, but she didn't care. Her eyes were riveted to the scene before her, the strange, compelling scene within the Ring.

Chains dangled from somewhere high in the ceiling, ending in leather cuffs with big metal buckles. Against the back wall stood three enormous wooden crosses. And bound to these crosses were two women, one man. The man had his shirt off, and a woman dressed all in black with hair dyed an impossibly bright scarlet was hitting his back with a small leather whip, raising fine red welts on his skin. With every slow, even stroke of the whip, the crowd called out, urging her on, making goose bumps rise on Devin's arms, on the back of her neck.

But what really interested Devin were the women.

The two young blondes were stripped down to bras and underwear, arms raised high over their heads, their wrists cuffed to the crosses. A pair of men spanked them with paddles in perfect synchronicity, moving with the beat of the heavy techno music.

Something in her stirred, awoke with a sharp cry of need as she watched. Amazing. Amazing that seeing this happen could make her body respond in this way. Amazing that she had never thought about this sort of thing before. Her pulse was racing, her legs trembling.

The two men, dressed entirely in black, wore leather pants and snug T-shirts; their attention was focused on the pair of women, their backs to the crowd. And when they smacked the women's flesh a cry arose from the wild group of onlookers. The music shifted and the men worked faster, in time with the new rhythm. Devin saw the ripple of muscles beneath their tight T-shirts as they lifted their arms and swung. The sound of the crowd became one long, continuous arc of noise. She could feel the aura of excitement all around her as the crowd fed it, fed her, making her pulse hammer in her veins. She couldn't take her eyes away from the scene before her.

Kimmie yelled into her ear, "What do you think?"

All Devin could do was shake her head. What could she say? It was too loud in there to try to explain to Kimmie everything that was going through her mind.

"Do you want to go?"

"What? No!" She wasn't going anywhere.

The two men finished and released the girls from their restraints, rubbed their arms, their wrists, took them to a back corner and sat them down on a bench. A young girl dressed in a red leather corset wrapped the women in blankets, gave them something to drink. Devin watched, mesmerized by the entire process. One of the men disappeared through a side door. The other turned around and a shock of heat roared through her.

He was beautiful.

Even in the flashing club lights, she could see the honeyed shade of his skin. His hair was a short, spiky shock of brown tipped with blond, as though he'd recently been in the sun. His close-shaven goatee, a few shades darker than his hair, made him look purely devilish. It was too dim and he was too far away for her to see his eyes. They seemed dark, glittering. He looked back at the desperate, wild crowd and gave a crooked grin and a saucy wink, as though he were very much aware that he was performing. And then he pulled his shirt off over his head.

She only had a moment to take in broad, muscled shoulders and tight six-pack abs before he turned around and started to pick up some items scattered around the floor: a crop, the two paddles he and the other man had used, a variety of multitailed whips; Devin wasn't sure what everything was called. All she knew was that this man made her entire body surge with need.

If only he would turn around again.

When he did, he looked right at her. Even among a crowd of hundreds, she knew it immediately. He looked at her and gave that small, cocky smile he'd given to the crowd of revelers before. But this time it was for her alone.

He moved forward, toward the front of the Ring, until he stood right in the middle of it. He stopped there and stared at her, locking his eyes on hers. Her stomach filled with butterflies. She couldn't believe he was looking at her, but the line of his hot gaze was perfectly clear.

She licked her suddenly dry lips. Her nipples went hard beneath her tight, stretchy top. His eyes seemed to instantly travel there, to almost caress her skin before his gaze returned to her face. That self-assured smile again, quirking just one corner of his mouth. Unbelievably sexy. He had a pair of heavy, black tribal designs tattooed around each bicep, those armbands she loved so much on a man. Sexy enough that lust sang in her veins, thrummed through her limbs.

The tattoos, the wicked goatee, him standing in the middle of this place, shirtless, he was the ultimate bad boy. She'd never been so attracted to a man in her life. The hot flood of music and the colored lights only seemed to add to the sensual aura as he stared her down, daring her somehow.

He beckoned with his head, his grin quirking a little more. Yes, daring her to join him in the Ring.

She couldn't do it, of course, no matter that every cell in her body screamed at her to go to him, to have this man touch her.

Impossible.

And then he walked right up to her, right up to the railing and put his hand out to her. She noticed then another tattoo on the inside of his left wrist, some sort of Chinese symbol done in heavy black lines.

She offered her hand to him before she had a chance to think about it. He took it in his, turned it, and laid a soft kiss in the center of her palm. A wave of lustful heat rushed through her body.

Wow.

He leaned in and yelled over the music, "I'm Shaye. Tell me your name." God, he was talking to her. His deep voice boomed over the noise of the club.

"Devin."

"Come play with me, Devin."

She pulled back and saw that evil grin on his face. He had perfect white teeth. His eyes were a dark and smoky hazel up close, with long, thick lashes.

"No, I . . . I can't."

"Of course you can. Just say yes."

He still held onto her hand. His was large and warm, the contact like an electrical current running up her arm and straight to her sex. But she couldn't bring herself to do what these people did in the Ring. Could she?

She felt dizzy suddenly with the possibility. This wasn't her. She was no innocent virgin, but this was too much, too intense, too wild. She'd come to watch, not to participate. And she wouldn't even be here if it weren't for Kimmie dragging her along tonight. She glanced around. Where was Kimmie?

But he was leaning in again, until his mouth was warm against her ear. "Come and play with me, little Devin. You know you want to. I can feel it from here."

His voice was a low purr. Sexy as hell, like everything else about him. And he was close enough that she could smell him; a little bit of clean male sweat mixed with some earthy fragrance. Sandalwood? She allowed herself to take one long inhale, savoring the scent of him. It made her shivery and hot inside. It made her confused.

"I can't. Really. I'm uh . . . I'm here with my friend. I have to go find her."

"Come back. Later tonight. Any night."

She started to shake her head. He tucked a card into her free hand.

"This is my cell. Call me if you'd ever like to play. Here. Or wherever. I want to see you."

She looked up at him and the grin was gone. His gaze was hot, burning right into her. He lifted her hand and kissed it again, sending that shiver of heat through her system once more.

The woman with the bright red hair came and tapped him on the shoulder, said something into his ear. He waved her off.

"I have to get back to work. Call me, Devin. Come and see me here. Promise me you will."

"I don't know . . ."

"Promise, Devin."

He hadn't let go of her hand. He gave it a small squeeze. Her pulse raced, hot and fast as lightning. He scared the hell out of her. She wanted him so much it hurt.

"I'll . . . maybe . . ."

"You will." His devastating grin spread across his face. He took a step back, dropped her hand, took another step before turning around and walking to the back of the Ring.

She was left breathless, shaken. Who the hell was this guy?

She looked down at the card he'd given her. Shaye Vincent. No title, just the name and a phone number in silver on a sleek black card.

When she looked up again he was already binding another young woman to the big wooden cross. She wanted to watch, yet somehow she couldn't bear it at the same time.

It's because you want to be the one bound and helpless.

She shook her head. This place was really getting to her.

This man was really getting to her.

It had to be the novelty factor. She'd never seen anything like this, any place like this. And he was unspeakably gorgeous.

Her eyes went back to him, to the sight of his strong, still shirtless back as he bent to bind the woman's ankles in what appeared to be leather shackles chained to metal loops in the floor.

She spent a brief moment imagining what it must be like to be bound in that way. To be rendered helpless. To give over control to someone. To Shaye.

She started to shake all over. She had to get out of there.

The club had filled up since she'd arrived. It took some work and a few carefully placed jabs of her elbow to make it to the edge of the crowd where she could breathe again. She hadn't seen Kimmie.

She made her way down from the loft that held the Ring to the main dance floor, which was enormous, but even here club-goers were practically on top of one another. People gyrated to the hard-hitting beat of the music. Go-go dancers on platforms, dressed in skimpy black leather and thigh-high boots for the evening's event, writhed and twined their bodies around poles.

She'd never find Kimmie here, and she really didn't want to wait. She'd go outside, catch a cab and call her friend later.

She made her way to the front door and shoved it open, letting herself out into the chilly San Francisco night. The damp air made her shiver as she stood beneath a street lamp while the club's bouncer flagged down a cab for her. She got in and slammed the door behind her, grateful for the heat of the car. She smoothed the hem of her short skirt down.

"Where to?"

"Eleven-fifty Capra Way."

"Ah, the Marina. Nice down there, huh?"

Why did she have to get the one cab driver in San Francisco who spoke English tonight? She didn't want to talk. She had too much to think about. But she didn't want to be rude, either.

Always the good girl.

"Yes, it's nice."

Luckily, he remained silent after that. She tried to organize in her mind all of the jarring images of the evening: the Ring itself, intimidating, fascinating. The people who went there to be abused by the

Dominants who worked there. Yes, she knew what they were called. She couldn't even remember how or why.

Mostly she couldn't get the image of Shaye out of her head. Of him standing there with that swaggering, crooked grin on his beautiful face. She knew men didn't particularly like to be described that way, but she couldn't think of another word that fit him as well. He *was* beautiful. And wicked looking in the most luscious way. She'd never seen another man who was quite as beautiful as he was.

The cab raced through the dark night, down Lombard Street now, with all its restaurants and bars, brightly lit neon signs whizzing past the windows in a blur of yellow, blue, pink. The streets were still lively at . . . she checked her watch. It was already almost one in the morning. How long had she stood at the edge of the Ring watching him? No wonder Kimmie had taken off.

Crap. Kimmie. She pulled her cell phone from her purse and dialed. Her friend's voice mail picked up.

"Hey, Kimmie, sorry I left, but I had to get out of there and I couldn't find you. Call me tomorrow, okay?"

She flipped her phone shut. She didn't want to talk about the club tonight, even to her best friend. She needed some time to absorb her feelings, her reaction to it.

The cab pulled up in front of her building, a classic San Francisco–style stucco, built in the twenties, as were so many others in this part of town. She paid the driver and went inside. Too edgy to wait for the elevator, she jogged up the four flights of carpeted stairs and let herself, breathless, into her apartment.

It was chilly inside and she flipped the heat on as she passed the thermostat in the hall. In her room, she kicked off her black stiletto heels, put them on her closet shelf where her shoes were all lined up in perfectly ordered rows. She quickly changed into her burgundy velvet robe, a vintage piece she'd found at one of the thrift stores on Haight Street. Hanging up her skirt in the closet, she put her black top into the laundry basket, then padded on slippered feet across the wood-floored hall to the bathroom. There she ran the water to wash her face, then decided she wanted the bar smells out of her hair and turned the shower on instead.

She carefully took her makeup off while the water heated, put her long, straight auburn hair up in a clip and stepped into the steaming blast of water.

This was one of the things she loved most about her apartment. Yes, the view of the Palace of Fine Arts only eight blocks away was gorgeous, and she loved the dark, gleaming hardwood floors, the bay window in the living room. She loved the ornate crown moldings in every room, the old black-and-white tile work in the kitchen, but she was absolutely in love with the bathroom. It was enormous and had the best water pressure and endless hot water, something one rarely found in these older buildings. She could stay in the shower forever. She loved the pure decadence of it. Loved the sensation of the water sluicing hot and silky over her skin.

She let her head fall back against the dark green tiles as the shower stall filled with steam. And she let her mind wander, remembering once more what she'd seen tonight.

Of course, the first image that came to mind was Shaye. His bare torso shadowed in the nightclub lights that defined and illuminated every ridge and plane of muscle. His flashing white teeth. His lips on her hand.

She shivered.

That had been one of the most erotic moments of her life.

Her body went warm and loose all over just thinking about it. And when she pictured the way Shaye had looked when he was working that girl with the paddle, the muscles of his arms and back rippling, the tattooed armbands gripping his flexing biceps, her sex pooled with molten heat. No, if she were being truthful, what really did it for her was imagining that *she* was the one he was doing it to. That it was her stripped nearly naked and on display for all those people. That it was her flesh being smacked with the paddle. By *him*.

She let out a groan and her hand wandered down her body, sliding over her breasts, over the hard peaks of her nipples, finally coming to rest between her thighs. There she rubbed her fingers teasingly over the lips of her sex, deliberately avoiding her tender, aching clit. And in her mind, it was Shaye's hand there, sliding over her mound, while the hot needles of water pelted her skin. She turned her body into the spray, so the wet heat fell on her breasts, slipped down her body, just as his hands would.

Shaye.

Her fantasy became more elaborate as she used her fingers to part her swollen pussy lips, to explore the waiting, expectant heat between them. In her mind, she was with Shaye at the Ring, with the flashing lights, the music pouring through the place, making her body vibrate with the beat. All around was the crowd, wild with anticipation. He led her to one of those long chains hanging from the ceiling, stretched her arms high above her head, cuffed her wrists firmly, then stripped her clothes from her until she was naked before the crowd. Before him.

She let her fingers brush her clit. Pleasure hummed through her body.

He would touch her there, would use his hands on her, running them over her bare skin, touching her breasts.

With her other hand she cupped one breast, slid the palm up over her nipple, squeezed gently, then harder. He wouldn't be gentle, would he? He would hold her breasts, squeeze and knead them. Pinch her nipples.

Yes.

She pinched, hard, and cried out at the hot streak of pleasure that shot straight to her sex. She spread her legs apart and pushed two fingers inside.

She'd never been so wet, so stricken with desire. She needed to come so badly it was almost painful.

She let her body rest against the tiles behind her, the cold surface a jarringly erotic contrast to the heat of the water, the heat of her fingers still working her sex. She saw him in her mind. He was behind her as she stood, her arms suspended over her head. Helpless. And he was shirtless, as he'd been tonight, pressing his muscular body up against her back, reaching around and moving his hand between her thighs, massaging her clit.

Yes!

She trembled on the verge of orgasm, tugged and pulled at her clit, trying to remember the scent of him while she moved her fingers inside herself, pumping. Her pussy was on fire, sensations thrumming through her body, while her mind whirled with flashes of Shaye, of the Ring, of the evil little whips she'd seen there. It all became a blur of image and sensation as the first wave of her climax washed over her. Her hand rubbed hard at her clit, driving her orgasm on. Her sex clenched and spasmed around the fingers of her other hand, still moving inside her. And still she came, wave after wave crashing over her in a powerful tide.

Finally she was left shaken and weak, leaning into the wall of the shower. Steam rose all around her in ghostly wisps. Her skin was burning hot from the water, from the fierce climax that had just ripped through her body.

And still, she couldn't get his face out of her mind.

Shaye.

She stood beneath the pounding spray of water for a long while, trying to catch her breath. What was it about him? What was it that had her fantasizing about being naked on display in public, about being hit with a paddle? She'd never had these thoughts before. And now it was all she could think about.

Her body was thrumming with need again already. She thought immediately of the vibrator she kept in her nightstand drawer. Yes, it would give her a fierce orgasm; it always did. But never had it delivered anything like the climax she'd just experienced, using only her hands and a vivid imagination.

Shaye.

What was it about this man?

She turned the water off and stepped from the shower, still trembling. She dried herself with a thick white towel, her skin sensitized, needy. Her nipples went hard as she brushed the soft terry cloth over her chest.

Yes, she needed the vibrator, and *now*. She had a feeling it was about to become her new best friend. And if she couldn't find a way to satisfy her need, to get Shaye out of her lust-addled head, she might never leave her apartment again.

She dropped the towel and crossed the hall back to her bedroom. Naked, she climbed into her antique four-poster bed, pulled the vibrator from its drawer and switched it on, lay back, spread her legs. Closing her eyes, she thought of *him* while the vibrator buzzed and the San Francisco fog swept past her windows.

And later, after she'd used the vibrator yet again, while her body lay, lambent and humming, and she drifted toward sleep, his face still filled her mind.

Her last thought, before her eyes fluttered closed, was that she would never see him again.

Or would she?

TWO

She dreamed of a dark, womblike place where water fell in warm cascades all around her, slick on her skin, like tiny fingers touching her, teasing her. And a commanding voice in her ear whispered, "Promise me."

She moved her legs apart to allow the teasing, sensual water to touch her there. It flowed in a silky stream between her thighs. And out of the darkness came a figure.

Shaye.

He was naked, she knew, even though she couldn't quite make out the details of his body in the dark. She waited for him, holding perfectly still. She knew it was what he wanted; for her to remain as still as possible, to await his command. To await his pleasure.

Her sex pulsed with anticipation.

The phone rang.

She came out of sleep fast, so fast she was too confused to find her cell phone right away. Following the insistent ring, she crawled out of bed, dug in the small purse she'd taken to the club with her the night before, flipped her phone open.

"Hello?"

"Are you still sleeping? God, it's almost ten."

"Kimmie?" She found her robe on a chair and slipped it on.

"Yeah, who else? What happened to you last night?"

"Nothing. I just . . . you wandered off and I couldn't find you."

"I told you I was going to get a drink at the bar downstairs. Then I met this guy and we danced for a while. When I went back upstairs you were gone."

"Sorry, I um . . ."

"How much did you drink last night, Devin?"

"What? Nothing. I didn't drink. I just slept really hard, I guess. I had this dream . . ." She searched for her fuzzy pink slippers, found them under the bed, slid her feet into them.

"You are really out of it. So, what did you think of the Ring?"

"It was . . . interesting."

"Interesting? I couldn't have dragged you away to save your life. You were totally fascinated."

"Okay, so I was fascinated."

"Don't be so defensive, Dev. I'm the one who took you there. I'm the last person to judge you for liking it."

"I know. I just . . . I'm kind of having a hard time with how much I liked it. And him."

"Him? Him who?"

"There was this guy there. He was gorgeous. No, it was more than that. Didn't you see him?"

"The guy with the goatee? Yeah, sure. They're all hot there; all the people who work in the Ring. They only hire beautiful people."

"He was different." She paused. "I talked to him."

"Did you?"

"He gave me his card. Asked me to come back."

"Are you going to?"

"No. I don't know. I don't think it's my thing, Kimmie. It's too much for me."

It felt like a lie. She knew it even as the words slipped out of her mouth.

"Well, if you want me to go with you, let me know."

"Kimmie? Have you ever . . . you know . . . been in the Ring? Done those things?"

Her friend's voice turned somber. "I've never been in the Ring. I've thought about it. But I really don't like the idea of being in public like that. But privately? Yes, I've done a few things."

"Like what?"

"I've been tied up, been spanked a few times. Nothing like what goes on there. It's fun, but I don't take it all that seriously." She paused. "It really got to you last night, didn't it?"

"Yes, I guess it did. And he really did, this guy. Shaye. The whole experience has me imagining things I've never thought of before."

But was that the truth? She remembered suddenly the story-like fantasies she'd had as a little girl, games she played in her head while she was in the bath. The most common theme was that she'd been captured by pirates, bound in rope, naked and helpless, then brought to the captain's quarters. Helpless, yes. That had been the key to the whole thing, hadn't it?

But she'd never really imagined what happened once she was in the captain's quarters. Her young mind hadn't been able to comprehend anything more. But she certainly could now.

Shaye would make an excellent pirate.

Her body began to heat up again, her thighs to tremble. This was ridiculous. She had to pull herself together.

"Still there Dev?"

"What? Yes. I was just thinking about everything. About last night. I don't think I'll go back. It just doesn't feel right."

But why, really, was she fighting it? Every cell in her body screamed for her to go to him. To Shaye. She was lying to Kimmie. Lying to herself.

"It's up to you. Look, I'd better get back to work. I'll talk to you later, okay?"

"Yes. Sure."

She snapped her cell phone shut and sat on the end of her bed. Her body was humming to life again, hot and needy, her sex drive working at warp speed. She didn't like the loss of control over her own body, her own thoughts. Yet at the same time, something in the back of her mind whispered for her to just let go for once.

Letting go was not her forte. She was someone who ran a perfectly ordered life, with everything in its place. A life in stark contrast to the one she had growing up. A life of chaos until she was old enough to take on all of the responsibilities that should have been her mother's. A life that had created in her a driving need to maintain control, to fight against the chaos.

It was one of the reasons she loved her work as a web designer; she had total control over what happened on the page. She loved the clearly defined language of the computer, the software she used to create her designs. She knew if she clicked on something, wrote the correct sequence of code, she could control the outcome every time. She knew what to expect. Everything nice and neat. This obsession was messy. Complicated. And giving in to it would mean a very definite loss of control.

She wasn't about to hand control over to anybody. Not even the beautiful and mysterious Shaye.

Her body surged with lust just letting his name roll through her mind. Her sex clenched in needy anticipation.

Damn it.

How was she going to force herself to stay away from him? She hated that she didn't have a concrete answer, couldn't assure herself of the outcome.

Mysterious, yes. And frightening. And so incredibly tempting she could barely stand it. Her mind whirled with the possibilities. She'd just met the man. Once. Why was it she couldn't stop thinking about him? About the lovely, wicked things he wanted to do to her? But how could she ever let him? This was crazy. She'd never been more confused in her life.

Shaye Vincent, in their one brief meeting, had knocked her whole world off its axis. And right now she wasn't sure how she'd ever regain her balance.

She usually took Saturdays off, but Devin had turned to work as a desperate means of escape from the images battering at her. Still, her mind kept wandering from her computer screen. She'd been sitting there for more than two hours, yet all she could see was his face, those dark hazel eyes, that sexy, crooked grin, and the glossy sheen of sweat over the ripple of muscles . . .

Devin sighed. She was never going to get any work done this way. She closed her graphics program, then shut her computer down. She didn't know what to do with herself. Her sex was throbbing with heat and she felt too restless to stay in her apartment all day, but she wasn't in the mood to call Kimmie or any of her other friends. She knew she wasn't in a normal frame of mind and didn't want to have to explain herself to anyone.

Throwing a heavy sweater on over her T-shirt and jeans, she grabbed her purse and headed downstairs and out into the cool afternoon. She took off in the direction of Chestnut Street, a few blocks away. She'd find a cup of coffee and walk with it, maybe head down to the Palace of Fine Arts at the end of the street. A good, long walk should cool off her lusty thoughts. And she'd always found the serene, swan-filled pond and the beautiful neo-Roman structure to be a peaceful place. She often went there to think, to work out design issues in her head while strolling around the park-like setting or feeding bread crumbs to the ducks and swans.

She found her favorite coffee spot and ordered a latte to go. The street was already crowded with traffic, locals and tourists thronging the sidewalks. She paused to glance into the shop windows, letting the crowds flow around her. The Marina district was famous for its colorful boutiques and cafés, but she found she couldn't concentrate on the clothes and books in the windows. His face was still foremost in her mind. His gorgeous face, along with other fleeting thoughts she tried to push away. Wondering what his hands would feel like on her skin, his lips pressed against hers, what it might be like to let him spank her with that black paddle . . .

She took a long swig of the hot coffee, trying once more to chase the images away, but it was no use. She realized there was nothing she could do to get him out of her head, except give it some time.

Or else see him again.

Dangerous.

Yes. He was dangerous. He was dangerous to her sanity already. How much worse would it be if she saw him? But now that it had occurred to her, she could barely think of anything else. All she had to do was show up at the club next Friday night. She could go by herself, just watch him through the crowd. See if he was still as intriguing in person as he was in her imagination. Why not? She didn't even have to talk to him, let him know she was there, if she didn't want to.

She'd want to. Who was she kidding? She was going, dangerous or not. For once in her life, she'd do something totally illogical. Something on a whim, without thinking it through. It was about time she challenged herself. She ignored the underlying suspicion nagging at her brain, the one that told her going to see Shaye could have long-term consequences. But what the hell, he was only a man, like any other.

Wasn't he?

Nine o'clock on Friday night. She'd put it off, arguing with herself tonight after arguing with herself all week. But finally, she'd taken a long, hot bath, dried herself, put on her makeup, going a little heavier on the eyeliner than usual. She found a short, black wraparound skirt in her closet, a black stretchy tank top, black stiletto-heel boots she'd bought last winter but hardly worn, because they were so high. She realized she was dressing for the event. And somehow dressing itself felt like some sort of ritual, as though she were preparing herself for him.

She frankly loved the idea.

She zipped up the boots and stood, her heart hammering in her chest. She felt daring, a little wild. All she was doing was going to a club alone, something she'd never done before, but plenty of other people did all the time. She took a deep breath, then moved down the short hallway, her heels clattering on the wood floor. She grabbed her leather jacket and turned the knob on her front door when her cell phone rang. She flipped it open.

"Hello?"

"Hey, it's me."

"Hi, Kimmie."

"What are you doing? There's this band playing at that new place on Fillmore. I got us on the list. Wanna go?"

"I . . . um . . . not tonight. Thanks, though."

"Are you okay? What's up?"

Devin bit her lip. "I just need to get caught up on some work."

"Are you sure? You sound weird, Dev."

She cleared her throat, tried to clear away the heaviness of the lies on her tongue. "Yeah, I'm fine. I'm just tired and want to stay home."

"Okay. I'll ask Renee to come with me, then."

"I'll call you tomorrow."

"Get some rest. You don't sound so good."

"I'm fine. And I will. Bye, Kimmie."

"Bye."

This was the first time she'd ever lied to her best friend about anything. It felt weird. But she also thought if she told anyone about what she was doing she'd feel . . . she wasn't sure what. Maybe too foolish for chasing a guy down like this? Too unlike herself? Either way, she had to do this on her own.

She opened the door and went downstairs, walked a few short blocks to Lombard Street and hailed a cab, climbed in and slammed the door shut.

"Where are you headed?" the cabbie asked.

"Take me to Club X."

The hard throb of music and black-clad crowd of gy-rating dancers were the same as the week before, but there was a new aura of excitement for her the moment she entered the club. She felt open, raw, as though anyone who looked at her knew why she was there. Yet at the same time she had a sense of being utterly isolated from all of it, from the lights, the music, the people. Of being in her own head.

She checked her coat, then made her way across the main dance floor, through the heat of hundreds of bodies. The place was crowded already and it was still early. Things wouldn't really pick up until around midnight. She glanced at the bar, but realized she didn't want a drink. She needed to be clearheaded. Or as clear as she could be right now, with her lust-addled brain directing her.

He couldn't possibly look as good as she remembered. Still, her pulse raced at a thousand miles an hour as she pressed through the dense crush of bodies, catching whiffs of sweat and perfume as she went, the sharp scent of alcohol. She made her way up the stairs to the loft above the dance floor, pushed through the crowd already surrounding the Ring. Somehow she managed to get right to the front, until the metal bar which separated the Ring from the rest of the club was pressed against her stomach. People jostled her on either side and it took a moment for her to get her balance. She looked up, and saw *him*.

Shaye walked to the center of the Ring to look at tonight's crowd. It was packed already, even though it wasn't ten yet. That was good. He liked to work in front of a crowd. It gave him a hell of a thrill, which was why he worked here almost every weekend. And of course, he loved working the girls who came here, the innocent ones who wanted to try just a little spanking, to get flogged in front of their friends. Cheap thrill. But not for him. For him it was the real thing. If only they knew the evil thoughts that went through his head when he stripped them down to their underwear and gave them the first paddling of their lives. Virgin flesh.

He surveyed the throng already surrounding the enclosed dungeon area of the loft, looking for prospects. The girls often had to be enticed, flirted with, cajoled into entering the Ring. That was easy for him, almost too easy. But he didn't care. All he cared about was that exchange of energy, of sensation and response. That's what he got off on. He didn't even have to sleep with them, rarely took any of these girls home. It had been months since any of them had captured his attention in that way, and none had ever managed to hold it for long. He wasn't built for permanence. Yeah, he was a chip off the old block, wasn't he?

He pulled his shirt over his head, threw it on a bench and moved toward the railing, still scanning. He loved it all, the powerful vibe of the people, the scent of leather and sweat and the faint aroma of fear when a new girl stepped into the Ring with him. He loved the pounding throb of the music that he used to create a rhythm in his swing. He loved the feel of tender young flesh beneath his hands. Couldn't get enough of it.

He moved his gaze from one end of the crowd to the other, slowly. And then he saw her.

That girl from last Friday night. Devin, she'd said her name was, and he hadn't forgotten it, had thought of her all week, hoping she'd come back. Beautiful girl, sweet-looking face. Innocent, even though she was a bit older than most of the others. But he loved that. There was a lot more to her, he could tell from her eyes. He moved closer. She hadn't seen him yet.

He watched as she glanced around, as her hands gripped the railing in front of her, and he went hard just looking at her fine-boned hands, at her lush red mouth. He'd love to kiss that mouth, to really kiss her, to feel her melt under him.

Shit. Where the hell had that come from? But there was no doubt he was getting hard just looking at this girl.

All dressed in wicked black tonight, her short skirt showing off long, lean legs. He knew if he spun her around, her ass would be flawless. He moved in to get a closer look, and while she had her head turned away he quietly slipped his hand over hers.

"Hey."

"Oh. Hi." Her face broke into a sunny smile. There was no pretense of the seductress here. No, she was simply happy to see him. She hid it quickly enough, but he'd seen it. Too late to pretend.

"You came back."

"Well, I . . . I was here, you know . . ."

"It's okay. I like it that you came to see me." He gave her hand a squeeze and watched her blush. Charming. "Does this mean you've come to play?"

"Oh, no! I mean, I came to watch. That's all."

Better than nothing. Pretty damn good, in fact, knowing she would watch him tonight. His strong streak of exhibitionism would love that. Not as much as he would if he could get his hands on her, but it was a start.

"Stay right here, then. Things will get started soon. Are you sure you won't join me?"

She nodded, her auburn hair swinging. Looked like heavy silk. He wanted to touch it.

Shit.

Instead he lifted her hand and brushed a kiss across it, felt her small shiver. He smiled.

"I have to work now. Promise me you won't go anywhere without telling me."

"Yes. I promise."

He left her, strode back into the Ring, prepared his work area, lining up on a bench toward the back of the room the usual array of floggers, paddles, straps. His whole body was still buzzing with the faint, sweet taste of her flesh on his lips.

The first girl came into the ring and Daniel, the ring master, sent her Shaye's way. Nice-looking girl. Young, blonde, pretty but hollow. Not nearly as attractive as Devin. Still, he took her to his station, to one of the X-shaped St. Andrew's crosses, stripped her down to her bra, bound her to the cross at wrists and ankles, with her bare back to him. He went right to work on her, starting an easy rhythm with a light flogger, nothing that would hurt too much, just getting her warmed up. He focused on the music, watched the girl's breathing, pausing to check in and make sure she was okay. But half his mind was on the other girl, the one watching from the sidelines. The one who made his blood boil like no one had in a very long time.

Devin watched the muscles flex in his arms, his shoulders, his back, loved the way the heavy lines of his tattoos moved with each ripple of flesh. He was strongly built, heavily muscled without the unnatural look of one of those bodybuilders. He moved gracefully for a man of his size and build. Every stroke was smooth, in beat with the music, which was some techno trance piece. The blonde girl was quiet, her body swaying just a little beneath the strike of the flogger he was using.

And Devin's blood was humming through her veins in that same cadence.

She wished it were her up there, stripped down and under his hands.

No, no, no. Too much, too foolhardy. Too unlike her. Hers was a life of perfect order, and this seemed like some form of bedlam to her. Yet she couldn't look away. Couldn't stop her body's reaction to what she was seeing.

She took a moment to glance at some of the other people playing in the Ring, but none of them held the fascination for her Shaye did. Watching him made her shiver all over, made her heat up inside. Made her imagine scenes she'd never dreamed of before.

Dangerous, her brain reminded her. She didn't want to listen to it right now. But neither was she brave enough to fight against it completely, no matter how much she wanted to.

Watching him again, her body warming up, a kind of molten heat made her arms and legs tingle, go weak. And her sex was absolutely on fire with need.

What would it be like to spread my legs and let him touch me. . . ?

God, she really had to get herself under control! Control was key. It always had been. It was how she had survived her childhood, the weakness that was her mother. She wasn't going to allow any man to take that from her.

But why was she even thinking about these things? She was just watching him, had barely exchanged a dozen words with him. Still, her body wanted him more than she had wanted any man in her life.

He moved around the girl, switching from flogger to paddle now. He pulled up the girl's short plaid skirt and swatted her round bottom. Devin went hot all over and squeezed her thighs together. She couldn't tear her gaze away from him, from what he was doing to this girl. Her hands tightened around the metal railing.

If he asked her to come into the Ring with him now she wouldn't be able to refuse.

Peering through the dim and pulsing light of the club, through the alternating lights and shadows, she saw the flex of his hand as he gripped the paddle, the ripple of muscle in his shoulder as he pulled back to swing, the smooth golden texture of his skin. With every strike he landed on the girl's flesh, her own body surged with need. Desire flooded her system, until she could hardly stand to watch any longer. As he landed each strike, she felt almost as though the sensation reverberated through her own body. Over and over, in time with the music, which seemed to flood her head with sound.

Her panties were absolutely soaked.

He finished with the girl and the same woman from the week before, the one in the red corset, took the girl away to a bench at the back of the room. He set his wicked tools of pleasure down, used a towel to wipe the sweat from his forehead. Then he walked right over to her and took her hand.

"Come play with me, Devin."

The scent of him filled her nostrils, making her weak and shivery. She shook her head mutely.

Say no, Devin. Say no.

He leaned in, closer, until his mouth, that lush, masculine mouth, was only inches from hers. His breath was sweet, minty. If she moved in only a few inches she could kiss him.

God.

"Come on, Devin. I know you want to." His voice was quiet, yet she could hear him over the pounding music, the crowd of people. And at this moment, there was no one else in the world but the two of them.

He went on. "I can see it, you know. In the rise and fall of your breath, in the gleam of excitement in your eyes. I can *feel* it, coming off you in waves. You want this. You can't tell me you don't."

She could only shake her head. She knew if she spoke she would have no control over what came out of her mouth.

His fingers curled around her hand and he lifted it, held her palm to his bare chest.

"Can you feel it? That's my heart beating with need for you. I swear it."

His voice was ragged with desire. She thought she might pass out.

"Come with me, Devin. It's okay. You'll be in my hands. I'll keep you safe. And I'll make you feel better than you ever have in your life."

The truth of his words hit her like a warm blow to the chest. The heat spread, infused her body, her throbbing sex. She couldn't say no. And so she said, "Yes."

THREE

He felt her tremble, her soft little hand still in his as he led her through the gate and into the Ring. A cry went up from the crowd as he brought her in, the excitement of new flesh. Yes, he always felt it, too, and the crowd loved it. But why was his heart hammering in his chest as though this were his first time?

Jesus. He had to get himself under control.

It was this girl, this beautiful girl, who was really scared to be here. Yet she had agreed to this, had wanted it. Still wanted it beneath the fear, he could tell. She held on tight to his hand. And the heat of her, the scent of her perfume, was driving him crazy.

Just do your thing.

He'd do his job, as he always did. But tonight would be different with her. He knew that already. He didn't want to think too much about it.

He led her to a pair of leather cuffs suspended from a chain toward the back of the room. He didn't want her right out in front, as he usually did, playing to the crowd. He wanted Devin to himself.

What the hell was wrong with him?

Just focus on her. Yes, easy enough when he looked at her, that perfect, porcelain skin, her flushed cheeks. Her green eyes were glossy, huge, her lashes long and dark, picking up some of the colored lights on the tips. He was going to strip some of her clothes off her perfect little figure. The noise of the crowd faded into the background as he reached out and brushed his fingertips across the fabric covering her stomach. She gave an answering shiver.

His cock twitched when he pulled her top over her head and her black lace-clad breasts came into view. Not too large, but so damn perfect. He watched her take in a few deep breaths. She was nervous as hell. But he could almost smell her desire. The flush on her cheeks had spread down over her chest. Oh yes, she wanted this, was every bit as excited as he was.

He spanned his hands around her tiny waist, just let them rest there for a moment, needing that contact to read her. Jesus, her skin was baby-smooth under his hands. What would the rest of her feel like?

She looked up at him and those emerald eyes caught his, held him. She was really and truly scared.

"It's okay. I'll take care of you. Can you trust me, Devin?"

"I . . . I think so. I'm just . . . I've never done anything like this before."

"But you want to, don't you?"

She paused, then nodded her head.

He leaned in and inhaled the scent of her. Like flowers and sex. He moved in closer, until he could speak right into her ear. "Relax. Put yourself in my hands. Turn yourself over to me. You can do it. Okay?"

"Yes."

God, just her tremulous voice had him hard and almost panting.

Do your job, man.

Yes, his job. "Devin, we need to go over your safe words. Do you know what that is?"

"Safe words?"

"If things get too intense for you, you need to tell me. If you need me to slow down, go easier on you, if you're experiencing any sort of discomfort, even if it's just that the cuffs are too tight, say 'yellow.' If you want the scene to stop completely, say 'red.' And I will stop, I promise you. Do you understand?"

She shrugged, trying for a nonchalance that was entirely transparent to him. She was still trying to hang on to some control, but it was gone already, had been since the moment she'd agreed to come into the Ring with him. "It sounds easy enough."

Easy enough for her. He was the one who had to hold it together.

He laid his hands on her shoulders, ran them down over her arms. The skin there was just as soft as her waist had been. He took one wrist in his hand, raised it over her head and buckled her into the soft leather of the cuff. Her small gasp of surprise pleased him somehow. He did the same with her other hand. By the time he had her completely bound she was breathing hard, every breath making her breasts swell against the confines of that sexy black bra.

"Calm down, Devin. It's okay." He took her chin in his hand and tilted her face. Her eyes were huge, her lush, red lips parted. It would be so easy to kiss her now, just slide his tongue into the wet heat of her mouth . . .

Jesus. Get it together.

He sucked in a breath. "We'll start out easy. Okay?"

She nodded.

He moved around behind her and smoothed his hands over her back. He could barely restrain himself from slipping his hands around the front of her to cup the soft mounds of her breasts. Unbearable hard-on at the thought. But her ass could be his. He moved his hands down, slid her skirt up until he uncovered the black lace panties that matched the bra. Her ass was every bit as perfect as he'd known it would be. But he'd get to that later.

He let the hem of her skirt fall around the tops of her thighs and picked up the small flogger he used on the new girls. It was light enough to get some good sensation, but not enough to hurt unless he really wanted it to. He wanted to hurt her; of course he did. But he wanted her to like it, and he knew for that he had to bring her into it slowly.

He started with a gentle stroking of the leather thongs over her flesh. After a minute he saw her let out a breath, saw her shoulders loosen up. He kept up the easy rhythm, watching the tension in her body shift. She was breathing harder, but it wasn't fear or pain. He could feel her arousal coming off her in waves as though it were a palpable thing. His body answered in kind, but he ordered himself to calm, to focus on nothing but her.

Another few minutes of that slow, easy stroke, then he gave her one good smack. She yelped.

He moved around to the front of her, lifted her face in his hand so he could see her eyes. They were lit up, like green sea glass. And there was a small smile on her face.

That smile went through him like the pure heat of the sun and landed in a warm knot in the pit of his stomach. He tried to shake the sensation away. But looking into her eyes, with the scent of her perfume surrounding him, infusing him, he couldn't do it. The heat traveled through his body, making his cock hard. He couldn't help himself. He bent down and kissed her.

She was half out of her head and she knew it. But when his lips met hers the entire world faded away. God, his mouth was soft and hot. She leaned in, wanting more, felt one of his hands slide around the back of her neck, his fingers burying in her hair. She opened her lips, inviting him inside, but he pulled back, leaving her needy and panting.

He slipped his hand up, over her cheek, looked into her eyes. His were shadowed, unreadable. But she could sense the heavy rhythm of his breath.

She had never been in such an exquisite state of arousal in her life.

"Are you ready for more?"

"Yes."

If only he would kiss her again. Kiss her and kiss her and never stop. But he moved back around behind her once more. She steadied her racing pulse, ready and wanting the soft kiss of his little whip almost as much she wanted his lips on hers. She didn't know why it felt so good, but it did. She'd been scared only the first minute or two before her body had relaxed into it as though familiar with the cadence of his strokes. And there was no real pain. For some reason she didn't understand, she knew she wouldn't mind if there was.

He started again right away with the flogger, the leather hitting her skin, releasing its earthy scent. Her body moved right into it, loving the sensation, loving even more that it was *him* doing this to her.

Over and over, while her mind went into a sort of trance of buzzing desire. Then one hard, sharp smack. She gasped, melted, smiled. A cry rose from the crowd. She realized she'd forgotten all about them, about the hundreds of people watching. And this sudden realization sent a surge of excitement through her.

His face was next to her ear suddenly. "How are you doing? Do you want more?"

"Yes. Please."

Was this really her here with him, doing these things, asking for more? But she couldn't find it within herself to care. All she knew was sensation, being under his hands. It was too good to stop.

This time he hit her harder. Her body seemed to absorb the sensation, to turn it into pure pleasure. And after a while she found if she opened her eyes and focused on the crowd, their energy fed her. Fed her pleasure, fed her desire.

She had no idea how long she'd been there when he stopped and wrapped an arm around her waist, his palm flattening on her bare stomach. Fire flooded her and she wished he'd move his hand lower. Right here, in front of all these people. She didn't care. She only knew what she needed.

"Jesus, what you do to me, Devin." His voice was rough. He was breathing as hard as she was. He sounded like a man who'd just had sex.

God.

She moaned, let the weight of her body hang against the leather cuffs holding her up.

"I think you're done."

"No!"

He laughed. "Oh yes, you are. You're too far gone to know it, but that's my job, to take care of you."

Yes, take care of me . . .

She knew she wasn't thinking straight. She didn't care.

He unbuckled her and her legs went weak. She fell into his arms. Nothing had ever felt better to her.

"Ah, I've got you, my girl."

My girl. Sweet.

He held her for a moment, buried his face in her hair. Her body was alive, electric, lit up with need. He half-carried her to the padded bench against the back wall. The girl in the red corset approached and she knew he was going to leave her there with the girl.

"Shaye . . . please."

He knelt on the floor in front of her, rubbed her arms. "What is it? What do you need? Are you cold? Thirsty?"

She shook her head. "Don't go away."

He stared at her, his hazel eyes smoky, serious. He bit down on his lip, his strong white teeth coming down on the soft flesh, sinking into it. She wanted him to kiss her again.

Finally he said, "You are fucking amazing, Devin. But I have to go to work. Melissa will take care of you."

She shook her head. Why did she feel like crying? And then, to her horror, one big, fat tear slid down her cheek.

"Jesus," he muttered, then pulled her into his arms. "Shh, you're okay, you're just crashing. It usually only happens with heavy play. You'll be okay in a while."

She felt okay with his strong arms around her, crushed against his chest, his bare skin right up against hers. Better than okay. As long as he didn't get up and leave.

Again he said, "I have to get back to work."

She shook her head mutely, tilted her head up and pressed her lips to his. She heard a moan from him before he opened his lips and his sweet tongue slid into her mouth. She pulled it in, pulled in his breath. Her arms went around his neck. His kiss was hard and wet. She was wet, too, had never been so wet in her life.

He stopped, pulled back. "Damn it, Devin. I'm not supposed to do this with the club girls."

She managed between panting breaths, "I'm not another club girl."

He looked into her eyes. He bit his lip again, making her want to put her tongue there, to lick that tender spot. She shivered.

He let out a long breath, ran a hand back through his hair. "Fuck it. I'm taking you out of here."

He helped her to her feet, and with one arm looped around her waist, said to the red-corseted girl, "Melissa, get her shirt for me, will you? I'm taking the rest of the night off. Tell the others."

The girl did as he asked, and he helped Devin back into her top. Then he led her from the Ring, down the stairs, almost carrying her through the press of bodies and the thundering music. He stopped to get her coat, draped it around her shoulders and led her from the club, into the cold night.

Outside she pulled the frosty air into her lungs, trying to get her brain working while he talked to the doorman, who sent another guy off at a run to retrieve Shaye's car. They stood in silence, his arm still firmly around her. She was surprised when the kid from the club pulled up in a silver BMW. This was Shaye's car? Somehow she'd assumed he was one of those classic club guys, who drove some junker and lived with six roommates in a flat off Haight Street. Not that it mattered.

He helped her into the passenger seat, went around and got in.

"I'll take you home. And it'll be whatever you want it to be. Tell me where you live."

She gave him the address and he shifted the small, sleek car into first gear and took off. The night seemed heavy with silence after the pounding music of the club. She felt enveloped by it, as though they were isolated from the rest of the world, just the two of them driving through the darkness.

Every now and then he glanced over at her as he drove, but they didn't speak. She was glad. She was afraid too much talking would break this sensual spell. She wasn't ready to give it up.

They reached her building and he found a spot in front. All gentleman again, he came around to her side of the car, opened her door, helped her out. She was a bit wobbly on her feet and he steadied her, his strong arm looping around her waist, so that she was right up against him. She caught a whiff of that masculine, woodsy scent and it went straight to her sex, soaking her.

"Here, give me your keys, Devin."

She pulled them from her pocket and handed them over. It felt good to let him take over, take care of everything.

"*. . . that's my job, to take care of you.*"

Yes. So nice.

She gave him her apartment number and he bundled her into the ancient elevator that held the papery, moldy scent of old books. She'd been to Paris once and had visited the catacombs beneath the city, those ancient caves lined with the skulls and bones of thousands. The elevator smelled exactly like the dim entranceway there. She hadn't found the place frightening, but rather fascinating and even beautiful in its own way. Did that make her morbid? Or simply someone who was attracted to the unusual? Perhaps it wasn't so odd after all, what she'd done tonight. That this supremely kinky man was here with her. That she was about to . . . what? She shivered all over just imagining what might take place.

He didn't let go of her as the elevator creaked up to her floor, his body deliciously solid against hers. The doors slid open and he moved with her down the hallway, found her door and inserted the key. The door swung open and he pulled her inside.

It was warm in her apartment; she must have left the heat on. In the dark it seemed womblike. Safe, yet incredibly sexy at the same time. Shaye was still holding on to her. She didn't ever want him to let go.

"Devin." His voice was a deep whisper.

"Yes?"

"Tell me if you want me to go and I will."

"I want you to stay."

He pulled her closer, until she swore she could feel the hammering beat of his heart through the clothing which separated them. She peered through the dark, could see the silhouette of his face only inches from hers.

Please kiss me.

"Are you sure? I want you to be sure. Because it isn't really fair of me to ask this right now, after you've been played for the first time."

"I know what I want."

Please touch me.

"Jesus, Devin."

He crushed her body to his and kissed her, hard. She opened to him immediately and his hot, slippery tongue found hers. Her sex clenched, her whole body trembled with need while they stood just inside her door, making out like a couple of lust-crazed teenagers.

He drove his tongue into her mouth and his hands were everywhere, sliding her coat from her shoulders, moving his mouth away only long enough to tear his shirt over his head, then hers. Then he was on her again, his lips seeking out her neck and fastening on the tender flesh there. She shivered with desire as he licked and sucked. Holding onto him, her fingers dug into his shoulders. She wanted her clothes off, wanted to be naked with him.

"Devin," he crooned against her neck, his voice igniting a new fire within her.

Pushing her back up against the door, he kissed his way down the front of her body. He drew his hands over her breasts and her nipples went hard against his palms even through the heavy lace of her bra. Her sex was drenched, wanting him to touch her there. His kisses were hot, sending heat lancing through her body, straight to her core. It was even better when he opened his mouth and dragged his tongue over her skin.

"Shaye . . . please . . ."

He seemed to know just what she meant. With quick, clever fingers he undid the clasp on her bra and it fell away, leaving her naked and needy. He worked his way back up her body, pushed her breasts together with his hands and bent to tease her nipples with his hot, wet tongue. God, it felt good, so good she almost needed to come just from this. Then he took one nipple into his mouth and sucked so hard it hurt. But the pain was pleasure at the same time and she only wanted more.

He moved to tease the other nipple in the same way, biting, pulling it hard into his mouth, making her moan. She ran her hands over his broad shoulders. He was so big, so well muscled. She could hardly wait to see what the rest of him looked like, felt like.

Yes.

And then he lifted her skirt, pushed the edge of her soaking panties aside and sank down to brush his lips across her aching sex. She arced toward him.

"So damn sweet, Devin. Like warm honey," he murmured. "I have to know, have to taste you. Spread a little more for me. Yes, that's it."

And then he dove in, fingers and tongue and lips, probing, stroking, then finally sucking on her clit until she thought she'd explode.

When he pushed his fingers inside her she did. She came, hard, in a flash of brilliant, blinding pleasure. She was hot all over, shaking, as her sex clenched and she fought not to cry out.

He stood slowly, snaking his way up her body. Every place his bare skin touched hers was like a tiny climax in itself. Finally, he reached her face and caressed her flushed cheeks with his hands, his mouth, a soft fluttering of small kisses.

"Jesus, you are too perfect, Devin. So damn responsive. And I'm so hard for you." He pressed his hips into hers, and she felt the solid ridge of his cock beneath his jeans. She knew instantly she had to have him inside her. *Now.*

"I need you, Shaye. Please."

"Ah, you ask so nicely. So prettily. But I can't do this, Devin. As much as I want you. It's irresponsible of me to have you now, like this."

Panic went off like a thunderbolt in her chest. "Why?"

"I told you earlier, it would be taking advantage of you, after play-ing you tonight." He kissed her then, a soft brush of his lips against hers. "Don't think I don't want you. I want you so much it hurts. But I will suffer so that you can think about it after you've had time to calm down, to come back to earth."

She started to shake her head, but he silenced her with another kiss. His lips were sweet, soft against hers. She was so confused!

He pressed his erection into her again, the hard ridge sinking into the flesh of her belly.

His voice was a rough whisper. "You see how much I want you? How I need to fuck you? But I won't. It's my job to remain in control. But I can still give you pleasure tonight. Is that what you want, Devin?"

She wanted him, all of him. But she understood what he was doing and why.

"Yes. I want you to stay with me. Please."

His hands were on her breasts again, teasing her taut nipples. "Then I'll stay. And I'll bring you pleasure. I'll make you come, over and over. Until you beg for me. And only then will I know that's what you really want."

He pinched her nipples and she yelped. But the pain quickly turned to burning desire.

"Yes, that's it. You can take it. You'll take a lot more tonight. Are you ready?"

Was she? Right now she felt ready for anything he wanted to do to her. She was in his hands. She was too far gone, too filled with aching lust, to think about anything else. Tonight she belonged to him.

"Yes. I'm ready."

FOUR

He didn't know how he'd manage to keep himself under control tonight, but he had to do it. Keep it all together, yes, but he also had to be here with her, present in the moment.

He hadn't been so turned on, so fucking out of control, over any woman, ever. He had to have her. In whatever way he could without completely breaking the code he lived by as a dominant. That meant he was responsible for her well-being while she was under his hands. But all he could think about right now was putting his hands on her. And frankly, putting his cock in her, but that was out of the question tonight. He could hold back that much. Oh, but he would touch her all over. All that porcelain skin that looked so cool, but was so hot beneath his fingertips.

He couldn't let himself think about how hot and silky her pussy was. How wet and ready. Too much. No, just think about pleasing her. About making her come apart.

As his eyes adjusted to the darkened room, he could see the outline of her hot little body. And he could hear the panting edge in her breath. Just the sound of it made him throb for her.

He wrapped a hand up in her long, silky hair, twisting until he felt the strands pull against her skull. A move meant to make her yield to him, yes, but he had to touch that glorious hair, like strands of dark fire. She moaned. He knew he had her, could do anything he wanted, and she wouldn't deny him. It was taking everything he had to keep it together, not to take advantage of her vulnerable state.

He pulled her head back, baring her long, slender throat. He bent and tasted her skin again, sucked a bit of that tender flesh into his mouth. Almost as sweet as her hard little clit had been. Another long, hard throb in his cock at the thought.

Fuck. Pull yourself together.

He picked her up with a deep growl and carried her to the sofa, laid her down and slipped the scrap of lace panties over her long legs. She looked so soft and open lying there. And again he had to beat back the animal in him that wanted to jump on her and fuck her senseless.

He pulled in a few deep breaths, trying to ignore that floral scent of hers that drove him crazy. Once he had himself under control, he began a slow exploration of her lush little body. Her skin was like pale satin in the blue moonlight coming through the living room window, and just as smooth. He ran his palms over her stomach, her thighs. Her muscles tensed everywhere he touched and she squirmed a little under his hands. What would she feel like under him, under his body, his cock pushing into her?

"Just feel me, Devin," he murmured to her. "Just focus on the sensation. Let the rest go."

Another quiet moan from her. Then a sharp intake of breath when he cupped her breasts in his hands. They were gorgeous. About the most perfect breasts he'd ever seen on a woman. And her nipples were coming up hard again under his palms. Too tempting. He pinched them between fingers and thumbs, smiled when she squealed. Even more at the sharp, panting breath that betrayed her pleasure.

"You like that, don't you? You like the pain."

"Yes." The word was a single quiet breath.

He squeezed her nipples harder, then gave a sharp pull.

"Oh!"

"What is it, Devin? Tell me what you're feeling."

"Like I'm . . . oh God . . ."

"Tell me." He twisted the hard nubs in his fingers.

"I . . . it hurts. But it feels too good."

He pinched harder and heard her groan. "I knew you'd like the pain. I could see that in you the moment I laid eyes on you."

Jesus, her body responded to everything, pleasure or pain, in the same way. And he was rock hard, touching her, hearing her moans. He leaned in and took one nipple between his teeth and bit down.

"Ah!" She arched off the sofa, into his mouth.

Yes, she loved it.

He sat back and looked at her for a moment. There was so much he wanted to do to this woman. For the first time in his life he was at a loss where to begin.

He pulled in another deep breath, ordered himself to calm down. Then he slipped one hand between her thighs, into that damp heat. His cock gave a hard twitch. He could not believe how wet she was. She writhed, spread her lovely thighs for him. Almost too much for him to take, but he had to do it, had to make her come. There was nothing he wanted more in the world right now.

He went to work right away with both hands. One hand inside her, moving his fingers in and out. The other hand teased her clit, tugged and pinched. She was panting in seconds. After only a minute he felt the hard clench of her inner walls around his plunging fingers. Heard her long sigh. Her body shook as though a small earthquake ran through it and her hands fisted in her own hair.

Too fucking beautiful. But he was hardly done with her.

He leaned in and kissed her fevered forehead, whispered, "Devin, do you have any toys?"

"Toys?" Her voice was still shaky from her climax.

"A vibrator?"

"Yes. In my nightstand."

"I'll be right back. Don't move."

As he walked down the narrow hallway he heard her mutter, "As if I could."

He found the bedroom easily enough, turned on a bedside lamp. And was pleased to see the big antique bed with its four carved wooden posts. *Nice.* Plenty he could do in a bed like that. But he'd have to think about it later. Next to the bed was a small nightstand, another antique from the look of it. And in the top drawer was a nice collection of toys. He found one of those butterfly vibrators that women loved so much, but what he really wanted was something more phallic. He shuffled a paperback book aside and found it, a large pink vibrator, textured all over with a raised dot pattern. Nice piece of equipment. His cock burned with lust just thinking about what he could do to her with this thing.

He returned to the living room and found she was right where he'd left her. Good girl.

He knelt on the floor beside the sofa. She was watching him, those green eyes impossible to really see in the dim wash of moonlight. But he could tell by the cadence of her breath that she was right there with him.

He used his hands to part her thighs. Skin like a baby's. Jesus.

Concentrate.

He let his fingers tease for a moment at her slick hole. "You're so damn wet, I could slide this thing right in."

"Yes. Do it. Please." An edge of desperation in her voice. He knew exactly how she felt.

He switched the vibrator on and let the tip rest against her clit. She groaned and he pulled it away. Let her lay there and pant. Let her want it before he pressed it again over her mound. Just when she started to squirm, he moved it away again.

"Please, Shaye."

God, he loved that begging tone. "Please what?"

"Please touch me."

"Like this?"

"Oh yes . . ."

Pleasure rippled through her like a long beat of thunder. It hit her core like a blow. Her body convulsed with the first wave of climax. He pulled away once more.

How could he do this to her? Pure torture. Of course, that was his specialty, wasn't it?

Her body was shaking with that keen edge of orgasm.

"Breathe into it, Devin. Ride it out."

"I can't."

"You can. And you will. For me."

For him. Yes.

She could do it for him, do anything for him.

She gritted her teeth when he touched the vibe to her clit again, sending jarring rumbles of pure pleasure through her.

"Hold on to it, Devin," he commanded her.

She pulled in a gasping breath, blew it out. And just when she thought she had it under control, he pinched her nipple, hard. She came up off the couch, her whole body rising, burning.

"Calm, Devin."

Calm? God, she was completely gone and she knew it.

Just let me come. Make me come!

But all she did was moan aloud. She was trembling all over.

"Focus on my voice. Do you hear me?"

"Yes."

"Hold it back as long as you can. And when you're sure you can't hold it any longer, you'll have to ask for it."

She groaned again. "Can it be now?"

A small, evil laugh from him. "No."

His hand on her thigh, moving her legs even farther apart. Then he laid the tip of the vibrator on her clit. His touch was light; all she could feel was the gentlest vibration, but pleasure coiled like a serpent in her sex, spread out, made her arms and legs shake with need.

At the same time he pinched the tender skin at the juncture of her hip and thigh. So painful, but the pain turned immediately to pleasure, impossibly ramping up the sensation between her legs.

"Please . . ."

"Not yet. Hang on. I know you can do it."

He pressed the vibe a little more firmly against her and she bit her lip. Her climax threatened with a sharply honed edge, the pleasure achingly intense.

"I can hear your breath, Devin. I can hear your need in it. Do you need to come? Tell me."

"Yes. I need to come."

"Ask nicely."

He moved the vibrator, then slid it into her, holding it so the heel of his hand ground onto her swollen clit at the same time. Her sex clenched hard around the vibe. Pleasure moved through her in rippling waves. Burning hot, scorching.

"Please!"

Please, please, please . . .

"Yes, now. Come for me, Devin. Come into my hands."

He moved the vibrator, sliding it in and out of her, circled her clit with his hard palm. And she came undone.

Her climax slammed into her like a wall of pleasure, moved through her sex, her limbs, her head, like a honeyed tide.

So good . . .

He kept at it, pumping the vibrator into her, his hand grinding into her clit. Her body shook with the force of it. Pleasure washed over her, drowning her. She became nothing but sensation, the focal point her sex, his hand, the pulsing vibrator buried deep inside her.

"Shaye . . . oh God . . ."

Still he worked her, drawing out the last quivering sensations, until she was too weak to move.

Finally the last trembling threads of her orgasm faded away. He seemed to know instinctively when it was over and pulled her into his arms, into his lap as he sat on the sofa. She leaned her head against his chest and inhaled deeply of his scent, so dark and earthy, so *him*.

Her body was in love with him already.

What had made her even think that? But she was too lambent with the afterglow of a shattering orgasm to think about it—or to think about anything, really.

He stroked her hair, her cheek, her shoulder. So nice. So sweet. Such a contrast to the wanton, wicked way he had treated her body only moments ago. She loved that, the contrast of sexual abandon and this . . . tenderness. What else could she call it?

Devastating.

Oh yes. He was the kind of man a girl could really fall for. Except she wasn't that kind of girl. This night with him did not make her submissive. She'd been the strong one for far too long. She'd had to be. Nothing would ever change that, not even this man with the amazing hands, the sensual instincts that read her body like an open book.

"Devin?"

"Hmm?"

"What's wrong?"

"What? Nothing."

"Then why did you just close up?"

"I don't know what you mean."

"Your whole body tensed up, you crossed your arms over your breasts . . ."

"Did I?"

A long moment of silence, then, "Do you want to talk to me about it, whatever it is you're thinking?"

"I . . . no. It's nothing."

But that wasn't true. Maybe it was what he'd done to her tonight, the playing, as he called it, the orgasms. The tenderness of him now. But she wanted to tell him. Wanted to tell him what she was thinking, about what had happened to her to make her feel like letting go of control was some sort of sin, some failure on her part. But she hardly knew him.

His voice was a quiet rumble, with her ear still pressed against his chest. "It's something. But you don't have to tell me now."

She sighed and relaxed into him again. He felt too good. They stayed there for a long time, until she almost drifted off to sleep, her limbs languorous, her mind hazy. Then he began to stroke her skin, his hands drifting slowly over her arms, her shoulders. She let her muscles unwind, melted into his touch while he slid one hand over her waist, her hip. It was so easy to open for him, so that he could stroke the inside of her thigh, stoking the banked fire of lust between her legs.

He pushed her down, so that she was lying back against the arm of the couch. With one hand he caressed her breasts, while with the other he cupped her mound. She moaned, her sleepy body absorbing the sensation. Desire buzzed through her system, yet she could barely move.

"Yes, that's it, Devin. Just lay back and let me do my work on you."

He slipped one finger into her soaking wet cleft and her hips arched toward his touch.

"I love that, to see you respond. To know you like it when I do these things to you." He pushed two more fingers into her, making her sex clench with need. "Yes, you love that, don't you, when I fuck you with my hand like this?"

"Yes!"

"But you'd love it even more if I really fucked you, wouldn't you?"

"Yes . . . please, Shaye."

"That's the one thing I won't do tonight. But I need to know you want it."

God, the rough texture of his voice was the sexiest thing she'd ever heard. She ground her hips, impaling herself harder on his fingers.

"How do you want it, Devin? Tell me."

"I want it hard. I need it."

"Like this?" He moved his hand so that his thumb pressed onto her swollen clit while he pumped his fingers hard into her.

"Yes!"

Her body trembled, on the brink of orgasm already. When he pinched her nipple painfully she exploded, her climax rocking her body. Shards of sensation shot through her, blinding hot. She cried out as she shivered with pleasure.

His voice was a ragged whisper. "Jesus, to watch you come, to know I make you come so damn hard . . . you're killing me, girl."

She could barely take in his words. Didn't matter, anyway. All that mattered was the rapture of climax after climax, being here with him like this. She lay across his lap, half out of her head and fighting an inner battle between the sharp, aching desire to please him and the need to stay in control.

But who the hell was she kidding? There was nothing about tonight that had to do with her being in control. As frightening as that was, it felt good, too. He was right about that.

Without really thinking about it, she slipped off the sofa, onto her knees on the floor, her hands on his strong thighs. She looked up at him, saw him smile.

"Shaye. Let me please you." Yes, even saying the words to him filled some empty place in her.

He stroked her cheek with his thumb, trailed down to her mouth and ran the pad of his thumb over her lips. Her tongue darted out to taste him. He moaned softly and pushed his thumb into her mouth. She took it in, sucking gently.

"Jesus, Devin."

She ran her hands boldly up his jeans-clad thighs, loving the solid texture of muscle beneath the fabric. She moved upward until she felt the bulge of his erect cock. God, he was big. Her sex flooded with wet heat once more. Focusing on him, she unbuckled his leather belt, slipped his zipper down and found he was bare underneath.

Lovely.

She curled her fingers around the thick shaft. It was like iron in her hand, iron sheathed in silk. And just below the head, the underside of his cock was pierced with a small steel ring. He dug his fingers into her hair as she lowered her head and took him into her mouth.

Sweet flesh, so hard, so hot. The ring felt strange in her mouth, strange but wonderful. She could only imagine the sensations that ring would cause if he was inside her. She slid her lips down his shaft, heard his groan of pleasure. She would have smiled if her mouth hadn't been so full.

With her fingers clasping the base of his cock, she moved up, then down, then up again, sucking, licking, curling her tongue around the heavy head, playing with the metal ring. His hips ground in time with her strokes, the ring sliding over her tongue, his cock plunging deeply into her throat. Her eyes watered, but she wanted to take all of him, wanted to make him feel as good as he'd made her feel tonight.

She moved faster, sucked hard on the rigid flesh. His breath was a rasping pant, his fingers pulled hard on her hair, hurting a little. But she loved it, wanted the pain, as though, she realized, it cleansed her of any culpability. The pain took away her need for responsibility, allowed her to give herself over to him.

God, had she needed to let go so badly? Tears stung her eyes, even as she continued to suck him, to pump him with her mouth. His muscles tensed, he let out a groan and he pulled her mouth from him.

"Shaye?"

His voice was rough, panting. "I won't come tonight. This is not for me. That's not why I'm here."

"Did I . . . you didn't like it?"

He groaned. "Jesus, Devin. If I liked it any more I'd fucking explode all over your face. I almost did. But I have to keep some control tonight. I owe you that."

"You don't owe me anything."

He reached down and pulled her back into his lap.

"Devin, control is a big part of being a dominant. I love that you want to do this for me, but I cannot come while I'm in this role, while your well-being is in my hands. It's irresponsible."

"But isn't that torture for you?"

He laughed, a raw sound. "Hell yes. But that's how it has to be."

"It's the reason why you won't sleep with me?"

"Yes."

"Will you stay here with me tonight, anyway?"

"Only if you promise to keep your hands off me. I don't think I can hold back any longer. Even I have my limits. Come on, I'll tuck you in."

She started to get up, but he gripped her more tightly in his arms and stood, then carried her to the bedroom. There he set her on the bed, helped her pull back the covers and get in. He stripped his jeans off and in the dim reflection of moon and stars coming through the parted curtains of her window, she saw that he was half hard still. Her sex clenched, wanting him, needing him. But she understood the rules, and she would stick to them rather than risk him leaving her.

He climbed in beside her, his body hard and hot as he rolled her onto her side and curled around behind her. The rigid shaft of his cock pressed against her back. She tried to relax, but the object of her desire was all too close. Despite her exhaustion, her body heated again, her sex burning with need.

"Shaye?"

"Is this what you need again, Devin?"

He slipped a hand around the front of her body and right into the vee between her thighs.

"Yes!"

"You're so goddamn wet. Jesus."

He moved his hand and rolled away from her. She moaned in frustration.

"I'll tell you, Devin, this is killing me, not to fuck you. Not to shove my cock deep into you. Come here."

He rolled her over onto her stomach, pulled her up onto her knees, so that her ass was in the air.

"Move your legs apart. I want to see your pussy. Yeah, just like that."

He leaned in and she felt his warm breath on her before he shoved his tongue inside her. A bolt of pure pleasure shot through her. But the groan she heard was his.

He moved away, then his hand came down on her ass in a hard, stinging slap. She gasped in surprise, then moved into his hand, into the pain. She didn't want to think about why, didn't care right now.

"I'm going to spank the hell out of you. I need to."

She whimpered, spread her thighs a little wider.

"Oh, you are perfect," he murmured.

He smacked her again, a hard and fast volley of slaps that made her skin tingle and hurt. Her sex was absolutely dripping. Harder and harder he spanked her, until she could barely take it, could barely breathe. Just when the pain became too much to bear, he slipped his hand between her thighs and went to work on her clit, pinching and tugging with his fingers.

He was working her so hard, her clit, her ass, she couldn't think, couldn't breathe. She was a being of pure sensation, all of it blending together, pain and desire. When she came this time it was like breaking shards of glass—that sharp, that shattering. Pleasure ripped through her body at a thousand miles an hour. She came so hard she couldn't even scream.

When it was over, she collapsed onto her stomach. She was shivering all over. After a few moments she became aware of the ragged cadence of his breathing, of the heat of his big body near hers.

"Fuck, Devin. You really are going to be the end of me."

Maybe she should be worried, she thought, but she felt a deep sense of pleasure at his words, at knowing she affected him with the same impact he did her.

After one night with this man, her sense of self was shifting. Certainly what she knew of herself as a sexual being. And she was pretty damn sure other parts of her life were about to change.

Tomorrow she might feel differently, might feel that intense need for control once more. But for tonight, she chose to give it all over to him.

Shaye.

He might very well be the end of her, too.

FIVE

Devin lay curled up next to him, silent tears sliding down her flushed cheeks. Shaye wiped them away with careful fingers, pushed her long, wild hair from her face. This was part of his job, too, caring for the bottom when they crashed. He was always able to do it with no emotional involvement at all. Just do his job, take care of the girl until she calmed down. He could do it in his sleep. Why was this girl so different?

He *felt* her tears, damn it! What the hell was that about? But he had to think only of her right now.

"Shh, Devin. You're okay," he crooned to her. "You're just crashing. We talked about this earlier, remember?"

She nodded her head, whispered, "Yes."

"You'll be okay in a little while. Just let it happen, this crash. Crash into me. Into my arms. I've got you."

He pulled her closer, trying to ignore the hammering of his pulse in his veins. The heat coming off her was incredible. That and the sweet scent of her hair, making him want to keep her safe. From everything. Maybe even from him. That was part of his job as a Dom, too. Wasn't it?

But it went far beyond that with her. There was more here than that ever-present sense of responsibility. Something about her . . .

She was sexy as hell, no doubt about it. But beneath that was an intrinsic innocence he hadn't seen in even the youngest girls who came to the club, the brand-new twenty-one-year-olds. The innocence he saw in Devin wasn't necessarily virginal. No, there was something in her eyes, something about the way she'd given up that power struggle so easily, even though it was obviously against her nature. She was still strong. He never saw the ability to submit as something weak, anyway. But there was definitely something special about her.

It was almost too much to think about, with her warm in his arms, her scent all around him and his heart thundering in his chest as though he'd just run a marathon. And his poor, neglected cock still as hard as ever.

It occurred to him then that he wanted to take her out of the Ring, to Sanctuary. To that most exclusive of BDSM clubs, which he'd belonged to for almost three years. Why the hell was he even considering such a move?

Devin was worthy of that place. He had never taken a girl there before. But again, Devin was special. On so many levels, it scared the shit out of him. But once he had it in his head that he had to take her to Sanctuary, he couldn't stop thinking about it.

He fell asleep in her four-poster bed, with images of presenting Devin at Sanctuary. With the half-formed idea of how he would propose it to her, taking her to this most formal and extreme place.

Could she handle it? He knew she could. The bigger question now was, could he handle it? Could he take her to Sanctuary, knowing what it could mean to them both?

• • •

Devin expected to wake up alone. Still, she kept perfectly still, not daring to open her eyes, wanting to stay in that dream place where she imagined he had stayed with her. So real. So real she could almost smell him, feel the heat of his body.

With a sigh she opened her eyes, and found him watching her, his hazel gaze dark and intense on her face.

"Shaye."

"Good morning, little one."

Ah, so nice, that nickname. Made her melt all over.

"Good morning."

He smiled. "You sound surprised."

"I am. I didn't think you'd be here."

"I wouldn't have left without saying good-bye. And there's something I want to talk with you about, once you've had a chance to really wake up."

"Mmm . . . impossible without coffee, and I don't keep it in the house. I go down to the Marina every morning and buy it there."

"Up with you, then. Let's get showered and dressed."

Why did she love that he told her what they were going to do, rather than ask her? Wasn't that strange for a woman like herself? She'd been running her own life—and her mother's—since she was ten years old. But she sat up and watched him get out of bed, stark naked and as gorgeously put together as any piece of classic statuary, his cock semihard. Her mouth watered. She got up and followed him, naked herself, into the bathroom.

He was already turning the hot water on in the shower. He stepped in and pulled her with him, moving her right into him beneath the warm spray.

She'd always had a thing about water. It seemed a sensual thing to her. And to be standing here with him, the smooth, wet heat falling all around them, was almost too much for her. Her legs shook with need, her sex pulsing with desire the moment he touched her. She looked up at him, at the droplets clinging to his lashes. His eyes were as dark and unreadable as ever, but his mouth seemed just a little bit softer. She stretched up on her toes and kissed him.

His mouth was every bit as soft as it looked, and a hundred times sweeter. He didn't open to her right away, just kissed her lips over and over until she thought she would drown in her need for him.

He grabbed the soap and slid it over her skin: her back, her shoulders, her stomach, and finally her breasts. Her nipples peaked so hard they hurt. And as he slipped his soapy hands over her body, she felt utterly cared for in a way that was entirely new to her.

They didn't speak. This was a moment of just being together under the hot spray, that white noise of falling water all around them, embraced by the wisps of steam. A sweet moment, thoroughly sensual.

"Shaye . . . please . . ."

He whispered in her ear, "Yes, I know what you need. Here, turn around."

With his hands on her waist he helped her turn so her back was to him, pressed up against the front of his body. His cock was hard as steel against the small of her back. She opened her legs without even thinking about it.

He reached around her, her body still crushed against his. As his arm slipped over the soapy surface of her skin, she noticed again the small tattoo on the inside of his wrist. She grasped his arm, pulled it closer so she could really look at it, could run her fingers over it.

"Tell me what it means, Shaye."

His voice was low and smoky in her ear. "It's the Chinese symbol for power."

His answer hit her hard. Yes, that made perfect sense. This man radiated power. But she didn't have time to think about it before he slipped his hand between her thighs. He pressed two fingers into her and her sex clamped around them. With his thumb he circled her aching clit, making her shiver, on the verge of climax in moments.

Yes, power indeed.

Behind her his voice was soft and husky, right next to her ear. "Come, Devin. Come for me. Right into my hand."

And she did, her body rocked by the force of it as pleasure shot through her. She bucked her hips into his hand, cried out. He held her tightly in his arms while she trembled all over.

"That's it," he murmured. "Good girl."

Another quick flash of pleasure at that. *Good girl.*

He let her catch her breath, then, "Come on now. If I touch you again I'll come all over you like some teenager."

"Yes, please." Had that really been her, that smoky voice, begging him like that?

He laughed. "You challenge my control, girl. But it's time to get dressed, get out of here and get you some coffee."

They rinsed, then stepped from the shower to dry off. He dried her himself, the nubby texture of the towel rubbing over her skin a sensual experience that made her want him more than ever. She realized then that no matter how many times he made her come, she wouldn't be satisfied until she felt him in her body. Her sex gave a sharp squeeze at the thought.

God, he was turning her into a nymphomaniac.

Finally they managed to get dressed. They took the stairs down rather than waiting for the old elevator. Outside there was a brisk, salt-scented wind, but Shaye looped an arm over her shoulders, keeping her warm at his side as they walked.

Was this supposed to feel so much like a relationship, walking out on a Sunday morning to get coffee?

They reached her favorite spot two blocks away, a tiny café called Insomnia. There he ordered for them both and paid for the coffee, and they took a seat at a small table next to the window. Outside the city was waking up, the stores opening. The first tourists of the morning strolled by in their shorts and their San Francisco sweatshirts while Devin and Shaye sipped their coffee in companionable silence. He was the first man she could remember ever feeling this comfortable with, that they could be together without talking, yet there was never any sign of tension, of needing to fill the silence.

"So, what did you want to talk to me about?"

His hazel eyes locked on hers. They glowed with deep shades of amber and chocolate, and a tantalizing sheen of green. "There's a place I want to take you, a special place."

"Oh?"

"I know you're new to this, to the whole bondage and discipline thing. But I think you'd love this place. I know already you can handle it."

"What is it, this place?"

He drank from his paper cup, swallowed, and she was momentarily distracted by the working of the muscles in his throat. "Think of it as being like the Ring, but for a more sophisticated crowd. Sexual sophisticates you could call them."

"I'm hardly that sexually sophisticated."

"Maybe not in the sense they are. But you have what it takes. I can see it in you, Devin."

Even his vague description sounded enticing, if a bit frightening. But if he wanted her to go anywhere with him, she would. She didn't want to think about why. "Tell me what it's like."

"It's a sort of secret society, so I can't tell you much until you agree to go. But it's in this old mansion. A beautiful, elegant place. The crowd ranges in age, but we'd be at the younger end of the spectrum. The people are beautiful. And it's pretty intense, I'll tell you that."

"Intense how?" But without even knowing any more details, the idea was making her heart pound in anticipation.

"Intense in that these people are very serious about what they do, about what *we* do. Sort of Old Guard. Formal. There are a lot of rules. You would have to remain silent unless spoken to. That kind of thing."

"Would you . . . put one of those collars on me?"

He paused, seemed to think for a very long time while he bit down on the plush flesh of his lower lip, making her want to kiss him again.

"Maybe. Eventually." Another pause, then, "The collar means something to these people. To me. It's not merely a symbol, part of a costume. But yes, if I take you there, I would have to collar you before we went back again. That's how it works. I would present you to the group the first time, for consideration. Theirs, yours, mine. After that . . . yes, there would be a collar. But we would talk about it first. We would both have to understand exactly what it means."

He stopped, shrugged, looked a bit flustered. His eyes were shuttered, and she couldn't read what was going on in his head. She wasn't even sure what was going on in her own head, about this collaring thing, how talking about it made him appear nervous and unsure, something she'd assumed he never was. But she couldn't help but imagine him putting a collar around her neck. The idea made her warm and shivery inside.

"I want to go." She knew it with a certainty that didn't surprise her, somehow, even though it should have.

"Take some time to think about it, Devin."

"I don't have to."

"Do it anyway."

He smiled at her, but she could see he was serious and wouldn't accept her answer just yet.

"Okay. I'll think about it."

"Talk to me now. Tell me about your life."

"It's not very exciting."

"You're the most exciting woman I've come across in a long time."

The way he looked at her when he said it, the way his gaze was locked on hers, almost made her believe him. Then he reached over and brushed the back of her hand with his fingertips. "Tell me."

A quiet order, but one she wasn't about to ignore.

"I'm a graphic designer. I design Web sites, logos, whatever the client wants."

"Do you enjoy your work?"

"I'm my own boss, in control of my pace. The business is doing well, so I don't have to stress about money. And I get to do something I love. I get to create. I love it."

"That's a rare thing, to love what you do."

"And what do you do, aside from abusing young girls in the Ring?"

He grinned crookedly. "I do that for fun. I make my living in the Financial District. Corporate gig. I actually like it. Numbers turn me on."

"You *are* kinky."

He laughed. "You don't even know the half of it. But you will."

God, how could he make her blood run hot, her sex clench, with a simple comment? She had to pull herself together in this public place, before she did something stupid, like slide to her knees at his feet and beg him to touch her, to make her come again.

God.

She took a sip of her coffee, letting the heat of it clear her throat. "Tell me something else, Shaye. Tell me about your family, about growing up. Tell me about your parents."

He shook his head, was silent for a moment. Then he said quietly, "My mother's gone, died when I was six."

"God, I'm sorry. And your father?"

"I don't talk to him much. He's kind of an asshole." He went quiet again, and a range of emotions flashed quickly across his features before he got them under control. His face relaxed. "I'd rather hear about you. What was growing up like for you?"

"It sucked, to tell you the truth. My dad left us a long time ago, when I was almost ten. And Mom just . . . never recovered. She's always been a mess, really. We moved a lot. Always in California, but we must have lived in twelve different cities by the time I got out of high school. I was always the adult in the relationship, had to make sure the bills got paid, that there was food in the house. There wasn't always money in the checking account for rent, which is why we moved so much, I guess. Mom found another husband to take care of her when I was nineteen, so I got away, put myself through college."

"Shit, Devin."

She shook her head. "No, don't feel sorry for me. It made me who I am, made me strong."

He said quietly, "That explains a lot about why you're so controlled. About why yielding to me is so necessary for you."

She hated that he could read her so easily, but she loved that about him at the same time. Frightening and comforting simultaneously. Yes, she did need to yield to him. Whether she liked the idea or not. She could feel her body melting even now, just thinking about that need. She dropped her gaze to the table.

"No, Devin. Look at me. It's okay."

He raised her chin in his hand, that slow burn running over her skin at his touch. His gaze was dark, penetrating, as though he could see right inside her.

"I want to go, Shaye," she whispered, knowing he understood exactly what she meant.

He slid his hand down, took her hand in his, and that current of hot electricity ran through her veins. He felt it, too. She could tell by the way his eyes glittered, by the way he held her gaze. Finally, he smiled, that dazzling flash of strong white teeth. Her pulse was absolutely racing.

"Then we'll go. We'll go to Sanctuary. Next Saturday night. Be ready, Devin, for the night of your life."

It had been the longest week of his life. He'd gone to work, done his job, come home and talked to Devin on the phone. But he hadn't seen her. He knew—hell, was afraid—that if he saw her he'd tear her clothes off and fuck her senseless, and still wouldn't be able to get the need for her out of his system. He could not allow himself to lose control that way. Not with her. Not with anyone.

They'd talked a lot about what would be expected of her at Sanctuary. That she had to be naked, which didn't seem to worry her at all. No reason why it should. She had an amazing body, lithe and lean, like a dancer. Gorgeous. He'd told her that she'd be on her knees much of the time, had described to her the submissive position she must assume when kneeling at his feet. Told her to expect that others might touch her, examine her. She would be a slave at Sanctuary; he'd been clear with her about that. And her response had been a long pause in which all he heard through the phone was her quick, panting breath. That told him all he needed to know about whether or not she was ready to go there, to Sanctuary, to this most extreme BDSM environment. But was *he*?

He had never taken another woman there. Had never wanted to. His membership at Sanctuary had so far been as an observer, other than the few times he'd been invited by a fellow Dom or Domme to join a scene, to play their submissives.

Taking a sub to Sanctuary was not like going to any other BDSM club. It was more than the scening, more than the heavily charged atmosphere. If Devin accepted Sanctuary, if the members there accepted her, then their next visit would mean a collaring, that ritual which, in this lifestyle, signified as much of a commitment as marriage did in normal society.

He hardly knew her.

He felt as though he'd known her forever the first moment he'd seen her.

This was fucking insane.

But he was taking her there. And the idea made his whole body surge with lust and an intense sense of needing to protect her, to own her, that he'd never felt before.

Oh yes, he was a control freak, no doubt about it, but owning her? What the hell was that about? He was a chip off the old block, he kept reminding himself. Just like his father, he never committed to a woman. He was his own man. He didn't need anyone. Need equaled weakness. He'd witnessed what that kind of need could do to a person, seen it when his mother had died, in the way his father had totally fallen apart for a few years. He'd also seen how his dad had regained control of his life, had hung on to that control by never loving another woman. And Shaye had learned his lesson well.

His need for Devin was frankly scaring the shit out of him.

If he was smart he'd never talk to her again, never see her. But he couldn't do that. And tonight, he would take her to Sanctuary. He kept telling himself it was nothing more than indulging his desire to play there, in that amazing place. That Devin was merely a girl who could handle it. But that was pure bullshit, and he knew it. Taking her there was a test. But whether he was testing Devin or himself, he wasn't really sure.

SIX

Shaye had told her how to prepare herself, and she'd found a deep sense of ritual in bathing, smoothing lotion onto her skin, dabbing perfume behind her ears, in the hollow of her throat, behind her knees.

How did one dress for an evening in which she knew she would be naked?

She found a short, soft-knit black skirt that wrapped around and tied at her waist, paired it with a stretchy black top and left off her bra and panties. What was the point? And she felt gloriously naked beneath her clothing. Her high black pumps completed the outfit, which left her with a few minutes in which she had nothing to do but wait. To imagine. To focus on the tremors running through her body like a series of small earthquakes.

She stood by the window in her living room, looking out as the fog drifted across the night sky. There was no moon tonight to illuminate the streets below. But she knew the city was still there, as endlessly busy as always. Yet she felt entirely insulated from the bustle and the life there. The anticipation of the night ahead made her feel separate from everyday life, from other people, from everyone but Shaye.

Her heart gave a good, hard thud when he rang the bell. It was time.

She opened the door. God, he looked too good in his leather trench coat. She took a deep breath, took in the earthy scent of the leather along with the warm, woodsy scent of Shaye himself.

"Are you ready, Devin?"

He held out a hand to her and she took it. His fingers curled around hers possessively and immediately her sex went warm and liquid. She couldn't speak. She nodded her head. How was it possible that she felt as though her mind was sinking into that dark, warm place already? Into subspace, Shaye had told her it was called. But she gave herself over to it. To him, as he pulled her through the door, took care to lock it behind them before they rode the old elevator down. The moldy scent of the Paris catacombs smelled like sex to her tonight. Or maybe it was Shaye standing next to her, a protective arm around her waist.

He put her carefully into his car, that shining little BMW that felt like pure luxury inside. But even sexier than his sleek car was his profile as he drove. His dark goatee made him look like the devil himself tonight.

They were silent as the car glided over the rough San Francisco streets, up onto Nob Hill, one of the most exclusive sections in the city. The quaint Victorians gave way there to mansions done in every architectural style, each one more grand than the next.

Shaye downshifted and turned onto a narrow side street. She watched the way his hand caressed the gear shift, remembered with a shiver of desire how that hand had felt on her skin, between her legs . . .

"We're here, Devin. Are you ready? Do you remember everything I told you?"

She looked up to see high, wrought-iron gates sliding back sound-lessly in front of the car. So enormous. So stately. Her throat went dry. But when Shaye reached over and smoothed his fingers over the back of her hand she calmed.

"Okay?" he asked her.

She nodded. "Yes. I'm okay. I'm ready."

He took his hand back, gunned the engine and drove through the gates.

The house, if one could even call it that, was beautiful. Four stories of brick, with graceful white columns. A wide staircase that led to an imposing pair of doors flanked by uniformed attendants. Magnificent. The place reminded her of the antebellum mansions in the South. But there was something more Gothic about it, more New Orleans Garden District.

Shaye stopped the car in front and a valet opened Devin's door for her, helped her out and handed her to Shaye. She was shaking all over. With fear of what lay ahead, but just as much with excited anticipation.

He laid a hand on the back of her neck, leaned in and said quietly, "Here we go, Devin."

He led her up the stairs, her heels clicking on the steps. Marble, she thought, glancing down.

One of the doormen greeted Shaye. "Good evening, Mr. Vincent."

He swung open the heavy front door and they stepped into a foyer. Two naked and collared women stood in front of them. They approached Devin and immediately began to undress her. Panic flooded her.

"Shaye?"

"Shh. It's okay. You're to be naked tonight, remember? And you must be silent." He smoothed a hand over her hair, tilted her chin and brushed a quick, hot kiss over her lips. "Be good, Devin. There is no room for error here, in this place. You must follow the rules. Do as I say. Tell me you understand, and do it right."

Yes, don't speak.

She nodded her head, somehow comforted by knowing she'd done it correctly. By having rules to follow in this strange place. Rules to fall into. It made it easier somehow.

The two girls had stripped her bare, removed her shoes, and Shaye's hand was on the back of her neck again, squeezing.

"Head down, yes, that's good. And clasp your hands behind your back. Come."

She followed him, feeling more naked than she ever had in her life, with her clasped hands making her back arch, her breasts thrusting forward. The idea of what she was doing in this place was overwhelming, yet again she was comforted by knowing what was expected of her, by being able to let go of control and simply do as she was told. And her sex was as hot and damp as it had ever been, her nipples two stiff and aching peaks.

He led her through another pair of doors and she was hit by a wall of sensation: music, voices, the scent of expensive perfume and even more expensive scotch. All she could see was the marble floor beneath her feet as Shaye led her into what must have been the center of the room, to a spot where a large circle of gleaming black broke the expanse of white marble. He took her to the very center and had her stand on a pattern of gold stars set into the floor.

"Down, Devin."

His voice was commanding, his hand on the back of her neck exerting a gentle pressure. She went right down. Gave herself over to the sinking sensation as her knees hit the hard, cool floor. Her mind emptied out as though a stopper had been pulled. All she could do was breathe in, breathe out, and wait to do whatever he wanted her to. Automatically, she assumed the position he had told her would be required of her tonight: knees spread, back arched, palms face up on the top of her thighs. She kept her head down.

She was dimly aware of a hush settling over the room, of a crowd of people pressing in. The music faded, went silent.

Then, Shaye's voice, deep and formal. "I present Devin to Sanctuary."

A pause, and then the jarring sound of applause made her tremble as he lifted her chin and said quietly, "Head up now, Devin, so everyone can see how beautiful you are."

God, to look at the faces of the people around her! It was thrilling and terrifying all at once. To be so objectified! And yet a sharp thrill of excitement ran through her, charging her system with energy, with a deep, stabbing need.

It was a few moments before she could catch her breath. And then she was able to focus a bit, to take in the scene around her.

Other submissives—slaves, she supposed—naked and on their knees, as she was. Beautiful, all of them. An expanse of naked flesh, gleaming eyes, parted lips. Yes, to be one of them! She envied their collars, made of leather, chrome, heavy chain. She couldn't take her eyes off them. The others, their masters and mistresses, were clothed, but she couldn't really pay them any attention. She was too intrigued by these mirrors of her own yielding need.

Slowly, she came to realize the crowd had closed in, that people were talking about her.

"She's a lovely girl, Shaye. Spectacular breasts."

"Beautiful. Love her red hair."

"Wherever did you find one so innocent? Yet look at the way she goes down on her knees as though it's the most natural thing in the world. She's meant for this."

"You'll have to let me get my hands on her some day, eh, Shaye?"

Her head was spinning. And then they began to touch her. Shocking, even though he'd told her to expect it. Hands on her thighs, her shoulders, touching her hair. When a woman pried her lips open with her fingers, then her teeth, she gasped, but Shaye was quick to lay a reassuring hand on her head. "Shh, Devin. Just take it. You can do it."

Yes, anything for him, even this humiliation. She would think later about that small part of her that loved it.

More hands on her, her nipples peaking hard as someone lifted and weighed her breasts. Then a low, female voice.

"Time for the real test, don't you think, Shaye?"

"The honor is yours, Alana."

Devin was surrounded by a faint cloud of perfume, dark and spicy, then a woman's soft fingers slipped between her thighs and slid right into her wet heat.

Her breath came out in a soft *Oh*. She didn't dare move, but her body shook all over. With shock, with desire.

The woman's voice again. "Perfect."

Then those same soft fingers lifting her chin. She stared into a pair of sharp blue eyes set into a beautiful, feminine face with high cheekbones, full scarlet lips. The face of a woman of perhaps a well-held fifty.

The woman said, "You are a little beauty, aren't you? I approve. He'd be wise to collar you quickly." She smiled, released Devin's chin.

Collar me. Yes!

She wasn't quite sure she understood what that meant. To be owned, yes, but what else?

Suddenly she couldn't stand the idea of anyone else touching her. And as though he could read her thoughts, Shaye laid a hand on the back of her neck once more. She knew it was him, knew his sure, warm touch. Her muscles let loose again and she relaxed into his hand.

"Up now, Devin, and we'll watch a scene together."

She rose to her feet, dizzy, and Shaye steadied her. Was this really happening?

He led her across the floor. She kept her hands clasped behind her back, her head down, but still she caught glimpses of high, arched doorways, a fleur-de-lis pattern on the cream-and-gold wall-paper, enormous, ornate gilded mirrors, gorgeous antique furniture everywhere.

Through a wide hallway and into another marble-floored room. Shaye sat down on a low, velvet-covered love seat and she knew enough to settle to her knees at his feet. He leaned over her, his large hand snaking around her neck. "Watch now, Devin."

His hand drifted down, caressed her breast, and her nipple came up rock hard. A small, wicked laugh and a sharp pinch from him before he withdrew his hand and settled back into his chair. She wanted to cry, suddenly, so keen was her need for his touch. She pulled in a deep breath, commanded herself to calm.

The lights dimmed and then went brighter at one end of the room, which was set up as a kind of stage. Against a backdrop of an enormous marble fireplace, the mantle intricately carved, was a high, padded bench. Strapped to it on her back was a young woman with long waves of pale blonde hair. She had a tiny, delicate waist, large, full breasts. Devin ached just looking at her, shivered at the sight of the black leather gag across her mouth, stretching the woman's lips. She didn't know if the sight frightened her or made her want to be up there, to be that girl, displayed and subjugated before the crowd.

God.

Another naked woman stood to one side, a beautiful girl with dark, tawny skin and close-cut curling hair. She had the large, dark, luminous eyes of a doe. The beautiful and imposing Alana stood over the blonde on the table. She seemed to be entirely focused on her, to have blocked out the crowd, as she stroked the girl's body with her hands. Devin could see the blonde's nipples swell, felt her own sex swell in response. Then Alana picked up a small bristle brush from a tray offered by the darker girl and began to run it over the blonde's skin, which quickly turned pink. Devin could imagine what the brush must feel like, how it would bring the blood to the surface of the skin.

She watched as Alana drew the brush harder over the girl's skin: her breasts, stomach, thighs, until she was gasping and writhing on the table. Alana stopped.

The dark girl came to the table once more, a tall pillar candle in her hands, the flame flickering gently. Alana took the candle, nodded, and the girl retreated. She played with the candle for several minutes, swirling the melted wax as it pooled in the center. She bent over the blonde, whispered something to her, and Devin saw her nod. Alana held the candle over her prone body. Devin's heart clutched, then tumbled in her chest as Alana spilled a small pool of wax onto the girl's stomach. She arched, moaned. There was a small flutter of sound from the audience. Shaye's hand flexed on her shoulder.

"Watch now, Devin. This is something I'll do to you some day."

A prickle of delighted fear at that lovely threat.

Yes, anything for you.

She meant it, knew it down deep. How was it possible, with a man she barely knew? But she trusted him utterly, more than any man she'd ever known.

She watched as Alana paused a moment, holding the candle aloft, then let a stream of melted wax fall onto the blonde's breasts. This time the girl yelped and came up off the table hard.

Devin scooted closer to Shaye's leg, her blood pounding in her veins. Excitement coursed through her. She wanted that pain, wanted to feel what this woman was feeling. And the need itself frightened her.

Seeming to sense her panic, Shaye pulled Devin up and into his lap. She looked into his eyes and saw the desire there, the excitement that matched her own. And beneath her naked bottom she felt the hard ridge of his arousal pressing into her flesh.

God, to have him inside her now, even here, in front of all these people . . .

"Does this excite you, Devin?" he asked her quietly.

She nodded her head, her mouth too dry to answer.

"Watch. There's more to come."

She stayed in his lap, her body buzzing with lust at the solid feel of him, at his dizzying scent, at the scene going on before them like some sort of wickedly sensual theater. She swore she could smell the sweet, pungent scent of Shaye's excitement.

She needed him to touch her, to play her, to give her pain. She needed to please him, to show him how much she wanted this one thing. A soft little moan escaped her.

"I feel your need," he told her. "Do you feel mine?"

He shifted his hips, pressed his hard cock closer into her flesh. Steel hard, and she swore she could feel him throbbing even through the fabric of his slacks. She closed her eyes and let that strong pulse reverberate through her system.

Please . . .

"We'll go now."

Go? She wanted to cry. To ask him why they were leaving so soon. She'd been sure he would play with her here, in this amazing place, in this sanctuary of the sensually deviant. Yes, some part of her still viewed it that way, but it only made what they did more alluring.

He lifted her from his lap, stood beside her and whispered into her hair, "I have to get you out of here, Devin, before I lose all semblance of control. I need to take you someplace where I can touch you, where I can have you all to myself."

The disappointment blooming in her chest shifted, heated, until her sex was pulsing, her breasts aching. Suddenly she couldn't wait to leave, as fascinating as this place was to her.

She kept her head down, her eyes averted, her hands clasped demurely behind her back. Funny to think of any of this as "demure." Naked and under Shaye's command as she was, she was as ready to rut as a cat in heat.

They reached the foyer and the two slave girls quickly dressed her again, but she hardly noticed. All she could think about were his words: *touch you . . . have you all to myself.* Yes, that's exactly what she craved.

Shaye took her outside, one strong arm around her waist as they waited for the valet to bring his car around.

During the silent drive he kept a hand on her thigh when he wasn't busy shifting. She couldn't stop the faint trembling in her body. She was too excited. Beyond excited, really. She didn't know how to describe it. Even though Shaye hadn't played her at Sanctuary, even though she'd been little more than an observer, she felt as she did after he spanked her, made her come. Light-headed, exhilarated.

They arrived at her apartment and he slid the little BMW into a rare parking space, made her sit in the car while he went around the other side to help her out. He didn't take his hands off her as they rode the old elevator up. She thought he might kiss her in there. Wanted him to. But he just looked at her with that intense gaze of his, his eyes holding a golden glow, like dark honey lit from within.

Once in her apartment, she stood just inside the entrance while Shaye took off his trench coat and dropped it over the back of a chair. He came to her, and just as he had that first night, he backed her up against the door. But this time he simply stood and pressed the solid planes of his body against hers. Gripping her shoulders almost painfully, he looked hard into her eyes. His gaze was dark, searching. His eyes darted down to her mouth. He licked his lower lip and she thought he'd kiss her, but his gaze moved back to hers and his hands slid gently up to her face. He stroked her cheeks, her lips, her throat.

The intensity of his gaze confused her. And his tender touch made her heart throb in her chest, made her yearn even more for him to kiss her.

Leaning in a fraction of an inch, his breath was warm and sweet on her face. Her lips parted in invitation.

But he slid his hands down to her shoulders again, used his body to press her hard against the door at her back, gripped her shoulders again in that sharp grasp. She watched his face; his features had gone soft in a way she'd never seen before. She didn't know what it meant, only what she hoped it meant, this alternately brutal and tender touch. The expression on his face.

God, please just kiss me . . .

When he looked up at her again, held her face in his hands, she wanted to cry. Why was he doing this to her? Torturing her, holding back, making her mind and her body whirl with the possibilities?

He leaned in again, until she felt the whispering tickle of his dark goatee on her skin. His mouth was so close. She tilted her chin, but he shifted away, leaned his forehead against hers. She really did want to cry now.

She asked quietly, "Shaye . . . are you ever going to kiss me?"

"Yes."

He shifted and his mouth brushed against hers, just a soft feathering of lips. He did it again, and again, all the while holding her face in his hands as though she were a precious thing. His lips were so soft. How could any man have lips this soft and plush? And the gentleness of his kisses went right to her heart, making it swell and ache as much as her sex did, until she was a confused mass of sensation and emotion.

A small sob escaped her lips.

"Ah, Devin."

He took her face more firmly then, crushed his lips to hers, opened her mouth and dove inside.

His tongue was hot against hers, twining, searching. And she was no longer in the role of submissive. She was simply a woman with a man she needed, a man she was falling for like a thousand stars falling through the night sky.

Her arms went around his neck. As hard as he pressed her against the door, his big frame pressed against hers, it wasn't enough. She needed to be closer. She couldn't take it anymore.

She pulled back, and once more he gazed into her eyes as though he could see into her soul. Tears stung at the back of her eyes, brimmed against her lashes. Pulling her in closer, he held her head against his shoulder. She could feel the panting rhythm of his breath.

"Goddamn it, Devin. I can't do this to you. But I can't fucking help it anymore."

She lifted her head, shook it mutely. What did this mean? Would he leave her here, like this? Wanting, needy, breathless. A tear spilled down her cheek.

"I can't . . . hell, I can't *not* . . ." he muttered, before he bent and pressed his lips to hers once more.

The kiss was harder this time, his tongue driving into her mouth. His hands were everywhere: on her waist, sliding up over her ribs, cupping her breasts. He pressed his hips hard against her, his solid erection pushing into her belly. She moaned into the wet heat of his mouth as he began to pull her clothes off, then his own.

Soon they were entirely naked, still pressed up against the door. She couldn't believe how his body felt against hers, skin against skin.

Every nerve in her body was singing. Her sex pulsed with raw, aching desire as he slid one hand down, pushed two fingers inside her. Her hips bucked into his hand, and he shifted to press his thumb against her clit. He never took his mouth from hers; they breathed into each other. She thought briefly, wildly, that this was the most erotic moment of her life.

When she took his swollen cock in her hand he groaned. God, he was big. The velvet weight of it in her hand hit her like a blow that reverberated pure sex through her entire body.

She ran her other hand all over him: his arms, shoulders, buttocks. He was taut, steel-hard muscle everywhere she touched. Lovely.

He moved his mouth lower and sucked at that tender spot at the base of her neck, sending ripples of pleasure through her. And she gave his cock a long, slow stroke, then another, moving in rhythm with his fingers inside her, with the circling of his thumb against her clit. She was so close . . .

"Jesus, Devin."

"Please, Shaye. Please. I need you."

"Yes," he murmured, then grasped her ass in his big hands and lifted her. She wrapped her legs around him, her sex soft and open to the probing head of his cock. Then he slid right in, impaling her.

She gasped at the size of him, filling, stretching her. It hurt almost as much as it felt good. Didn't matter. The pain and the pleasure were all one thing to her.

He gave her a moment, held still, his cock buried deep inside her. They were both panting, and her body was filling up with desire like a flood of molten heat. When he moved his hips, pulling out of her, then sliding slowly back in, she moaned. So did he. Tremors of excitement ran through her, starting low in her sex, moving deeply into her body, spreading through her stomach, her breasts, her arms and legs.

Then he really began to pump into her. She held on tight to his shoulders, her body awash in pleasure, sharp stinging currents running through her like an electrical surge.

It wasn't long before that pleasure crested, peaked, until she couldn't hold back anymore. Her body exploded, her sex clenching, her breath coming in ragged gasps. And before it was over, Shaye groaned, his muscles tensing all over, and he pumped into her harder than ever, driving her climax on in deep, shuddering waves.

He collapsed with her against the door, still holding her up, still inside her body. She quivered all over with the last remnants of her orgasm. But his arms were still strong around her.

"Come on," he said. "I'm taking you to bed and doing this properly."

All she could do was smile as he carried her, still wrapped around his body like a snake, into her darkened bedroom.

SEVEN

Sunday morning. Shaye stretched, opened his eyes to the dim morning light. He glanced at the clock. Not quite eight. He was surprised he hadn't slept longer. He'd stayed up making love to Devin until nearly four.

Making love? Is that what it had been?

Jesus.

He was in deep fucking trouble here.

He glanced over at Devin's sleeping face. She was too beautiful to be believed. So damn innocent in sleep. Not much more than when she was awake, really, which was part of the attraction. But there was a hell of a lot more to it than that. Last night had proved it, if he hadn't known it before.

Why the hell had he slept with her? He'd known he shouldn't do it. Known he should never have taken her to Sanctuary. He knew what the rules were there: if he brought her there once, if she liked it, wanted it, then he would have to collar her before he took her back. He'd had the members' approval of her, no doubt about it. He could take her back. But if he did, it would mean she belonged to him. It would mean the kind of commitment he'd never made to a woman in his life. One he never should make.

He was his father's son, after all, wasn't he?

He'd really fucked up this time. And now Devin would have to pay the price as much as he would. He could see it in her. She didn't even try to hide her feelings. He knew last night had meant something to her. Hell, it had meant something to him, too. That was the problem.

As he watched her tranquil features, her long lashes fluttered, opened, and her liquid green eyes stared up at him. She smiled. It went through him like a knife to the heart.

"Hey."

"Hey." Her voice was soft with sleep. She raised her arms over her head, stretched, the sheet falling away to reveal one perfect breast, a flawless globe of milk-white flesh tipped in a hard, pink nub. His cock hardened.

Get yourself under control, man.

Yes, control. That's what was required here, before he gave into his need for this woman. A need that raced through his veins like fire. That hammered at his mind so he could barely think straight anymore.

He reached out, stroked a long strand of silky red hair from her face, but he had to pull his hand back at the jolt of emotion that went through him like an electric shock. He couldn't do this.

"Hey, I'm gonna go."

"Go?" She sat up in bed, the sheet falling completely away now. He tried not to look at the luscious mounds of her breasts.

"Yeah. I have work to do." He got out of bed and stood, feeling oddly naked, even though being naked had never bothered him before.

"But it's Sunday."

"Yeah, well . . ." His voice trailed off as he went into the living room, found his discarded clothes and slipped back into his boxers, his slacks. He drew his shirt over his arms, didn't bother to button it.

He went back into the bedroom. Devin was up now, wearing a short champagne-colored silk kimono that was falling off one shoulder. Her hair fell in a smooth curtain against the silk, a gorgeous contrast.

"Shaye? Is there something else going on?"

He could hear the edge of panic in her voice, felt it himself.

"I just have to go."

"I don't understand."

"Yeah, neither do I."

He started to turn away, to go back into the living room to find his shoes, but she put a hand on his arm.

"Shaye, you have to talk to me."

Fuck. She was right. He owed her better than this. He bit down hard on his lip.

"Okay. Okay." He turned back to face her, saw the emotion on her face. It made him feel like a criminal.

He scrubbed a hand over his hair. "Look, Devin, things are pretty damn intense between us. Too intense."

"What are you saying?"

"I'm saying that I'm not made for this stuff. Relationships. Commitment. And that's what it would have to be between us."

"Why not?"

A damn good question. He paused, blew out a long breath. "I was raised to be . . . I was raised with the idea that this is how a man operates. That committing myself to any one woman is suicide."

"That's ridiculous."

"Not if you grew up with my father."

She shook her head. "I'm sorry for whatever you went through with your dad. But that doesn't mean you have to buy into that idea."

He could feel the cold hardening inside him as his walls went up. "I've seen what can happen when you don't."

"Oh, Shaye . . ."

"Don't. I don't need anyone's pity, Devin. Especially yours." Why was he so angry suddenly? He had to get the hell out of there. "I need to go."

"Shaye, please."

But he hardly heard her through the heavy gray fog clouding his brain, his senses. He grabbed his shoes on the way out the door and almost ran the four floors down to his car. His hands shook as he tried to fit the key in the door. Finally he managed it, got in and sped off into the dark, damp morning.

Devin could not believe what had just happened. Last night had been the most supremely wonderful night of her life, and now . . . this.

Her chest ached as though she were weighted down with stones, and the tears fell, fast and furious.

What had he said about his father? She could piece it together well enough. That his father had turned into some kind of womanizer after his mother's death. That the man had vowed never to allow himself to be hurt by becoming attached to a woman who might leave, one way or another. She got that. But despite the way his father had raised him, Shaye did feel something for her. She knew it as thoroughly as she knew what was in her own heart.

What she didn't get was, if he felt anything even close to what she was feeling, how could he possibly walk away? How could he do this to her? To himself? And what, if anything, could she do now?

She was too hurt, too shattered, to even think straight. She needed help.

She picked up the phone and dialed Kimmie's number.

Her friend answered in a sleep-fogged voice. "Hello?"

"Kimmie, it's me. I'm sorry to wake you. I'm sorry—" Her voice broke on a sob.

"Devin? What's wrong? Are you okay?"

The tears poured over her hot cheeks. "No. I'm not okay. Right now I don't know if I ever will be again."

"Tell me what happened."

"Oh God, Kimmie, there's so much I haven't told you."

"You can tell me now, Dev."

"I don't even know where to start." She pulled a handful of tissues from the box beside her bed, blew her nose. "Remember that guy I saw at the Ring that night with you?"

"Yeah, the hot one with the goatee?"

"Yes. Kimmie, I've been seeing him and . . . we've been . . . I've done some experimenting with him . . . No, it's more than that, to be perfectly honest. I've gone into this . . . into the whole BDSM thing full force. And I love it. I feel like it's opened this part of myself I never even knew was there. A part that needed opening, you know? A part that needed to just let go for once. But there's so much more to it than even that. There's this incredible, intense connection. Something on a very deep level. Something unlike anything I've ever experienced before. And I . . . I've fallen so hard for him. And now he's gone."

"Oh honey."

"And the worst part is, I know he has feelings for me, too. I could see it in everything he did, everything he said. The way he looked at me. God." She had to pause, to take in a deep breath at the memory of his eyes, those deep, hazel eyes that held so much. The tears wanted to come again, but she held them back. "I know that's what drove him away, that he felt something for me. How fucking tragic is that?"

Kimmie was silent a moment. Then she said quietly, "Just because he left doesn't necessarily mean you have to let him go. You're a strong woman, Devin, not some passive mouse who just lies down and takes whatever the world dishes out. I mean, if you got nothing out of having to deal with your mother growing up, you got that. This doesn't have to be any different."

"I don't know this time. I feel weaker than I ever have in my life. Just . . . crushed by this."

"Love will do that to you, I guess. But you're still *you* on the inside, Dev."

Love? Is that what this was? This raging longing, this need for him that went far beyond the mere physicality of the chemistry between them?

God, I'm in love with him.

"You still there, Dev?"

"What? Yes. I'm just thinking about what you said. And you're right, Kimmie. God, you are so right. I have to find him, talk to him. Now. I'm sorry . . ."

"Don't be. I'd rather see you strong like this."

"I'll call you, let you know what happens."

"Don't worry about me right now. Just go."

Devin hung up the phone, threw on a pair of jeans and a sweater, grabbed her purse, her cell phone. She was already in the elevator, surrounded by the scent and memory of their anticipatory ride up last night, before she realized she had no idea where to look. She didn't even know where he lived. He'd never told her. This was crazy. Hopeless.

As the elevator made its descent, she sank to the floor and cried.

Shaye cruised up and down the hills of San Francisco, not even knowing where he was going. He didn't want to go home, didn't want to go anywhere except back to Devin. But that was the one thing he could not do. No matter how his body, his mind, his heart craved to just be with her. It meant something now, and so he had to let her go.

Didn't he?

He downshifted and made a right turn. Where the hell was he? Somewhere by Golden Gate Park, Stanyan Street. He could see the shadowed green of the trees looming ahead. He made a left onto Haight Street, home of the bohemian, the punks, the Goths, the homeless, the displaced.

That's how he felt right now. Displaced. And it was because he'd left Devin behind. Left behind the first and only woman he had ever loved.

Goddamn it!

He pounded his fist on the steering wheel. This was not fucking possible. This was *him*. His father's son. And the Vincent men did not love, not since his mother had left them.

The voice of reason in his head told him she had died. He knew that, damn it. But she'd left them all the same.

Suddenly, he remembered the sensation of his mother's arms around him, the scent of her: lemon verbena. Remembered the way she sang to him at night. It hadn't all been bad. In fact, while she'd been there, loving them both, it had been pretty damn good.

And now he was going to turn his back on the one woman to offer him love, to offer that kind of feminine comfort. And why? Because his father was an asshole who had shut down after his mom died. And had raised him to be the same kind of asshole.

Maybe he didn't need to be that anymore. Maybe Devin was already teaching him that he could be different, if only he was smart enough to pay attention. He pulled over in front of a thrift store, the colorful window display a sharp contrast to the empty, foggy morning, to the panicked desolation he felt inside. He pulled out his cell and dialed her number.

She'd taken the elevator back up to her apartment, made herself a cup of tea to warm her ice-cold hands, her aching and frozen heart. Now she stood by the window, looking out, but seeing nothing, trying to stop shaking. When her phone rang the sharp sound made her jump, her tea splashing on the hardwood floor. She pulled her cell from her jeans pocket and flipped it open.

"Hello?"

"Devin."

"Shaye?" Her heart tumbled in her chest.

"I need to talk to you."

His voice was commanding again, certain. She did her best to prevent her voice from quavering as it wanted to.

"Yes, I need to talk to you, too."

"I'm coming. Wait there for me. Will you do that?"

She gathered her strength around her, felt the sensation of her body filling up with it. And oddly enough, she drew even more from him. From Shaye. "Yes. I'll wait. But not forever."

"You have every right to be pissed at me. Furious. I understand that. And I'm going to try to get this all straightened out. Just . . . wait for me. I'll be there as soon as I can."

Twenty long, nerve-wracking minutes passed before she heard his knock on her door. When she opened it, the first thing she noticed was the torn expression on his face. She wanted to wrap her arms around him, to make him feel better, to make herself feel better. But she needed to hear what he had to say for himself first. She tucked her hands in her pockets and stood back.

"Come in."

He closed the door behind him, stalked over to the sofa but didn't sit down. He stood and stared at her, his eyes dark and so full of emotion she wanted to cry again.

Strong. Be strong.

Finally, he dropped his head, took in a deep, sighing breath, then raised his eyes to hers, locked there.

"I had no idea this would be so hard."

She took a step toward him. "What?"

"Being with you. Being with anyone. It's always been easy for me. Just have my fun, then move on. But I can't live like that anymore."

"What do you mean?" Her pulse was racing, her blood hot and thick in her veins.

He ran a hand through his short thatch of hair. "Fuck it, Devin. I love you. I'm in love with you."

Tears rose, clogged her throat. All she could do was shake her head, all strength draining out of her in a warm rush of longing.

"I know. It's insane. We hardly know each other. But it doesn't matter. What matters is that I'm finally feeling something, for the first time since my mom died. And it's because of you."

In two long strides he was across the room. He held her arms. "You're shaking, Devin. Say something."

She had to take a deep, gasping breath before she could speak. "Please don't say this unless you mean it, Shaye. Don't say this unless it means you're going to stay with me. I can't take it."

"Jesus. I'm sorry. I didn't want to hurt you. I never want to hurt you again." He paused, tightened his grip on her arms. "Do you love me, Devin?" His eyes were absolutely blazing.

She nodded her head slowly. "Yes. I love you. Goddamn it, you know I do!"

With that admission came her strength, flooding back into her in a wild rush.

He pulled her close, crushed her body to his. When she lifted her chin, his mouth came down hard on hers, bruising, punishing. But it was exactly what she needed. His mouth was sweet and demanding all at once, just like him. She wouldn't have him any other way.

He pulled back, held her face in his hands and gazed down at her.

"I want it all, Devin. I want to be with you, only you. I want to take you back to Sanctuary, to put my collar around your neck. To make you mine completely. Do you understand what that means?"

"Yes." Her heart was fluttering like a bird in her chest, needing to burst out, to fly. It meant he was hers, every bit as much as she belonged to him. Heart, body, soul.

He was the man of her dreams, lovely dreams she'd never even known she had. And Shaye had been the one to show her. It hadn't been an easy journey, but then, nothing worth having came easily, did it?

"You hurt me, Shaye. I don't like that you can do that. But I accept it, that there is this one thing I have absolutely no control over. I have to if I'm going to love you, if you're going to love me. It's a risk I'm willing to take."

"I realized the reason I left is that I couldn't handle that *you* could hurt *me*. That it's actually possible for the first time in my empty fucking life for any woman to have that much . . . power over me."

"That's why we have to trust each other. Why we have to trust that we won't abuse that power. It's the same way I have to trust you when we're in the roles of dominant and submissive. It's that same exchange of power that puts us on an even playing field, that balances it all out."

He stroked her flushed cheeks with his thumbs, the warmth of him seeping into her skin, then he bent his head and kissed her. This time it was a soft kiss, a tender kiss. A kiss filled with promise.

"I love you," he whispered against her mouth. "I love you. Jesus, I love you."

The tears stung her eyes again. Her heart filled, swelled. And her body curled into his as though it belonged there. She was certain now that it did.

Yes, he would take her back to Sanctuary, collar her; they would make that binding commitment to each other. But none of it could compare to that sense of absolute rightness she felt in his arms.

She had found her sanctuary with him.

WILD NIGHTS

JACI BURTON

To Charlie—
for wild nights. I love you.

ONE

Mike Nottingham cocked a brow at the gold foil-lined envelope sliding across the table. He glanced up at his friend Denver McKenzie. "What's this?"

Denver slashed a wicked smile and tipped his glass of scotch in a toast. "A gift. You look tense."

"Understatement." Every muscle in his body was wound tight. Getting away from work for four days had helped. The conference here in Las Vegas had been worth attending, and he'd learned a lot. But what he'd really been looking forward to was the vacation he so desperately needed. He glanced down at the envelope. "You got me a present."

"Yeah."

"I don't suppose there's a bottle of Jack Daniel's in there."

Den snorted. "You can get one of those yourself. What's in that envelope you can't."

"So what's in here?"

"Exclusive club. Invitation only."

Intrigued, Mike opened the envelope and pulled out the single embossed card, read it and glanced up at Denver. "Wild Nights?"

"Right up your alley. I figured since you had some time to kill while you're here, you'd want some fun. You're not really the showgirl or BunnyRanch type. I thought you might want something a little more out of the ordinary, and definitely private."

Den knew him well. Friends since their college days and through veterinary school, he and Denver went way back. Den knew Mike's predilection for the wild life. Even the name of the club fit Mike's personality. He did his job as a veterinarian in Oklahoma. He made nice with his customers and he loved his animals. But at night and on his own time, he liked to cut loose, especially sexually. So did Den. Which had a lot to do with why they'd become and stayed such good friends. The only other person he trusted with his secrets was his best friend and partner, Seth Jacobs.

"Present that card at the club entrance and you're in," Denver said. "Your name is already on the list."

Mike traced the raised lettering on the invitation with his fingertip. "I take it they know you well there?"

Den laughed. "I never miss a chance to visit Wild Nights whenever I'm in Vegas. Grace runs a very classy show. And the menu is as varied as your imagination."

"Grace?"

"Figured you'd zero in on that. Grace Wylde is the owner of Wild Nights." Den spelled her last name.

"Ah. Intriguing."

"Intriguing doesn't begin to describe her. Gorgeous, mysterious, keeps to herself a bit yet always makes you feel at home. And she's sexy as hell. I've never known a woman so comfortable in her own sexual skin."

"Really." And she owned a club like Wild Nights? A man's dream come true.

Den leaned back in the chair and shook his head. "Don't even think about it. She's completely untouchable."

"Happily married or with someone?"

Den laughed. "Not even close."

"Then she's not completely untouchable, Den. You and I both know that." They'd shared enough women over the years, women who at first look seemed like ice queens, but in the bedroom melted all over them.

"This one is. Many have tried. All have failed."

"I can't wait to meet her." Failure wasn't in Mike's vocabulary. There wasn't a woman he'd set his mind to having that he hadn't succeeded in seducing. The conference he'd come to Las Vegas to attend had ended and he'd already made plans to take an extra week off.

Wild Nights sounded like a perfect start to his vacation. A place to relax, unwind and see a little bit of the Vegas wild life. And he was intrigued by Grace Wylde. He never could resist a challenge.

He was ready for some action. He'd been good during the conference. Maybe at Wild Nights he'd find a spark, something to alleviate the restlessness that seemed to be a part of his everyday life. Because no matter what he did, no matter who he was with or what sexual games he played, he was never satisfied. He'd been with some amazing women, and he'd played every game in the book. If it existed sexually, he'd done it. He was always searching for the next big thrill, trying to top the last sexual conquest with something even better.

But now it had just become a game—an endless stream of women in and out of his life. Women who couldn't stand up to his challenges, although plenty had tried. He'd long ago stopped thinking of himself as a pervert or some kind of extremist. He was just looking for satisfaction.

So far, he hadn't found it. He'd just about decided it didn't exist, that sexual fulfillment would always lay beyond his grasp. Oh, he got off all right. He had good sex. Sometimes great sex. But he always felt like it lacked . . . something.

And he hadn't been able to figure out what that "something" was.

"Mike," Den said, capturing his attention again. "There will be plenty of others to play with at Wild Nights. You won't even get a shot at Grace. Don't even think about it."

But he was thinking about it. He hadn't even met her yet and she was already his target for tonight.

Look out Grace Wylde. If there was one thing that got him hot, it was a challenge.

No matter how many nights the doors opened to Wild Nights, Grace Wylde still got a thrill as if it were the very first time. Every night was opening night. Each time had to be absolutely perfect.

She surveyed the club, watched her staff behind the bar shine the glassware and inventory the alcohol. Her gaze drifted across the room to the dance floor where the DJ was preparing tonight's mix. He looked up, his headphones on, head bobbing up and down to whatever song played in his ears while he simultaneously did a light check. He grinned and gave her the thumbs-up sign. She smiled back at him and moved on.

Every table was clean and polished; not a single speck of dirt could be found on the parquet floors. Beyond the bar and dance floor were double doors leading to the private rooms. She greeted everyone. The staff, relaxed and joking around, waved at her as she walked by.

It seemed the only nervous one was her. Then again she had the most to lose. Wild Nights was her baby—had been for the past four years. It was incredibly successful, but she kept waiting for failure to occur, for no one to walk through those doors when the bouncers opened them. So far that hadn't happened. Lines of the uninvited waited outside, hoping against hope they'd have a chance to get in. But Grace was very particular about her clientele, catering to her clients but also careful about protecting her staff. She invited the best of the best, only those who could be trusted. She wanted people to enjoy her club, but she wanted it understood that her people must be kept safe. She loved her staff, and if any one of them was ever hurt, she'd never forgive herself.

Wild Nights was a place of fun. For her patrons, her staff and for her. Her clients paid a high price for that privilege, her staff was compensated extremely well to work here, and no one loitering outside was permitted entrance without an invitation and their name on the club list. No exceptions. Ever. And even those invited in were quickly escorted out the door if they didn't follow the rules. No second chances. The club ran smoothly because of her rules.

And she was proud to say that once in, no one wanted to get the boot. What they found inside Wild Nights was something they couldn't get anywhere else. Sexual freedom. No rules, no restrictions, only pleasure. If it was mutually consensual, it happened here.

Making her way back to the front entrance, she nodded at the bouncers who flicked open the deadbolts at the door and walked outside, ready to let in the regulars and the select few newcomers who possessed a coveted invitation and a place on tonight's list.

The games were about to begin.

Grace palmed her stomach, mentally calming the jitters and pasting on her best smile of greeting. People began to pour in. Some she knew because they came every night, some she recognized as regulars who showed up when their schedules allowed it, and others held invitations in hand signaling their first trip to Wild Nights. Those were the ones she'd make a concerted effort to cater to tonight.

Some were men and women who came alone, others were couples. She never asked the reasons people frequented Wild Nights. Everyone had their own individual desires, tastes and reasons for doing what they did. And those reasons were as personal as her own desires—she wouldn't dream of infringing on anyone's privacy.

Tonight there were five first timers—two men, one woman and a couple. She already knew their names and had read their short bios. One of her staff would escort them to the drawing room where she'd greet them, introduce herself and give them a brief orientation. Then they'd be free to enjoy the club and all its amenities. She hoped they liked what they saw and came back again. And again. Repeat business was very good for the club.

Once everyone was inside and Grace had said her quick hellos to the regulars, she headed toward the drawing room, breezing through the open doorway. One of the attendants closed it behind her. A quick glance sized up the newcomers. A very nervous couple in their early thirties swinging for the first time, one rich corporate exec who enjoyed being dominated, a female out for adventure—newly divorced and extremely pissed off at her philandering ex-husband—and a dark, enigmatic man who caught her eye right away.

He slanted a gaze her way and smiled. His bio was unremarkable, and he came recommended by one of her best customers, Denver McKenzie. But what was his story? Mystery—she liked that in a man.

"Good evening, everyone. My name is Grace Wylde and I'm the owner of Wild Nights. I'm very happy you decided to join us and hope you find something to your liking at the club."

One of the waitresses brought cocktails and handed them out. Grace took the glass of brandy Selena handed her. "Thank you, Selena."

Grace settled into one of the single upholstered chairs set in a circle in the drawing room, took a swallow of brandy, then began.

"Wild Nights caters to anything and everything you could possibly desire, sexually, as long as it's mutually consensual. Nothing is prohibited, as long as it's legal. We do not tolerate drug use, pedophilia or bestiality or the use of nonconsensual force. If any of my staff is abused in any way, you will be promptly escorted from the premises and held outside until the police arrive. Please know that I *will* press charges for assault on behalf of any of my staff members who are harmed. This is not a house of prostitution. No one is paid for their services. My staff like sexual pleasures and if they consent to have sex with you, then you are free to join them. You can also enjoy sex with any of the other guests at the club who agree to it. Safe sex is practiced and is a must—no exceptions. Condoms can be found in every room.

"There are many rooms and scenarios set up for your enjoyment, from straight sex to gay and lesbian, as well as fetishes, bondage and discipline, pain and torture, voyeurism and exhibitionism, ménage, oral and anal sex, masturbation . . . any one of a multitude of sexual pleasures await you.

"If you have any questions or concerns, my staff is set up throughout the club to assist you. You will see them wearing the appropriate Wild Nights shirts. There are video monitors set up in every room. Everything you do is watched. If you have a problem with that you are free to leave, but there is no corner, nook, cranny, closet, bathroom or room in this club that is not seen on video. This is for your protection as well as the safety of the staff."

She finished her spiel and took a sip of brandy, letting what she'd said soak in before continuing. "Does anyone have questions?"

"What's your favorite room?"

That from the tall, enigmatic man. Every night there was at least one like him who targeted her specifically. She could script it perfectly. As soon as she finished her speech he'd linger, hit on her, so confident in his own sexual prowess he'd expect her to select him as her partner for the evening. Granted, he was gorgeous. Well built, exuding sex appeal through midnight blue eyes that screamed sensuality.

But she chose her partners with care and she was never indiscriminate. This one had a lot to learn. She offered a half smile in response. "That, Mike, is my secret."

He arched a brow, cracked a smile and nodded.

"Any other questions?"

No one spoke up. "Then enjoy your evening."

As everyone stood to leave, she waited for him to approach, already prepared to let him down easy. She'd given her speech a thousand times before. She knew how to preserve a man's ego.

But he surprised her, linking his arms with the single woman, whispering something in her ear that caused her to tilt her head back and laugh. Without even a backward glance in Grace's direction, Mike Nottingham strolled from the room.

Grace was an expert at reading people, especially men. And she was never, ever incorrect. Her instincts were always right on. But she'd guessed wrong about Mike Nottingham.

Intriguing. Definitely intriguing.

Mike barely tuned in to the redhead on his arm, blathering on about her ex-husband's infidelities and how she was going to show him who could be wild and sexually crazy.

His mind, his entire body, was tuned into Grace Wylde.

Grace. Yeah, the name fit. She walked with it, talked with it—hell, she exuded it. He'd never seen a more beautiful woman. And he'd definitely been with his share of gorgeous ladies. But not one with raven hair and eyes the color of wild violets. Not one tall, slender, without the big tits and curvy body of a centerfold, but more like a ballerina. Small breasts, long legs, slim hips. She took his breath away, and it had been a damn long time since any woman had been able to do that.

His cock hardened just looking at her. She spoke of elegance, refined beauty, with a smoldering passion underneath just waiting to be uncovered.

And she was ready to blow him off in a millisecond. He'd sensed that when he'd asked her about her favorite room. He was no dumbass—he'd been playing this game far too long. The telltale smile gave her away. A woman like her must be hit on every night, and probably more than once. There wasn't a line she hadn't heard or had a snappy come-back for.

Time for retreat and reconnaissance. Time to just watch and figure out how to approach without her throwing an obstacle in his way. Because he wanted more than just to fuck her. He liked hearing the sound of her voice. He wanted to know the hows and whys of her involvement with Wild Nights. She was intriguing.

And Mike hadn't been intrigued in . . .

He wasn't sure he'd ever been intrigued by a woman. This was a first.

TWO

Though she spent the next hour mingling with her guests and making sure everyone was having a good time, Grace couldn't help but keep one eye on Mike Nottingham.

She expected him to approach her. He hadn't yet. He'd gone to the bar for a drink, spent some time talking to the bartender and a few of the staff, then hung out and chatted with some members. Not once had he sought her out or bothered her in any way.

For some odd reason, she was irritated by his seeming lack of interest. She *knew* he was interested in her—her instincts were never wrong, dammit. He was simply playing it cool and waiting for the right moment to pounce.

She continued to perform her normal routine—stopping at tables to visit her regulars, answering a question or two from those who approached her, even dancing with men or women who asked. As owner and hostess, she made herself available to her clientele, within reason of course. Anyone who came here on a regular basis knew her sexual boundaries. She did the choosing, and in that she was very particular. Partaking of the club's activities was a rare occurrence. Typically she liked to keep her own sexuality private, her partners anonymous.

But periodically she'd dally at the club. It was good for business. Patrons liked to see her taking part in the club's amenities. It fueled their fantasies of her. She knew it, the staff knew it, they all played it up.

She wasn't going to dally with Mike Nottingham, though. Mainly because it's what he wanted. And she never catered to men. They catered to her. It was part of her mystique. She did the choosing. She smiled at that.

"You have a beautiful smile."

She didn't jerk in surprise at the sound of Mike Nottingham's voice behind her. She knew he'd come around.

"Like a cat who just ate a bowl of cream."

Her smile didn't die. In fact, she kept it on when she turned to face him. Like it or not, he was a client. "Thank you. Are you having a good time?"

"Yes. You've created a hell of a niche market here."

"We stay busy."

"I can imagine."

He wasn't crowding her or invading her personal space. She liked that. Most men targeting her invaded her space and she hated feeling cornered. He kept a respectable distance, one hand holding his glass, the other resting on the bar.

"Find anything to your liking yet?" she asked.

He laughed. "Grace, everything here is to my liking. I love sex. That's why I'm here."

"Ah. Honesty. That's refreshing." His southern drawl was sexy. Rolling off his deep, husky voice, it singed her nerve endings. How long had it been since she'd played? Too long.

"But I like to take my time before I choose. I don't like to rush into anything."

"Really."

He nodded. "I might just want to look around tonight. I'm in no hurry."

Also different than a lot of the men who came here, usually with a hard-on before they came through the door, their cocks out before they moved from the bar to the playrooms. They'd have their dicks in the first willing woman before Grace could blink.

Maybe Mike got laid often. Though she got the idea he wasn't just after pussy, that he had more adventurous tastes.

"Any particular play you have in mind? Can I help you with something?"

He slanted a half-lidded gaze at her that admittedly got her panties wet. Practiced? Maybe. But either way, it worked.

"I haven't been to the playrooms yet, so I can't really say. I'll have to take a look around and see if anything gets me hard. But thank you for the offer."

The man smoldered. What would be wrong with a little one on one with him? He was damn fine looking and her pussy was quivering. She made no apologies to anyone for her sexuality, so what was holding her back? When she found a guy she wanted to fuck and she was in the mood, she went for it.

"Let me show you around."

His brows arched and he dipped his chin to look down at her. "Sure." He held his arm out and she took it, guiding him through the double doors from the main room into the playrooms, cognizant of how tall he was. She wasn't short by any stretch of the imagination, but Mike made her feel . . . petite.

His body was warm and he smelled . . . God, he smelled great. Like a fresh shower, not like those men who doused themselves in sickening cologne that gave her a headache. Mike smelled like soap. She breathed him in as they strolled down the hallway.

"Each room is marked so you know what it is before going in," she explained, pointing to the door marked, "Masturbation."

"Do you enjoy touching yourself?" he asked, his voice dropping down an octave.

Her nipples tightened. "Very much. Do you?"

"Every chance I get."

Verbal foreplay had always excited her. She paused and turned, tilting her head back so she could look at his eyes. "How do you do it? Only at home, or elsewhere?"

His lips curled in a knowing smile that made her want to climb on top of him and kiss him. "Like I said, every chance I get. At home, in the car, at work, outside . . . anywhere I get the urge, as long as I don't get caught."

She nodded and inhaled, her mind filled with visuals of him pleasuring himself. "Me, too. Sometimes I'll do it four or five times a day. Here at work, in the car when I'm driving somewhere. I even did it in my doctor's office one day. They make you wait so long in those exam rooms, though it really doesn't take me long to get myself off."

"Everyone knows their own body well. It's easy to make yourself come."

"True enough."

"I'd love to watch you give yourself an orgasm."

"I might like showing you." She turned and moved down the hallway, recognizing her body's signals. Flushed, breasts swollen, her nipples pebbling against her dress. Her panties were soaked and sticking to her moist cunt.

Yes, she was definitely going to have to play with Mike tonight. She needed an orgasm. Or five or six. She chanced a glance at his mouth as they moved to the next room, wondering how his full lips would feel latched on to her clit. Her pussy quivered and she wanted to stop right there, lift her skirt and let him lick her.

She hadn't had it this bad in a long time. She should have masturbated before she came to work tonight. Instead, she'd gotten involved in paperwork, gone to the gym for a lengthy workout, then had to hurry up and shower so she wouldn't be late. Now she was edgy and uncomfortable and in desperate need of release. Though the anticipation of what would happen tonight was nice.

"Spanking room?" she asked as they walked by yet another.

He grinned. "That could be fun."

She glanced down at his hands and felt a tingle of anticipation at the thought of them wandering over her ass. They moved on down the hallway and she nodded at a couple women who worked for her. They sized up Mike, their eyes widening with distinct interest. Not that she could blame them. With his dark good looks and lean, well-toned body, he was a prime specimen. He walked in a barely leashed predatory manner that she found quite compelling since it wasn't affected at all, but natural. He offered a friendly acknowledgment to the women, but kept his attention focused on Grace.

Nice.

"Same-sex rooms ahead," she said.

"Fun to watch but I'm completely hetero."

"What do you like, then?"

"Just about everything you'll suggest. That's why I'm here."

She had an idea he'd respond that way. "Been there, done that, in other words?"

He shrugged. "I haven't exactly been a monk in the past."

"I'm sure I could find something here to tempt you."

"Only if your name is Eve and you're holding an apple in your hand."

Now it was her turn to laugh. She stopped and turned to him. "I'm the challenge every man who comes to Wild Nights wants, Mike. But I'm not a prize."

Now he did lean in, though just enough to tantalize her with his scent. "No, you're not. You're a treasure worth exploring. A prize is something to show off in front of everyone. I don't see you like that."

"You don't."

"No. A man should take his time with a woman like you. But not here."

"No?"

He shook his head. "Someplace private, where we can get to know each other, explore each other. Without you being on display."

Okay, now she was really impressed. The typical man who pursued her wanted to show her off like a trophy, like they'd just won the lottery and she was the grand-prize fuck. They always suggested one of the showcase rooms, where they could exhibit their prowess in screwing the owner of Wild Nights. Total turnoff. Grace didn't mind a little exhibitionism, but on her terms, and she didn't want to be shown off like a prize deer during hunting season.

Which made Mike different than most men.

"Come with me." She held out her hand and led him down another hallway, through the door and to an elevator marked "Private." They passed some staff members along the way.

"David, I'm heading up to my suite. Please let the managers know where I can be reached in case of emergency."

David nodded. "Of course, Grace. Have a nice time."

She intended to. Mike had piqued her curiosity. Now she wanted some time to talk to see if her instincts about him were right. She punched the code and the elevator door opened. Mike stayed silent on the ride up to her penthouse. One of the advantages to living where she worked was that there was no commute. When she wanted some privacy all she had to do was take a short ride and she was home.

"Nice place," Mike said as they stepped inside her suite.

"Thank you." She didn't need to live extravagantly, preferring to put her money back into the club and bank the rest of the profits for later on. She didn't intend to be in this business forever. But she loved the view of Las Vegas afforded by the floor-to-ceiling windows in her living room, and the privacy of living high above the city.

Her décor was simple—beige and black. Nothing fussy. Standard furniture, comfortable couches and tables and chairs. She liked her living space livable—not pretentious.

"Would you like a drink?"

He stepped to the window. "Whatever you're having is fine."

She poured two brandies and handed one to him. "I love this view. Frenetic pace, dazzling lights, absolute madness down there. But still, it relaxes me." She took a sip of her drink, feeling it burn its way down and warm her.

"It's home to you. Anything that's home is relaxing."

She motioned him to the couch in front of the window, kicked off her shoes and sat, curling her legs under her. "Tell me what's home to you."

"Oklahoma. I'm a veterinarian. Own a practice with my best friend. We've been partners since our college days. I have a house in a small town and that's where I kick back and get away from it all."

"And you obviously love animals."

"Yeah, I do." He took a long swallow of the brandy. She watched his throat move as he tilted his head back. "I have a couple dogs and I'd eventually like to own a horse ranch."

Grace stared out the window. "I've never been on a horse in my life. But I'd love to ride someday."

"Come visit me sometime. I'll take you for a ride."

"I'll just bet you would." She teased, imagining the kind of ride Mike would take her on. "But I'm serious about the horses. I've always loved animals but I never had any pets."

"Why not?"

She shrugged. "My parents never allowed us to have any, and after I moved away from home my lifestyle wasn't conducive to keeping one."

"That's too bad. I was brought up around animals. I grew up on a farm."

"Interesting."

"Are you from Las Vegas?"

She laughed. "Oh, God no. I'm from Kentucky."

He arched a brow. "No trace of an accent."

"I left home at eighteen. That was a while ago. There's no part of the Kentucky girl left in me."

He reached out and grabbed a tendril of hair from the side of her face, letting it slide through his fingers. "You know what they say. You can take a girl out of the country, but you can't take the country out of the girl."

"Trust me. This girl has no country left in her. I left their morality and their holier-than-thou standards and prejudices on the doorstep the day I walked out. There's nothing of them left in me."

"Bitter?"

His voice was soft. No accusation. "Not at all. I just didn't want what they were selling."

"Which was?"

"Hypocrisy."

Mike nodded. "Now, that I understand. Those who preach one thing and practice another."

"Exactly." She took another drink and sighed, wondering why she'd revealed so much about herself to a stranger. She never talked about her past with anyone. Some of her close friends at Wild Nights didn't know where she'd come from. "Your glass is empty. Let me refill it." She reached for his glass, but he laid his hand over hers.

"I'm fine right now, thanks." He laid his glass on the side table, but didn't let go of her hand. His thumb drew lazy circles over her palm. The sensation was wild. Amazing for someone as jaded as her. It was just her hand. She usually needed much more stimulation to get her going.

"I'm not promising you anything by this," she said, needing him to understand.

His lips curled in a wicked, sexy half smile. "I just want to spend time with you, Grace. There are plenty of women I can fuck. I like you. I like talking to you. Just relax, okay?"

"Sorry. I'm used to meeting men whose sole objective is to fuck the panties right off me. It's a defense mechanism to set the ground rules right away."

"Consider them set. No promises. I won't ask you to bear my children or move to Oklahoma with me tomorrow."

She snorted. Dear God, when was the last time she did that? "That was funny." He was right. She needed to lighten up.

"How long have you lived out here?" he asked, content to roll right back into talking.

"Ten years. I came out here right out of high school. Went to college and worked nights to support myself."

"Damn hard life for a kid all alone."

She shrugged. "I managed. I made friends and scored a couple really well-paying jobs. I knew exactly what I wanted."

"Pretty impressive for someone so young."

"It's important to have goals."

"And what were your goals?"

"To start up Wild Nights."

His brows lifted. "You knew even then?"

She nodded. "I grew up in a repressed family. Sexuality wasn't discussed. The town I lived in was littered with hypocrites who preached abstinence and morality and practiced adultery and indiscriminate sex. It was ludicrous."

"And you were confused as hell, I imagine."

She nodded. "Understatement. I had this raging libido and everyone telling me that what I felt inside was bad, evil. And it wasn't bad. I knew it wasn't. How could something that felt so good be wrong? What was so bad about expressing one's sexuality?"

"Nothing."

"I was determined to get the hell out of there before I ended up pregnant and married and trapped at eighteen. No way was I going the route of so many of my friends. They were brainwashed into believing that bullshit. I knew I was destined for something else. I felt stifled there and I couldn't wait until I was old enough to make a run for it.

"So as soon as I graduated high school I packed up and left. I'd worked a part-time job in school and banked every spare cent I could. Enough for a bus ticket to Las Vegas and money to last a month. I was lucky—I landed a job and a place to live and worked my ass off in school and at work for several years, with my eye always on the prize."

"Wild Nights."

She smiled. "Wild Nights."

"So you've realized your dream, Grace. Are you content?"

She started to answer with a yes, then realized no one had ever asked her that question before.

Was she content with her life? Could she honestly say she was happy?

"Truthfully, Mike? I don't know."

THREE

Mike was surprised at Grace's honesty. And absolutely stunned by her. Everything about her. Her story, her beauty. Her tenacity and drive.

"You're an amazing woman, Grace. You've put your life on hold to realize your dream."

"My dream is my life. Or at least it has been for the past twelve years."

"I did the same thing with my practice. Between school and setting up my business, there wasn't room for anything else for a long time."

"But you've found time to play, haven't you?" she asked, shifting on the couch so she could draw nearer to him.

He knew what she was doing. She was trying to change the subject because she felt like she'd revealed too much. Fair enough. He owed her for her honesty.

"I've played plenty. Too much, I think."

She stilled, then leaned back a little, frowning. "Too much?"

"I've played the game for so many years I think I've become desensitized to it all. So I find myself looking for the next big thrill, and finally coming to realize there isn't one."

She relaxed her shoulders. "Ah. Yes, I understand."

"I've done it all, Grace. It's hard to get excited about it anymore. It's like I'm pushing the sexual envelope, looking for the next conquest before I've even finished the one I'm with."

"And it's not fun anymore," she replied, nodding.

He laughed. "Well, sex is always fun. But lately it's been a little . . . unsatisfying."

She crossed her arms. "I know the feeling."

"Really?" He couldn't believe he was telling her this. Or that she of all people was a kindred spirit. Grace was like a shrink—easy to talk to. He didn't really spend a lot of time talking to women. When he was alone with a woman, talking typically wasn't something they did. Then again, she was a stranger. A beautiful, intelligent, eloquent stranger, and different from most of the women he knew.

After tonight he'd never see her again, so why not? It wasn't like he had anyone else remotely close to open up to about things like sex. No way would his male friends understand how a man who got as much pussy as he did could possibly be dissatisfied with his sex life.

"People always wonder about me," she said. "Why I opened this club. How I must have suffered some sexual trauma that made me want to explore the wild side of sex, when the truth of the matter is, I always felt sex should be openly celebrated. I've always enjoyed it. There is no dark history in my life—no rape, no incest, no horrors in my past that caused me to want to investigate my deviant side. I just love sex. That's why I moved here and started this club.

"As I mentioned, I was dissatisfied with those who preached morality, that sex was something to be hidden as if it were bad. There's nothing bad about sex as long as it's consensual.

"But the problem is, when you engage in so much open and free sexuality, when you can have anything you want anytime you want it, you become desensitized to it. Then what does it take to be satisfied?"

"Is that why you don't partake of the fun and games at Wild Nights?" he asked, curious whether it was choice or just part of the mystique.

She shifted, stared out at the lights of Las Vegas again. "Partly. I have responsibilities at the club and if I spend all my time engaged, I can't cater to my clientele. But yes, I've also become a bit jaded. I used to play a lot more than I do now. Because I've done it all. It doesn't have the allure it once did."

"When you've experienced everything, and more than once, there's no thrill."

She looked at him. "Yes. That's it exactly. I sometimes wonder if I'll ever find the one man who'll be able to touch me the way no man has been able to touch me before."

He smiled. "Oh, that guy."

"What guy?"

"The perfect man. He doesn't exist."

She returned his smile. "Nor does that perfect woman you're looking for."

"We're both alike, Grace. Looking for something or someone who can't be found."

"So what do we do about that?"

God she was beautiful. Her hair shined like blue-black magic in the lights from the strip. The silk of her skirt and top clung to her body like shrink-wrap, molding to her breasts and hips. He wanted a taste, a touch, to sink inside her and see if she held the magic key to what was missing in his life. He hadn't felt this comfortable with a woman in too long.

Or maybe he just wanted to avoid what was going on downstairs. Maybe it didn't have the allure he thought it would. In that, he'd been honest with her.

What he really wanted to explore was sitting right next to him. Grace had fired his engines in a big way. Her intellect, her free spirit, her honesty and her beauty—all of them intrigued him more than any woman had in a long time.

"One night. Give me one night with you. No promises other than enjoying each other."

"We both know we're not going to find what we're looking for," she said, her gaze betraying nothing of her emotions at the moment.

"I know, but I like being with you. Isn't that enough?"

"Is it?"

"I've been honest with you, Grace. That's really all I can offer."

He watched her face as she absorbed his words, wondering if she'd toss him out and deny him, and herself, a chance for a night together. She knew him. Okay, that was wrong. She didn't know *him*, but he figured she knew hundreds of guys just like him. Men who'd had lots of women. She probably thought he was looking at her as just another conquest.

When he first came here tonight that's exactly what she'd been. Another challenge. But she'd rocked him back on his heels and gut punched everything he thought he wanted. She saw right through his bullshit. He needed a woman like that.

She stood. "Let's just take this slow, see how things go."

He nodded, instinctively understanding that was important to her. "However you want to set the ground rules."

"I don't really like rules, per se . . . and I haven't said yes to anything yet."

Her voice had gone smoky and the atmosphere in the room changed in an instant. From polite conversation to something more elemental—something definitely darker, with more promise.

"I think I want you to sit over there—in that chair." She motioned with her head to the black leather chair directly across from her.

Mike moved, sat down and placed his arms on the chair, keeping his gaze riveted on Grace. She moved to the other side of the room and flipped a switch, filling the room with soft, sexy jazz music, then headed back toward him, all long limbs and polished refinement. Even in the way she walked, she hitched his pulse up a notch. Nothing hurried, nothing hesitant in her movements. She stopped a foot in front of him and parted her legs.

"Don't move. Don't get up and don't touch me unless I ask you to."

"However you want it." His cock twitched in anticipation of what was to come. His heart began to pump a fast beat and the room grew warmer. He didn't know what kind of game she was gearing up to play, but he was definitely all in.

"People rush into sex, as if fucking is the grand prize," she started. "No one takes the time for mystery, for teasing or seduction. All the joy leading up to sex has gone by the wayside, and it's such a shame, because the buildup can be as intense as the act itself."

She sucked her bottom lip between her teeth and smoothed her hands up her arms, then across her neck and collarbone. Light, fingertip touches, avoiding her breasts. Slow and easy, like an exploration. Mike took a breath, waiting for her to fondle herself, to caress the hard points of her nipples peeking through the thin silk of her blouse. *He* knew she wanted to touch them. *He* wanted to touch them, could almost feel the tight buds between his fingers. Instead, she skimmed her hands down over her waist.

"The fine art of taking one's time in pleasing a lover has been lost in the haste for ultimate satisfaction. We forget to simply touch, breathe, watch."

Mike was definitely watching. Riveted, wondering what she was going to do next. A slow dance of seduction so unlike what he was used to with sex. Grace was right. It was usually a rush of mouths and hands and bodies tangling together—a race to penetration and orgasm. There was no time taken to explore. No agonizing temptation. Nothing like what he was forced to endure as she skimmed her hand across her ribcage, then dipped it inside her skirt.

Her eyelids fluttered closed as she found the target. Still clothed, all he could do was envision her hand covering her pussy. Was she bare down there or was there a tuft of dark hair over her mound? Would she glisten completely naked under his gaze, her body open and bare in the moonlight?

He'd never been so desperate to see before.

But he could smell her. All woman. He took a deep breath. She was so close he picked up the scent of her musky, deep desire.

"Ahh," she moaned. "So warm. My skin is soft, wet, aching for touch. My pussy quivers in anticipation of a climax." She opened her eyes and met his gaze. "I need to come, Mike."

She felt everything. He could only imagine, and his synapses were firing overtime. All he could see was her hand moving up and down under her skirt. It was driving him crazy. He wanted to lean her back against the couch, lift her silk skirt and plant his mouth over her steaming cunt, then lick her until she screamed, flooding his mouth with her come.

But this was her game, and she was in charge. It would be so easy to take his cock out and jack off watching her, but he wanted this to be for her. He wanted her to be the center of attention and no matter how rock hard his dick got, no matter how tightly his balls knotted up, he wasn't going to get off. Not yet, anyway.

That was going to happen later, when he was inside her. So he was just going to have to grip the edge of the chair with both hands and ride this out for as long as it took. Or as long as she took. And frankly, drinking in the sight of her, watching her move her hand farther down between her legs, not being able to see but knowing exactly what she was doing . . .

It was insane. Fucking hot and crazy. He'd wanted to do something he'd never done before? This was it. This wasn't "Get down to it and fuck hard." It wasn't "Do it ten different ways upside down or hanging from the ceiling." This was slow seduction. A woman who knew her body and how to pleasure herself and her man. A torturous tease, fully clothed.

Yeah, he'd never had it like this before. He dug his fingers into the thick leather chair and hung on for the ride. Her face flushed, the lights from the city casting her in a blue glow as she moved her hips in a sinuous rhythm to the slow, rhythmic jazz playing on the radio. She was like a classy stripper, only no clothes were coming off and it was driving him to the brink. She taunted him with what he couldn't see—just the stroking movements of her hand under her skirt.

But then he heard it—the sound of her fingers slipping inside her pussy. Wet, sucking sounds as she fucked herself, followed by her low moan.

Fuck!

"Do you hear it?" she asked, her voice tight with strain.

"Yes."

"My pussy's so wet, Mike."

"Tell me how many fingers you have inside yourself."

"Two. It feels so good. Oh, it feels so damn good."

Her lips were parted and she was breathing through her mouth now. Panting, actually. He wanted to be where she was. He wanted his fingers inside her, making her feel that good. He wasn't sure he'd ever wanted anything more in his life.

The undulations under her skirt grew faster. She tucked her other hand in her skirt, then shifted her hips forward.

"My clit's swollen."

"Tell me what you're doing." He had to know. His cock was near bursting. He'd never felt such pain before, so much excitement.

"Fucking myself. One hand. Rubbing my clit with the other."

She could barely speak through her panting breaths now. He found himself fighting for breath, too, as he watched her, forcing himself to keep his seat instead of leaping out of it to tear her skirt away and bury his face in her pussy. The scent of her was driving him mad. He hadn't come in his pants since he was a kid, but she was bringing him pretty close.

"Oh, oh, God I need to—"

"Do it, Grace. Come for me." He couldn't wait one more goddamn minute, and if she didn't have an orgasm soon, he wasn't sure he could hold to his part of the bargain.

She squeezed her eyes shut, tilted her head back and let out a cry as she released, her hands moving fast and furious under her skirt. Mike drank in every sound, every jerk her body made as she shuddered and moaned through her climax. It was amazing, ratcheting up his excitement like nothing he'd ever seen.

When she was finished she opened her eyes and looked at him, pulled her hands out of her skirt and licked her lips, blowing out a deep breath.

"Wow," she whispered, then sat on the couch and dipped her chin to her chest. She was still panting.

He was still hard. Aching, painfully hard.

And in awe of a woman who could make him feel things he hadn't felt in far too long. He moved out of his chair and next to her, lifting her hand and bringing it to his lips. The scent of her pussy was all over her. Sweet, musky, driving into his senses and wrapping around his brain.

He kissed her hand, licked her fingertips. Sweet, salty flavor on his tongue as he sucked each digit into his mouth. She didn't take her gaze from his lips as he licked her clean, her violet eyes going dark as she watched him.

"You were incredible," he finally said. "I've never experienced anything like it."

Her gaze drifted to his lap, where the outline of his swollen cock was more than evident against his jeans. He was big. Really big. It wasn't like he could hide it. He'd been teased about the Nottingham Monster ever since he hit puberty. After a while the teasing became admiration from women, jealousy from other guys.

Her eyes widened before moving back up to his face.

"I've never done that for a man before."

He arched a brow. "Seriously?"

"I don't lie, Mike. Especially about sex."

"Then, thank you. Because I really enjoyed it. I've never seen anything so hot."

She tilted her head, her expression skeptical. "With your kind of experience? I find that hard to believe."

He still had hold of her hand and placed it over his throbbing shaft. "Experience has nothing to do with turn-ons, Grace. Experience has nothing to do with finding something new and exciting that gives you a rush. You've been around the block a few times. You should know that.

"What you did just now made me so goddamn hot I almost came without touching myself. I'm so hard right now it hurts. Feel me. I'm hot, I'm aching and I need you. And I'm not lying about that."

FOUR

Grace hadn't intended to put on that show of masturbation. She hadn't planned for any of this to happen, but it had. And now that it had, she wanted more.

She laid her palm over the rigid length of Mike's sizeable cock, feeling the sweet slide of wetness between her legs in response. Masturbating for him had been an incredible experience and brought about an orgasm so intense she could barely remain standing through it. She hadn't come that hard in far too long.

But it had been all her. Mike's restraint amazed her. He hadn't leaped out of the chair to join in. He didn't even unzip his pants to jack off. He'd just watched. And that was the biggest turn-on of all. She got off on his hot eyes, the way he followed the movements of her hand. He wasn't out for himself—he was invested in her pleasure, in her orgasm. She'd never enjoyed teasing a man so much, had never become so aroused pleasuring herself—both for her own benefit and for someone else's.

And now that she had, she could well imagine his patience had worn thin. His cock was steel beneath the denim of his jeans, pulsing and rigid and hot. He was ready for a good fuck. Hard and deep and fast. Probably right here on the couch and right now.

She couldn't really blame him, since she'd teased him so badly.

"I know what you're thinking," he said.

Her gaze swept from his shaft to his eyes. "You do?"

He nodded. "Yeah."

"Okay. Tell me what I'm thinking."

"I'd wager the men you meet want to fuck you long and hard. When they get a chance with you, they want to assure you they're the best the fuck you've ever had."

She resisted the laugh bubbling up in the back of her throat. "Uh, you might be right about that." Actually, that was exactly what happened with most men she met at the club. That's why she rarely selected strangers and kept to men she knew, men she could count on to give her the release she needed, then discreetly leave. She didn't have time for he-men shows of prowess.

"I don't think that's what you need."

"You don't."

He shook his head and stood, reaching for her hand. "No."

Curious as to what he thought she did need, she slipped her hand in his and allowed him to pull her to her feet.

"Show me to your bedroom."

Bedroom? Now that was a first. She'd been taken on the couch, bent over by the window, on the kitchen counter and table, on the floor and across the coffee table—typically anywhere *but* the bedroom. In fact, if a helicopter from the *National Enquirer* were hovering by her picture window while she was being fucked, snapping photos for the next cover story, that would make the men who screwed her ecstatic. She was, after all, a prize and had to be shown off.

Her bedroom was her private sanctuary. She couldn't remember the last time she'd actually had a man in there. Entertaining was usually done in the living room, even with the men she knew. Yet she found herself leading Mike down the hallway to the double doors to her bedroom.

He opened them and pulled her inside, flipping on the light.

"King-size bed?"

"Yeah. Just in case I want to have two or three people in the bed with me."

He arched a brow, then laughed. Okay, so he doubted she was serious about that. He was right—she wasn't. For someone who enjoyed sex as much as she did, or at least as much as she had over the past years, she really hadn't had much lately.

Burnout. That had to be it. Too much stimulation for too long. Just like Mike had said—she'd seen it all, done it all, and it had lost its allure.

So why was the simple act of holding Mike's hand making her toes curl? Why, when he dragged her against his chest, did her heart slam against her ribs? She was hardly new at this seduction thing. Yet feeling her body pressed to his made her nipples harden and her breath catch. Being in his arms felt . . . right, felt good, stirred her into a rippling awareness of every movement, every touch of his fingers along her back.

Why did the simple scent of his soap cause her senses to go haywire?

Why did she feel a rush of panic when he bent his lips to hers? Because this wasn't scripted, because she didn't know exactly what was going to happen and how? Because so far tonight Mike Nottingham had proven to be anything *but* predictable?

The brush of his mouth was a slow assault, not at all what she was used to. It wasn't an attack, it was sweet. Just a whisper of a kiss—meant to entice, not ravage. He paused, his breath warm against her lips. It was a question. Mike was asking, not taking, placing the onus on her to make the decision whether to go further or put the brakes on.

A millisecond of indecision crossed her mind. The way he made her feel was dangerous. She could stop and they could simply talk. She enjoyed talking to him.

But why? When she'd wanted sex with a man before, she'd had it. She'd never been afraid of her feelings. Mike was a stranger. An attractive, sexy, compelling man, but not one she intended to see beyond tonight. So why wouldn't she indulge her desires?

She moved in and breached that last inch separating them, giving him her answer with a contented sigh into his open mouth. His lips were full and parted farther as she pressed her mouth over his.

Grace kept waiting for him to tighten his hold over her, to slam her into the wall or pull her skirt up to slide his hand over her pussy or throw her onto the bed so he could press into her. He did none of those things. Instead, he rubbed his hands over her back, massaging the muscles there in light circles, his mouth doing slow, gentle, magical things with his kiss.

He was tender, taking his time, enthralling her with a kiss unlike anything she could remember experiencing. Her sex life was about driving lust and hard passion—not this slow, exquisite seduction of her senses. The men she was used to taking to her bed gave her fast, intense fucks and quick orgasms—Mike didn't seem to be in any hurry to touch her breasts or insinuate himself between her legs.

But she was pulsing everywhere. Her nipples were tight and hot and aching and her pussy quivered in anticipation.

And still, he kissed her, notching her arousal to a fevered frenzy. She clutched his arms and dug her nails in, licking at his tongue as he lazily continued mapping her body with caresses.

She finally couldn't stand it and tore her mouth away. She leaned back and searched his face, confused by this languorous journey he was taking her on.

"Mike."

"Yes."

"What are you doing?"

Now that she was arched backward in his arms, he swept his palm up her belly and ribs, letting his hand come to rest under her breast. Her heart pounded against his fingers. "I'm touching you. Do you know how good your body feels against my hand?"

"Uh, no." But she knew how damn good it felt to be touched by him. So why was she about to complain? Because he wasn't throwing her down and shoving his cock inside her? What was wrong with her?

"Relax, Grace. We have all night."

She sucked in a breath. Relax. Right. She should do that. Stop thinking about past experiences and enjoy the journey.

But somewhere along the way she'd lost control of the situation. Mike had taken the reins and he was in charge now. Not that she was uncomfortable. Well, she was uncomfortable. Profoundly uncomfortable. But in an aroused, delicious, swept-away kind of way.

She gasped when he picked her up and cradled her against his chest. That she hadn't expected. He made her feel fragile, womanly— cared for. As if she would break if he manhandled her too roughly. He carried her to the bed and deposited her in the center.

Now they were getting somewhere. Now they were getting to the disrobing, and inserting of peg A into slot B. The fun part. The part where she got to feel that huge cock of his in her pussy. The part where she came. And he came.

Except Mike wasn't taking his clothes off. He didn't remove his shirt and jeans, just kicked off his shoes and climbed onto the bed, lying down on his side next to her. He palmed her neck and leaned over her, then started kissing her again, the same kind of oh-my-God intense, slow, incredibly soft kisses that made her insides turn to melted butter. The kind of kisses that made her think about jumping on top of him, unzipping his pants and impaling herself on his cock, then rubbing her clit against his hard flesh until she screamed.

She whimpered against his lips and started a half turn so she could grab him and inch closer, but he planted his hand on her belly and kept her pinned on her back.

"Stay there. I want to undress you."

Used to being more of a participant in sex, she plucked at his fingers. Mike laughed and held his hand firmly on her stomach. "Grace. Let me."

His deep voice was a command, not a request. She stopped struggling, giving herself up to the sensation of his hand gliding along her hip. He bunched the material of her skirt in his hand and pulled, raising her dress. Cool air breezed across her skin. She shivered at the dark look in his eyes as her flesh was revealed—first her thighs, then the panties covering her sex.

Once again he surprised her. He looked hungry, his jaw clenched tight like an animal ready to pounce. She thought he'd touch her pussy. He didn't. Just raised her dress and stared at her body, then looked at her face and kissed her again, taking her to that blissful place that was both agony and ecstasy. She felt his hand at her chest, undoing the buttons of her blouse. Slow, unbearably slow, he unbuttoned her, then pulled aside the silk, baring her breasts. She wore only an underwire bra, but no cups.

"Damn, that's sexy." His warm breath sailed across her breast, puckering her nipple.

She shuddered, then cried out when he covered the bud with his lips, sucking the tip between his teeth. With a gentle tug, he pulled her nipple into his mouth, then bathed it with his tongue. Over and over again, like his kisses, loving her nipple, then covering her breast with his hand.

Grace had very small breasts—not the kind men usually went crazy over. But Mike was paying very thorough attention to them. He took her to the peak of torment by licking and sucking one, then did the same thing to the other, his dark head bent over her as he focused his attention on each nipple until she arched her back to feed them to him.

When he finally raised his head, she lifted herself up on her elbows, both her nipples erect, wet points, aching with pleasurable tenderness. Her pussy was wet and throbbing and she hoped he planned to fuck her soon because she was about to self combust.

"I want you naked," was all he said, his lips curling in a hint of a smile.

He lifted her and pulled her blouse off, unhooked her bra and tossed both garments onto a nearby chair. Then he pushed her back onto the mattress and slipped his hand under her to pull her skirt off, taking his time to draw the silk down her legs. He followed the fabric, moving between her legs and spreading them, then staring at her again.

Still, he was fully clothed and she wore only her black panties.

"You have an incredibly beautiful body."

"Thank you." For heaven's sake, she was blushing! She felt the heat creep into her face and couldn't believe it. She never blushed. Though she hardly considered herself gorgeous, she knew she had pretty hair and unusual violet eyes, which more than made up for her small breasts and lack of curves. She'd long ago accepted that she wasn't hideous but she was no raving beauty. Yet, the way Mike looked at her made her feel like the most beautiful woman in the world. And that was an incredibly heady feeling.

"I'll bet your pussy is as pretty as the rest of you." He slipped his fingers under the skimpy strings at her hips and drew the panties down, but only part way. She lifted, wanting to help him, willing to do anything to get naked, then to get him naked, but he was bound and determined, obviously, to do this his way. He leaned in and pressed a kiss to her hipbone.

Could a woman die from arousal? From an overabundance of stimulation? Because it was happening. His mouth was . . . right there . . . so close and yet he was teasing her with soft kisses to her belly, her hips, dragging her panties down an inch at a time.

"Mike, please." She couldn't breathe. She was getting light-headed. She wished she was stronger because she swore she'd flip him onto his back and rape him at this point. A quick glance between his legs told her his erection was still there. Oh, man, was it still there.

"Please what, darlin'?"

His words, mumbled against her inner thigh. So close she could feel his breath at her pussy. So close, if he flicked his tongue out he'd touch her there. She'd go off in a heartbeat if he did.

She couldn't even answer him. He knew what she wanted, what she was asking for. She didn't have to tell him.

"God, you smell good," he said, taking her panties down another inch.

She was dying. Really dying this time, because he kissed right above her sex, and she prayed he was going to move down, follow the trail of her panties.

"Why are you doing this?" She didn't realize until he stilled that she'd said the words aloud.

"Because you deserve it."

She wasn't sure if it was a compliment or not, because at the moment she felt tortured, as if she were enduring some kind of punishment. Was he doing this because she'd teased him by touching herself and not letting him see?

Or was she just so lost in desire she was no longer rational?

Honestly, she didn't know.

But when she felt cool air waft across her clit, she no longer cared. She was bare, and he was pulling her panties down, leaving them at her thighs, but that was fine. Her sex was naked and his mouth was there—right there, and her gaze was riveted as he pressed a kiss to her pussy. Her clit quivered, her sex on fire as she poised, waited and watched.

Then his mouth covered her clit and she couldn't help the strangled cry that fell from her lips. She'd never felt anything so good.

He sucked her clit and licked it at the same time, rolling his tongue over the throbbing bud with a wet heat that sent her skyrocketing into orgasm. Her eyes widened and she gasped, shocked at the lightning bolt zapping her insides into molten lava. How could he do this to her? How could he make her feel this crashing pleasure with soft kisses and gentle tugs on her clit? It never happened like this. But, oh God, it was happening now.

She came fast. Her climax caught her unprepared and she grabbed on to his hair and pulled him against her, lifting her hips and letting out moans she couldn't control. He moved down to suck at her pussy, sliding his tongue inside to lap at the juices that seeped from her. Pulses quivered inside her long after that initial rush. She didn't even have time to come down from that first orgasm before he had her heated up and climbing again, his tongue like liquid heat and moving all over her, lapping her up from one end to the other.

He was a magic man, a sorcerer, and she gave herself up to him, relaxing the tension that had taken hold of her, letting the questions about him, about herself, fly away. She was going to have what she wanted with Mike tonight, and not think about anything else.

"Again," she begged, lifting her hips, demanding more of his mouth against her, his tongue pleasuring her.

But she didn't just get his mouth. She felt his fingers along her pussy lips and then inside her. One, then two. Not hard, but gentle, sliding inside her with a soft, rhythmic motion as he sucked her clit.

Yeah, he was magic all right. She closed her eyes and absorbed the sensations, letting him lead her to a shuddering climax again. When she went, her pussy gripped his fingers in a tight vise and she rocked against them, unabashedly enjoying the place he'd taken her to.

Grace couldn't wait to take his thick cock inside her.

She was ready to be fucked.

FIVE

Restraint wasn't a big word in Mike's vocabulary. Nor was it something he'd ever consider a huge turn-on, unless it meant silk scarves used to tie a woman to his bed while he pleasured her.

But restraining his baser urges and focusing his attention on making sex good for Grace was more arousing than he imagined.

From the moment she let him into her bedroom, he'd wanted to strip her and fuck her. But he knew, just knew, that's what every guy did to her. And he didn't want to be like the other guys. He didn't want to toss her on the bed, raise her skirt and drive his cock hard inside her. Well, he did. He really did. But something stopped him.

Why her pleasure was suddenly more important than his own was a freaking mystery he wasn't about to delve into tonight. Poking at his psyche wasn't his favorite pastime. In fact, he typically avoided it like a plague.

But her response was an incredible reward. He'd never been so invested in a woman's orgasm like he'd been in Grace's. Hearing her, feeling her, tasting her, had made him harder than watching her masturbate. It had spurred him on to take her there again and again. And now she was spread out before him, ready for more.

If he had to wait one more minute to be inside her he was going to explode. He jumped off the bed and pulled his shirt over his head, then yanked the zipper of his jeans down. The way she watched him made his cock press up against the already too-tight denim, made it hard to jerk them down over his erection. It sprang out, hot and hard and pointing right at her. Her eyes widened, like most women's did when faced with the size of him.

She was so tiny. Could she take him? God, he hoped so. If she backed away now he might actually break down and cry like a baby. He'd been hard for more than an hour and his balls were drawn tight and ready to explode. He crawled up beside her, staying on his knees, waiting for her reaction.

She sat up and wrapped both hands around him. He sucked in a breath as she stroked him, the softness of her palms like a balm to his tortured flesh. Her hands were so small, just like the rest of her. She made him feel like a giant.

Yet she knew what she was doing, rolling her hands over each other, squeezing the wide crest of his dick, then gliding her thumb across it in such a gentle way it made him shudder. Drops of pearly liquid oozed from the tip and she played with them, sliding her fingers through the silken fluid. She lifted her fingers to her mouth and tasted him, making a sound of contentment in the back of her throat that nearly caused him to erupt in her hand.

He pulled her hands away, had to stop her before he finished right there, just like that, with her touching him as if she were worshipping an idol.

He leaned onto the floor and grabbed for a condom package out of his jeans, tearing it open and taking care of business. She was waiting for him, feet planted on the bed and legs parted.

She had the prettiest damn pussy he'd ever seen. Bare, smooth as the silk she'd been wearing. He wanted to bend down and taste her again, but the need to be inside her outweighed the urge to suck on her clit until she screamed for him again.

Now he had to force himself to hold back, to take it slow, so he didn't hurt her. No acrobatics, no slamming into her, no acting like all those men she'd had before.

As much as he was aching, this was for Grace.

He pressed down on top of her, careful to keep his weight off her slender frame. His cock nestled along her bare sex, his balls riding in the cleft of her pussy. He surged forward, wanting to tease her a bit, to make sure she was fully ready for him before he filled her.

He took her mouth. Could he ever get enough of the taste of her? The brandy lingered, spicy and hot on her mouth. He sucked her tongue, then licked the soft velvet recesses until she whimpered, arching against him in a wordless plea.

Oh, he liked that. Her begging for his cock. He liked her wanting it as much as he did.

She pulled her lips away and leaned back, searching his face, her eyes drugged with passion.

"Mike."

"Yeah, darlin'?"

"Don't you think we've waited long enough?"

She gripped his arms, raking her nails down his skin. Dug them into his flesh. It felt good, gave him chills. The kind that made his cock lurch forward against her. She let out a gasp and surged up, trying to capture his dick.

"Yeah, I think we have waited long enough." Though he'd damn well enjoyed the tease. More than he'd ever thought possible. He lifted, positioned his cock head between her pussy lips and pushed in, just a little, watching for signs that it was too much for her. She sucked him in like a vortex of wet heat. Too good. Too damn good.

"More," she said, her breath warm against his cheek. He turned to her, watching her eyes, looking for hesitation, for anything that would tell him this wasn't what she wanted. All he saw was glittering desire and need.

He drove forward another inch, feeling her pussy lips spread, her body a heated welcome. God, she was so fucking tight, squeezing him past the point of endurance. Sweat broke out on his brow as he surged farther and her cunt pulsed around him, wetness seeping from her and onto his thighs. He stilled, waiting for her to adjust.

Grace frowned, pulling at him. "Stop that."

He knew it, knew he was going to be too big for her. He started to withdraw, but she dug her nails into his forearm.

"Don't you dare pull out," she said.

"You told me to stop."

With a disgusted sigh, she said, "Stop going so slow. I'm not going to break."

"I'm big."

"I noticed."

He felt the pulses of her pussy in response.

"I can handle you."

With a low growl, he let loose the last of his restraint and thrust forward. She was right. She was wet and more than able to take all of him.

She moaned, lifted, her pussy gripping him so tight he knew he wasn't going to last long. And for a man who prided himself on control, that was a damn hard truth to admit to himself. But he'd held out as long as he could; his balls ached, filled with come and ready to erupt. Grace's pussy was small and tight and with every thrust it clenched his cock in a stranglehold of sensation, her whimpers and moans increasing in intensity, demanding he give her more.

Still, he made love to her slow and easy, kissing her while he fucked her, licking at her tongue as he rubbed the tight little bud of her clit with the top of his dick. She was going to get off again before he let go, no matter what kind of agony it cost him.

She whimpered again, the begging little sound driving into his brain and making his cock harden more. He pumped long, even strokes into her, stilling to feel her quiver around him, then moved again. She tore her mouth from his and panted.

"Goddamn you, Mike, don't do this to me."

He smiled, kissed his way down her jaw and along her neck, licking at the pulse point there while he gathered her ass cheeks in his hands to draw her closer, wanting her clit tight up against his body while he rocked against her. He wasn't going to answer her—he knew what she needed.

"Oh God, yes," she said, her voice deep and gravely as she matched each thrust with raised hips and her nails along his back.

He lifted his head and looked at her, wanting to watch her when she came. Surprisingly, her eyes were open, too, the purple so dark it was almost black.

"I'm coming," she whispered, tightening her legs around him.

He gripped her ass and pulled harder, trying to crawl deeper inside her as she catapulted into her orgasm, her eyes widening. She screamed, her mouth wide open as she let loose the most beautiful cries he'd ever heard. He couldn't hold back then as an orgasm ripped from his spine and carried him along with her, emptying him from the inside out with shuddering, groaning pulses that poured out in waves of pounding pleasure.

He lifted the top half of his body off her, certain she couldn't breathe. She'd closed her eyes and lay there, panting. When she swept her lids open and smiled at him, he felt such relief he couldn't fathom it.

He held her for a while, stroking her, unable to get enough of the silken feel of her skin against his hands or the unique scent of her. He closed his eyes and breathed her in while they lay there together. She stayed quiet and seemed content to let him explore her arms, her ribcage, the soft swell of her hip and thigh. Her breathing was deep and even and he was going to enjoy savoring this while he could.

Finally, he rolled off and stepped into the bathroom, turning on the light and dragging his hand through his hair as he looked at himself in the mirror. He shook his head, pondering the change in him.

Different. It had been different with Grace. And that's all he wanted to think about right now. Anything else would have to wait.

He finished up and shut the light off, then crawled back into bed, pulling her toward him so her back was against his chest. Her deep, rhythmic breathing told him she was utterly relaxed. He ran his hand along her arm, her hip, then back up her ribs to cup her breast. He traced her nipple with his thumb, smiling when it hardened.

"Surely you couldn't possibly have any energy left," she said.

"You'd be surprised." He could fuck her all night. Being inside her had felt perfect. And it had energized him. Sex was rarely exhausting.

"You've done all the work. You should be tired."

He laughed. "Are you tired?"

She flipped over to face him and slid her hand around his rapidly hardening cock. "Is that a challenge?"

"It might be."

With a gentle push, he was on his back and she was on top of him, straddling him. Now there was a beautiful sight. Small, upturned breasts glowing in the light filtering in from the windows, her body bathed in the pink afterglow of their lovemaking, her lips puffy from his kisses and her hair messy and tousled from his hands in it.

He was fully hard now and she rocked against his erection with a devilish smile.

"I hope you can go without sleep then, Mike, because I never back down from a challenge."

At six a.m. Grace rolled over with a groan and cursed the red lights on her clock, wishing she could turn back time about nine or ten hours. Because that's when her bad decision-making had begun.

And it hadn't ended, because Mike was still in her bed. She flipped over and stared at his sleeping form, as alien to her as if she'd found a little green man from Mars sleeping next to her this morning.

She shook her head and crept out of bed, slipping into the bathroom as quietly as she could. She needed a shower and some time alone to think. Flipping on the faucet, she stepped inside the stall and let the steamy hot water pour over her head.

What had she done? Where had her mind gone, besides totally insane?

Men did not spend the night with her. Ever. Even men she knew. There was sex, and then they were gone. Grace slept alone, every single night. She always had.

Last night was the first time she'd slept with a man at her side, in her bed. She'd woken this morning snuggled against Mike, his arms wrapped tightly around her.

The worst thing about it was, it had felt like waking in heaven. She'd felt safe and protected.

And she'd never been so terrified. She'd been so careful with her life, keeping barriers between her professional life and personal one. When she occasionally chose men for sex play, she rarely brought them upstairs to her private quarters, and never, ever let someone into her bedroom.

Not to mention waking up in a man's arms.

Last night she'd broken every single one of her personal no-nos.

So why now and why with Mike Nottingham? What made him so different, so special, that she'd done every single thing she swore she'd never do?

She grabbed her shampoo and washed her hair, trying to reason it out while she scrubbed. Something happened that had never happened before—she'd lost control. She was always in charge of the night, of the situation, of the sex—everything. And last night Mike had taken over, and she had let him. Worse, she'd enjoyed letting him.

Squeezing her eyes shut, she rinsed shampoo from her hair, then applied conditioner and let it sit while she soaped her body and shaved her legs, pondering her dilemma. The problem with Mike was he was so different from the other men she knew. The ballsy braggarts, the ones who claimed they could take her to heaven and back and fuck her like she'd never been fucked before . . . those guys she could deal with because she was used to them. Someone like Mike—quiet, unassuming, but who really did take her to heaven and back by giving her the best sex of her life—and not by fucking her brains out, but by honest to God great lovemaking—he scared the beejeebers out of her.

Because she could care about a guy like him. A genuine, honest, sexy, dominant, alpha, hardworking, gorgeous, real man. There didn't seem to be anything phony about him. He was what he was, he made her feel magical, and just thinking about him made her toes curl, her nipples tighten and her pussy quiver.

God almighty, she had to get him out of her house in a hurry. Too much was at stake. Wild Nights was her baby, her life, everything she'd worked her ass off for. No man was going to insinuate his way into her heart and screw everything up. No man was going to make her start thinking about how lonely she'd been all these years and how nice it was not to wake up alone. No man was going to make her rethink her priorities. Oh no. She so wasn't going there. She'd been fine on her own since she was eighteen, and she'd continue to be okay without Mike Nottingham.

She finished rinsing and shut the shower off, grabbed a towel and stepped out, furiously drying herself as if she could somehow erase every trace of his touch from her body.

Okay, so maybe she'd blown all of this out of proportion. Mike was a great fuck and he wasn't the first or the last of those. He was nothing, really. And she felt nothing out of the ordinary for him. The fact that he was still here meant nothing. A momentary lapse in judgment. A quirk. An anomaly.

Until the bathroom door opened and he stepped in. All six foot something of him, naked, erect and looking sleepy, his thick, dark hair messy, with a goofy smile on his face and his deep blue eyes staring down at her in a sexy-as-hell manner that made her throat dry up.

"Mornin'," he said. "Hope I'm not in your way."

"Not at all," she managed, squeaking by him to finish drying off in her bedroom. Avoidance was good, since she wasn't prepared for her reaction to him.

Okay, so maybe she was affected just a bit.

Or a lot. Like one look at him and her heart was pounding, her pulse was racing and everything feminine in her body was screaming *Let's repeat last night all over again.*

Yeah, he had to go. Right now.

SIX

Mike took a quick shower, figuring Grace wouldn't mind. While in there, he noticed all the little doodads she used to make herself clean and pretty. Lotions and scrubby things and the like. The whole room smelled like her. Her soap, her shampoo, everything about her scent lingered in the expansive tile and glass stall. It made him want to hurry back to her, to bury his nose in her hair, inhale the woman, press his lips to her warm flesh and taste her again. His cock rose and swelled, thick with anticipation.

He rinsed and dried off, then padded into her bedroom to find her already dressed. He masked his disappointment with a smile.

So much for morning sex. He wished he'd gotten up before she had. He'd have liked to pull her under him first thing this morning. He'd woken up hard and aching, needing to be inside her again. As if the five times they'd done it last night—damn near all night, in fact—hadn't been enough.

And here he was, wandering around with an erection again. He wondered if he'd be forever hard around her.

She was wearing jeans and a red turtleneck sweater, her hair still damp. She looked fresh and very young without her makeup on. His cock twitched and her gaze drifted from his face to between his legs.

"Sorry, can't seem to help that around you."

"It's quite all right. I'd hardly find your erection insulting."

Her tight smile was anything but genuine. Something was wrong. He pulled on his jeans and tried to wrestle his unruly dick under control. "Would you like to go out for breakfast?"

She looked like he'd just asked her to witness open brain surgery. In fact, he was certain there was a green tinge to her face. She actually looked nauseous. "Uh, I can't. I have appointments. But thanks for asking."

He pulled on his shirt and sat on the bed to put on his shoes. "How about lunch?"

"I'm pretty busy the whole day."

She was a really bad liar. "Too bad. Dinner before the club opens tonight?"

"Oh, I couldn't possibly. I have to, um, go over supply and liquor orders with the managers before opening tonight. We're woefully behind on inventory and I don't want to run out."

Uh-huh. He sat up and stared at her. So, this was what getting dumped felt like. A strange and new sensation to be on the receiving end, since he was typically the one with all the excuses why he couldn't see a woman again.

Grace was giving him the brush-off. Clearly doing her level best to let him down easy.

Didn't it just figure? He'd found a woman he enjoyed and really wanted to see again. A woman he could actually see himself with—whether on a permanent basis, it was too early to tell, but he wanted to see her beyond just sex. He wanted to date her, to have meals together, take in the sights, go to the movies, just spend time with her. He wanted to see where things went.

And she didn't want to give him the goddamn time of day.

"I'd better get out of here, then, and let you start your day." He walked toward her, brushed her cheeks with a soft kiss, and grasped her arms to pull her close. "Thank you for last night," he whispered in her ear.

Her gaze darted up to his, her eyes so beautiful she took his breath away. The wariness in them intrigued him.

"You're welcome. I enjoyed it."

He wanted to stay, to kiss those incredibly kissable lips of hers. He wanted to convince her, to make her change her mind. But he didn't. He wasn't stupid. He turned away and walked to the elevator, pressed the button and, without a word, let himself out the door.

He wasn't about to give up though. Mike had glimpsed something in Grace's eyes—fear. Something about him scared her, and maybe that was a bad thing. But maybe that was a good thing, because he hadn't actually done anything to frighten her. If her fear was because she felt something between them, then that was definitely a good thing.

Still, it rankled that she'd hustled him out the door. He was always the one who ended things with a woman. Okay, he had a little finesse. He didn't intentionally set out to hurt a woman's feelings, and typically he let them know from the start that he had no desire for a relationship beyond one night or two, that he wasn't a settling down kind of guy. And if they didn't buy into it, if a woman thought she would change him or could prolong the attachment longer than he was interested in, then they got dumped in a hurry and he did it in a cold and heartless way. Because he was honest and there was no sense dragging out the inevitable.

Is that what Grace was doing? Cutting things off clean and quick so she didn't hurt his feelings? Making sure she didn't lead him on?

It felt shitty. Hell of a time for a rousing case of gut-wrenching empathy for all the women he'd done the same thing to.

Nevertheless, he knew the difference between someone who wasn't interested and someone who was.

Grace was interested. There was fire between them. Fire enough to give it one more shot, anyway. He wasn't a dumbass and he sure as hell wasn't a stalker. If she balked again and showed him the door, if she sent out clear signals that there was no chemistry between them, then he'd grab a clue and hightail it out of there.

But until then, he wasn't about to give up. Not when there was something he wanted.

And what he wanted was Grace.

So he needed a plan. And that meant he wasn't going to go back to the club tonight. He didn't want Grace to feel pressured. He'd wait until tomorrow night.

Mike returned to his hotel and made a few business calls, did some paperwork, then called Denver. He spent the afternoon and into the night hanging out with Denver at one of the casinos, losing more money at gambling than he really wanted to. But he wasn't focused, his thoughts centered more on Grace than on the cards in front of him.

"You're usually better at this," Den said when Mike lost yet another hand at blackjack. "In fact, you're typically pretty damn good. Right now you suck donkey dick."

Mike pushed back from the table and Den followed him to the bar. "Not my lucky day, I guess." He hoped his run of bad luck didn't continue, and he didn't mean at cards.

When the waitress brought them drinks, Den took a long swallow and squinted. "You went to Wild Nights last night. How did that go?"

"Good." Mike downed his whiskey in two short gulps and signaled the waitress for another.

"Good. That's all you're going to tell me? Details, man," Den said, laughing. "I need more than that."

Mike stared into his empty glass. "Nothing much to tell, really."

"You didn't."

Mike looked up. "Didn't what?"

"Last night. At the club. You fucked Grace, didn't you?"

He shook his head. "I don't want to talk about it."

"Don't give me that coy shit. That's something a woman would say. Tell me."

"I said I don't want to talk about it."

"Christ, Mike, what the fuck is wrong with you?"

What the fuck *was* wrong with him? He and Denver had shared more than just talk about women. They'd shared women. And Mike never cared before whether he kissed and told. So why was he being so close-lipped about Grace?

He laid his head in his hands. "I don't know what the hell is wrong with me."

"PMS?" Den offered.

Mike snorted. "Funny."

"She got to you, didn't she?"

He thought about denial. He was the poster boy for denial, he was so good at it. But maybe it was time to stop running from emotions. Maybe that's why he was so dissatisfied with his life. "Yeah, she got to me."

"Did you fuck her?"

"No. I made love to her."

"Jesus Christ. It's even worse than I thought."

He smiled and raised his head, looked at Den. "She's something special."

"She's just another pussy, Mike."

Had he ever been that much of an asshole? Yeah, he had. He'd never cared before. Women had meant nothing to him but a good fuck. He couldn't be mad at Den for acting like Den—hell, for saying the same thing he might have said yesterday. One night with Grace and suddenly he'd developed a conscience. Why?

"She just felt different to me."

Den shrugged. "I have no idea what you're talking about. They all feel the same to me."

"I can't explain it."

"And how does Grace feel about all this?"

Mike allowed a half smile as the waitress brought their drinks. He stared at the amber liquid. "She pretty much tossed me out on my ass as soon as daylight hit."

Den let out a loud laugh. "Payback is hell, isn't it, buddy?"

Mike nodded, then arched his brow. "Fuck you. Your day will come."

Den downed his drink, then slammed it on the table and signaled the waitress. He winked at Mike. "To end up like you? Mooning over a woman like a lovesick cow? I think I'd rather hang up my dick."

Mike snorted. "Famous last words."

Leaning back and grabbing a handful of peanuts, Den asked, "So now that she's given you the boot, what's the plan?" He popped the peanuts into his mouth.

"I'll go back tomorrow, feel her out."

"Want me to come?"

Mike shrugged. "That's up to you."

"I've been going to Wild Nights for a couple years now. I know Grace pretty well. Maybe I can help."

Reinforcements couldn't hurt. Then again, maybe it would. At this point he really didn't know how this was going to play out, but he was willing to use any means necessary to get another chance to explore his relationship with Grace.

Relationship. A foreign, typically unwelcome word in his vocabulary. He almost laughed out loud.

Goddamn, his perspective sure had changed a lot in the past twenty-four hours.

There was no doubt about it. Grace was pissed. The emotion shocked her so much she almost laughed out loud. But since she was knee-deep in clients at the moment, that wasn't a good idea.

She had no right to be upset. She'd gotten exactly what she wanted. Though she hadn't come right out and said the words, she'd pretty much delivered Mike an A-number-one, obvious-as-hell brush-off this morning. She'd turned down his offers of breakfast, lunch and dinner, and all but shoved him into the elevator with her foot on his ass.

Could she have been more rude? The cold chill of fear had turned her into an icy bitch, and her normal manners had flown right out the window. She'd been abrupt and ill-mannered and she'd spent the entire day feeling awful about how she'd treated him. He'd shown her a wonderful time last night and he hadn't deserved her behavior.

Maybe that's why she was kind of hoping she'd see him tonight. It was better that he hadn't come, though. He'd gotten the message, and there was no reason to prolong the inevitable. They had no future together. She had her business, which was her only goal for the future. Her plans didn't include a man. Relationships were too messy, too unpredictable.

She really had no business feeling disappointed that he hadn't shown up tonight. Yet, it was nearing midnight and she realized she'd actually expected him to show up. If that wasn't the ultimate in ego deflation, she didn't know what was.

Well, fine. This was better. And exactly what she wanted, and needed. No entanglements, no attachments, no emotional feelings for men she'd fucked.

"How 'bout it Grace? Is tonight our night?"

She lifted her gaze to Wayne Malone, one of the most attractive men she knew. Wicked smart and a self-made millionaire by the time he'd hit thirty, Wayne had been after her for over a year now. And she'd led him on one hell of a wild ride, enjoying the game of chase and not-quite-catch. She figured Wayne enjoyed it, too, which was why he kept coming back and spending all his wonderful money at her club.

"Not tonight, Wayne," she purred, tipping her fingernail under his chin and pressing a light kiss to his lips. "I have a headache."

He laughed, as if he'd already known her answer. He caressed her cheek. "Some other time, maybe."

"Maybe." But they both knew it was never going to happen. It rarely happened with her clientele. Her regulars were aware of how picky she was about fucking her clients. And the newcomers figured it out pretty fast.

But it had happened last night, hadn't it? She'd been so goddamn easy she was surprised Mike hadn't left fifty bucks on her nightstand. She'd spread her legs and whimpered and begged and damn near shouted out that she loved him. Then she'd come. And come. And come some more.

Her nipples hardened against her halter, her pussy clenching. But she felt empty.

It was ironic. Wild Nights was filled to capacity; there was a crowd outside waiting to get in. And Grace was lonely. Because the one man she wished had come tonight wasn't here.

SEVEN

Wild Nights was packed as usual the next evening. Grace was insanely busy, but still found herself often hovering near the front door. Mike wasn't coming. She might as well cast him from her thoughts and her life. It was over.

"Looking for someone?"

Grace turned at the familiar deep voice behind her. "Denver!" She hugged and kissed him, allowing him to pull her into his embrace. Denver was one of the few men she genuinely liked and trusted. A regular for a couple years, he was charming, sexy and wickedly dangerous to a woman's libido. She'd never had sex with him and he'd never hit on her. His casually charming demeanor made him easy to be around.

And, as she recalled, Denver was the one who'd garnered the invitation for Mike. Not that she was going to ask about him. Not at all.

"It's so nice to see you here. Are you alone tonight?" Damn. She just couldn't let it go, could she?

"I'm always alone, gorgeous. Why? Are you wanting company?" He arched dark brows above chocolate brown eyes that would melt any woman's panties right off. His sharp, angular features belonged on the cover of a fashion magazine, his lean, chiseled body encased in jeans and a tight T-shirt that showed off time well spent in the gym.

"Are you offering?" she shot back with a wink.

"I might be."

That would be a first. Though she wasn't at all interested. And Denver was an incredibly appealing man. But her thoughts were centered on one man alone.

"Hey, Den."

The one who'd just stepped up and spoken. The one who stole her breath with midnight black hair and blue eyes. The one smiling down at her.

"Grace."

She felt like a teenager, with sweaty palms and a racing pulse. "Mike. How nice to see you again."

Ugh. Too formal. She relaxed her shoulders and tried for a smile. He was just a client tonight. Nothing more.

Right. Tell that to her pussy, which was throbbing and moistening and quivering with happiness.

Down girl. Mike was off-limits.

"Nice to see you, too, Grace. The club is really full tonight. I practically had to offer up a limb to get in."

She laughed. "It's Friday night. Always one of our busiest."

"Glad I managed to pass the test, then."

She didn't mention she'd put him on the accept list. "I hope you enjoy your evening."

He nodded. "I intend to. Thanks."

"How about we head to the bar for a drink?" Denver asked Mike.

"Sounds good."

"There are some beautiful women here tonight. I'll introduce you."

"Talk to you later, Grace," Mike said, then wandered off with Denver. She turned and headed in the opposite direction. Danced a bit. Mingled a little, all the while keeping one eye turned toward Mike and Denver. It wasn't long before there was a throng of women crowded around the bar, fighting for their attention.

Grace would not—absolutely would not—be jealous. Her stomach was twisted in knots because . . . because . . . cocktail napkin inventory was low and they might run out.

Oh, sure. Because Wild Nights would go up in a ball of flames if they ran out of cocktail napkins tonight. Which they weren't even close to doing, anyway.

Disgusted, she left the bar and moved to the playrooms, checking on her clients and making sure everyone was having fun. Nearly every room was full, the sounds of sex and laughter everywhere. She stepped into a couple of the rooms, hoping to immerse herself in watching some of the action and get her mind off Mike.

A woman was chained facing the wall in the bondage room, a man lightly whipping her with a leather flogger. The woman moaned in equal parts pain and pleasure as the man first spanked, then slid his hands between her legs to cup and tease her pussy. In the orgy room, things were in full swing, the tangle of body parts hard to decipher as mouths met cocks and pussys and hands grabbed for the nearest sex organ. People were laughing and moaning and having a wonderful time. The musky smell of sex permeated the air around her. She sighed and moved on. There were no problems for her to attend to. As was typical, Wild Nights ran like a smoothly oiled machine.

With every step down the hallway, Grace grew more and more annoyed.

And curious about what was happening in the bar. Were Mike and Denver still there, or maybe on the dance floor with some of the ladies who'd been hovering around them? Or maybe, on their way to one of the playrooms with a few of the women.

Goddamit! How dare he make her think of him. She did not care what the hell Mike Nottingham did. She never should have put his name on the list. In fact, she should have barred him from the club. Then she would have been able to relax and enjoy her evening.

Screw that. She *would* have a good time tonight, whether he was here or not. She'd prove to herself she didn't care about him or what he did—or who he chose to do it with. Determined, she turned around and slammed straight into Denver's chest.

"Whoa, babe," Denver said. "Sorry."

She shook her head. "No, I'm sorry. I turned too fast." Despite vowing not to look, she couldn't help leaning around Denver enough to see Mike heading in their direction.

Damn. She felt weak in the knees just watching the predatory way he approached her. He was not going to affect her like this. She didn't need him, didn't feel a thing for him. He did not get to her in any way. Sex was sex and it didn't matter who she had it with.

Panicked, she laced her arm through Denver's and blurted, "How would you like to have sex with me?"

"Uh, what?" Denver's eyes went wide. "Say that again?"

Forcing a calm she didn't feel, she leaned into him. "I'm in the mood to play tonight. Are you game?"

She knew from the look on his face that what she was asking was incredibly unfair. Mike was Denver's friend.

Mike stepped up beside Denver and arched a brow. "Am I interrupting?"

Denver offered a halfsmile. "Grace just made me an . . . interesting offer."

"Is that right?"

"Yes," she said, taking control of the situation. "I asked Denver if he wanted to play with me tonight."

Mike looked at Denver, then at her. "I see."

Yes, he was going to see, all right. "I'm thinking the voyeur/ exhibition room, if you don't have a problem showing off."

Mike laughed. "Den loves to show off."

"Mike," Denver said, his gaze flitting between the two of them. "Do you have a problem with this?"

Mike shrugged and grinned. "Why would I? Grace is free to do whatever she wants, and so are you. I'll just take a seat in the viewing room and watch. It won't be the first time I've watched you with a woman."

"Are you sure?" Denver asked.

Mike nodded. "I'm sure. Hell, I get off on watching. You know that about me."

Den laughed. "Yeah, you will."

Mike was already turning around to leave. "You two have fun."

He pivoted and walked away. He was going to watch her and Denver having sex. Did he really not care, or was he putting on a show of bravado?

Wasn't this what she wanted? To prove to Mike, and to herself, that she was her own woman, in charge of her own destiny? It was necessary, for both of them, that this happen tonight. To put an end to any hope he might have for a real relationship. Wild Nights was her life—adventurous, unattached sex was what she did.

"Grace, are you certain this is what *you* want?"

She looked up at Denver, his gaze one of concern. He really was a beautiful man. She'd be well taken care of—and safe—with him. Which was probably why her instincts told her to choose him.

"Of course it is." She caressed his cheek. "It's been entirely too long since I've enjoyed the fun at Wild Nights, Denver. And you and I have never played with each other. Unless you have some objection."

"Are you kidding? A man would be insane to turn you down. My dick's already hard at the thought of touching you."

She laughed. "Then what are we waiting for?"

The pang in her stomach as she walked with Denver into the exhibition room was not guilt. It wasn't. She was free to do whatever she wanted, with whomever she wanted. If Mike wanted to watch, that was up to him. He was a paying client and if he got off on voyeurism, that was great. Good for him. She didn't care what he did to get his rocks off.

This wasn't the first time she'd been in the exhibitionist room. Grace occasionally enjoyed showing off for her clients. It was good for business. Her clientele liked watching her. It was important for them to see her participate.

And what better man to play with than Denver McKenzie? Tall, hot and sexy, she'd stopped in and watched Denver pleasure a woman or two in the past. He definitely knew what he was doing. He had magic hands and a great tongue. She'd envied the women he'd had, because they certainly seemed to enjoy the orgasms he gave them.

Tonight, she planned to do the same.

The exhibition room was set up like an open efficiency apartment, except it was just sofas, chairs, tables and a bed. Those using the room, and sometimes it was more than one couple or ménage, could choose either to watch or be watched, depending on their mood. Once in there, Denver took over, leading her into the living room portion and sitting her on the sofa. He kneeled in front of her and smiled.

"Relax. If there's anything you don't want me to do, or you just want me to stop, then say so so. I hear 'no' loud and clear."

She nodded, saw Mike step into the outer viewing room and cast her gaze back down at Denver. "I won't say no."

Denver's gaze went dark, his hands grazing along her ankles. "Good." His voice had gone deep and she felt a little thrill, though she wasn't sure if it was because Denver was rubbing her feet or because Mike had taken a seat in the front row of the voyeur room.

She could see Mike clearly. He'd settled in, leaned back in one of the wide chairs, his legs spread and his arms resting on the chair. He didn't seem uncomfortable or irritated. He seemed like anyone else watching their play—interested. Several other people had started to file in and take seats, but Grace ignored them, her gaze riveted on Mike. She wanted to know what he was thinking—was he angry, did he care at all, or did the fact that she was about to fuck his friend not matter?

And why did she care? Dammit, why did it matter to her what he thought, when it shouldn't? Wasn't this the reason she was in this room with Denver in the first place?

Focus, Grace. Focus on the man you're with, not the man on the other side of the window.

Tearing her gaze away from Mike, she looked down at Denver, watching him smooth his hands over her calves, kneading her muscles with a gentle squeeze.

"That feels good," she said.

"Spread your legs a little, baby," he said, using his shoulder to nudge her thigh.

Tonight she wore a short red dress, tight and clingy. She knew as soon as she spread her legs the dress would hike all the way up to her crotch. She did, and it did.

She hadn't worn panties.

"Damn," Denver whispered. "You have a pretty little pussy, Grace." He leaned forward, resting his arms on her thighs and pushing the hem of her dress up and over her hips. His warm breath washed across her thighs.

Grace couldn't help it—her gaze flitted to Mike again, wanting to gauge his reaction. Track lighting in the voyeur room showcased those watching for those exhibiting. It made it exciting for people on both sides. Mike's expression was clearly outlined, but once again he gave her no clue what he was thinking—there was neither anger nor pleasure on his face.

"Scoot your ass down this way a little," Denver urged, reaching under her to cup her ass cheeks and pull her forward. His hands were warm and she forced herself to look at the man pleasuring her, not the man watching.

Denver grinned. "Baby, go ahead and look at him if that turns you on."

"What?"

"Look at Mike."

"I'm not . . . I'm not looking at Mike."

Denver ran his palms over the inside of her thighs, his thumbs precariously close to her pussy. "Yeah, you are. I know you wish he was here instead of me."

She had muted the sound between the rooms. It was her choice whether to connect the audio portion of the two rooms or not, so at the moment Mike couldn't hear what was being said between her and Denver. She laid her hand on his head, smoothing her palm over the softness of his dark hair. "I don't wish anyone was here but you right now, Denver."

"You're not a very good liar, Grace. And I'm not emotionally invested in this, so quit worrying about hurting my feelings. You won't."

She didn't know what to say. Had she been subconsciously wishing Mike had dragged her in here? God, she didn't know the answer. "I'm sorry."

"Don't be, because I'm still going to make you come. And I'm still going to fuck you good and hard until I come. So believe me, baby, you have nothing to apologize for. You just look at Mike and make him wish he was in here with you instead of me."

Denver turned around and shot a quick glance at the window, then back at her. "Though I think he's probably already wishing that."

"Doesn't seem to be." She shouldn't care. Not when Denver was moving his hands so close to her clit, his thumbs making lazy, teasing circles around her pussy lips. She was wet, aching, needy.

"Trust me. He cares."

She didn't want Mike to care. Wasn't that the problem? She was so confused.

This whole thing wasn't clearing her head like she thought it would. Instead, she was spread out and Denver was crawling between her legs and Mike was watching.

And as Denver's lips pressed up against her sex, his tongue parting her and licking against her clit, arousal flamed hot and she moaned, flipping on the button to open the audio between the two rooms. She wanted Mike to hear her, wanted him to be as close to her excitement as he could get.

Yes, she was turned on now. But not because of what Denver was doing. Because Mike was watching, and she caught the telltale flicker of desire in his eyes. And dammit, she wanted him to want her, wanted him to want her so badly that the urge to tear through the window would be so great he'd have to use every ounce of his willpower to prevent himself from doing just that.

Did he want her that much? She hoped so, because every flick of Denver's tongue against her clit was Mike's. His fingers sliding into her pussy were Mike's fingers, and the orgasm bubbling up inside her was being brought about because she was locked on Mike's deep blue eyes, not Denver's brown ones.

She hated this, but she couldn't help herself. And when she couldn't hold back, when Denver pressed his hand over her belly, his fingers pumping hard and furiously into her cunt, when his mouth latched onto her clit and sucked hard and she came, she bit back Mike's name when she screamed, shuddering and crying out instead as waves of pleasure rocked her ass right off the couch.

And not once did she tear her gaze from Mike's. He didn't move, or stop looking at her. Not when Denver dragged her to her feet and pulled her dress off, covering her breasts with his hands and then his lips, tugging at her nipples until they were wet and rigid. Not when he pulled her over the back of the sofa and jerked his pants down, grabbed a condom and shoved his cock in her, impaling her with a hard thrust that made her cry out in pain and pleasure.

She wanted Mike behind her, fucking her like this, imagined his thick cock powering in and out of her with wild abandon, so hard it would make her hurt, bruising her with each driving thrust until she begged for more.

She saw the slight lift of Mike's chin, his nostrils flaring as Denver pushed into her so hard the couch scooted a few inches across the floor. She whimpered from the pleasure of it, but it was Mike giving her that enjoyment. Did he know that? Did he feel what she was going through, realize that she wanted him so much she could feel his cock inside her when another man was fucking her? Denver didn't exist for her anymore. The other people watching weren't there. There was only Mike and her, and the sweet pulsing of her pussy around the cock inside her.

"Harder," she said through gritted teeth, asking for more even though she couldn't take more. But she wasn't asking Denver for it.

"I need you," she pleaded. Did Mike understand? "Please."

She was panting now, mindless, wanting only the orgasm that hovered just out of her reach. "I need to come." She gripped the fabric of the sofa, tightening her fingers around the pillows. "Please make me come."

And yet knowing how much she needed it, feeling Denver behind her, she held back, unwilling to give it to anyone else. Denver growled against her back, shuddering as he orgasmed, pumping hard against her. She cried out as he lifted her with a punishing final thrust, then collapsed against her.

As soon as it was over, people filed out, onto the next activity, the next sex party—whatever thrilled them. Mike stayed, though. Denver pulled away, turned her around and kissed her forehead.

"You're an amazing woman, Grace."

She blinked her eyes closed for a second, then smiled up at him. "Thank you Denver. For . . . everything."

He winked. "Anytime, baby." He stepped out, stopping in the outer room to speak to Mike. He'd pushed the audio button first so Grace couldn't hear what they were saying. Mike nodded a few times and Denver squeezed his shoulder, then left.

That's when she realized she and Mike were alone, realized what she'd done, the signals she'd sent out to him. She hadn't come at the end with Denver because she felt guilty about having sex with him. Because Mike wasn't the one giving her the orgasm and she wanted it with him.

No. No, no, no. She would not do this, to him or to herself. What was wrong with her? Anger boiled up inside her. Anger and guilt. And she hated guilt. She was never guilty, especially about sex. That's what she'd run away from all those years ago, and she was not going through it again.

No goddamn man was going to make her feel this way.

She pulled on her clothes and stormed from the room.

EIGHT

For a few moments, Mike stood frozen, unable to move.

Whether it was the visual of watching Grace get fucked by Den that held him immobile, or Denver's words after that or the fierce expression of fear mixed with anger on Grace's face, he didn't know. All he knew was that he needed to sort this out before he went after her.

And he *was* going after her. They were going to get this figured out one way or another, tonight. No more mixed signals. He read the confusion on her face. One minute she seemed indifferent, the next sending him "fuck me" signals, the next angry as hell.

Then Den told him Grace was his for the taking, that she wasn't the least bit interested in screwing other guys. Yeah, right. Could have fooled him, since she'd just finished letting one of his best friends fuck her. Which was exactly what he'd said to Denver. He'd had to bite back the angry jealousy that had reared its ugly head. Hell he'd wanted to take a punch at Den, and that was completely out of character for him.

He never cared if Den fucked someone he knew. But he sure as hell had had an uptight moment when Grace told him she'd chosen Den.

A moment he'd had to get past in a hurry. Grace didn't belong to him and he knew that. She could choose anyone she wanted to. Hell, it was part of her job to do those things. So he'd let it go. And the view had been incredible. He'd even told Den afterward that it looked like he'd done a fine job fucking Grace. She seemed to enjoy the hell out of the experience.

Den had narrowed his gaze and told him he hadn't wanted to punch the shit out of him in a long time, but he was damn close. That Mike needed to start paying attention, because Denver wasn't often wrong, and he'd been wrong about Grace. She wasn't just another pussy—she cared about Mike, but she was confused. Then Den had the goddamn nerve to tell him to go easy on her.

Mike dragged his fingers through his hair, wondering if it had been such a good idea to come here tonight. Maybe he should have done what Grace wanted and stayed away. He didn't need this complication in his life. And he sure as hell didn't need to chase after a woman who clearly didn't want to be chased.

His relationships with women before had been simple. They went out, they both had mutually satisfying sex with no attachments and no emotion, and then they went their separate ways. No sticky entanglements, no involvements, nothing.

Why was it so goddamn complex with Grace? And why didn't he just walk away when the going got tough? That's what he usually did.

They had to wrap this up so neither one of them was confused or had the wrong idea. And he didn't like leaving things the way they'd left them—unfinished.

With his throbbing dick pressing insistently against his jeans, he stood, adjusted and headed through the doorway Grace had just exited. The hall led to her private elevator. He punched the intercom and waited.

"What?"

Her voice. Pretty damned irritated, too.

"Let me up."

She hesitated. He heard a weary sigh. Then the elevator started whirring, making its way to his floor. He stepped in and in a few seconds he was standing in her living room again. She was at the wide windows overlooking the city, her back turned to him, a glass of brandy in her hand. She didn't even turn around when he walked toward her.

"Did you enjoy the show tonight?" she asked.

"Sure. Who wouldn't have?"

He heard her soft laugh.

"But I'd have enjoyed it more if I'd been the one on the other side of the window instead of Denver."

"I do what I want, when I want, with whomever I want."

"Yes, I know." He poured himself a drink and moved next to her. "Grace, I don't expect you to change your life for me. I would be ten times an asshole if I did that. You are who you are, and I admire you for everything you've done with Wild Nights. You have nothing to prove to me."

She tilted her head toward him, then down. "I'm sorry about tonight. I felt I had something to prove. To you, to myself, maybe. I don't really know." When she looked up at him again, she shook her head. "Being with you scared me."

"Why?"

She slid down to the carpet, kicked off her shoes and stared out at the lights again. "You stayed the night. I've never let a man spend the night with me before. Having you wake up next to me . . . felt good."

"Ah." He knew that feeling. This whole episode with Grace was a lesson in the bizarre for a man who'd never once cared about a woman before. "I'm having a few revelations myself."

"You are?"

"Yeah." He reached for a tendril of her hair, just liking the feel of soft silk between his fingers. "I fuck women, Grace. I don't have relationships. I don't form attachments. I don't care. With you . . . it feels different. Believe me, I wish it didn't. I've put more effort into . . . whatever the hell this is between us . . . in the past couple days than I have with any other woman before. Frankly, it scares the shit out of me. It would be a lot easier for me to walk away, to go back to my life and do what I do best, than to continue with this . . . with you."

"Why do you, then?"

He shrugged. "I like a challenge."

"You just don't like being dumped."

He laughed. "You bet your ass I don't like it."

"I'll bet you've dumped a ton of women in your lifetime, haven't you?" She reached up on the table for the brandy and refilled their glasses.

"Too many. Though I was always honest. I never led a woman on. I don't believe in that."

She nodded. "Good for you. I don't believe in it, either. Upfront honesty is always the best way."

"Then dump them."

Her lips quirked. "Hell of a pair, aren't we?"

"Maybe that's why we're well matched. Neither of us have an expectation of falling in love, of forever. Whatever exists is for right now, and for whatever excites us at the moment." And she did excite him. Admittedly, watching her come apart for Den, watching his friend sink his cock into her, and all the while her eyes were fixed on him . . . that had gotten his dick hard. Grace was a one-of-a-kind woman. And he wanted a little longer with her.

Hell no, he wasn't expecting forever. Grace wasn't a settling down kind of woman—he knew that. And God knows he wasn't. But he had a few more days before he had to go back to work. He couldn't think of anyone more fun or more exciting to spend that time with.

"I think I can handle right now," she said, setting her glass on the floor next to the window. "I'm really good with right now."

He put his glass next to hers. "You didn't have an orgasm when Den fucked you."

She shook her head. "No."

"Why not?"

"Because I wanted you to make me come."

It didn't take telling him twice. He'd wanted that from the minute he'd seen her at the club tonight. "Lay back and lift your skirt."

With a hot smile she scooted back and leaned against the side of the couch, hiking her skirt up over her hips, the same way she'd done for Den. Only this time there was no hesitation, no frown on her face. She spread her legs and he rolled over on his stomach, crawling between her thighs. The sweet musky scent of her pussy drew him in like an irresistible lure, inviting him to taste, to touch.

He pressed his fingers on the insides of her thighs, feeling her tremble at the first touch. He kissed along her thigh, absorbing her scent and the softness of her skin against his lips. At the first swipe of his tongue along her flesh, she tangled her fingers in his hair and lifted her hips, offering up her pussy to his mouth.

Oh yeah. He loved her eagerness, her need, the way she twisted underneath him and held tight to his hair as if she was afraid he was going to move away.

Not a chance, babe. He wasn't going anywhere until she screamed and flooded his face with her come. That she saved this for him meant something, when she could have come with Den. He was going to make this good for her. He covered her clit and sex, sucking light and easy and mixing it up with a roll of his tongue around her clit, not touching it directly.

"Mike." His name rushed out of her mouth out in a whispered exhale, a pleading sound he found oh so sexy. He wanted to make her do it again, so he kept up the movements of his tongue, his mouth staying latched onto her cunt, refusing to let go. He wasn't going to give her a break, sliding two fingers inside her at the same time.

Her pussy latched onto his fingers in a clenching grip, then squeezed and released, making him wish it was his dick inside her getting that treatment. She was wet and hot inside, getting wetter with every thrust of his fingers, every lick of his tongue against her clit.

"Please," she said, pulling at his hair with both hands now, tightening around his fingers. He closed his lips around the hard bud and sucked, taking her over the edge. She came with a gush of wetness against his fingers, pushing her sex against his face and shuddering as she cried out.

"I'm coming! Oh yes, suck my clit!"

She was beautiful when she came. Uninhibited, reveling in her orgasm and completely wild. She rode the entire climax with unashamed abandon until her butt relaxed against the floor and she let out a breath of completion, releasing his hair and smiling down at him.

"Thank you," she said, her voice soft and low.

He stood, then held out his hand and pulled her to her feet. "You're welcome."

Her face was flushed, her lips parted and he had to have her mouth. He leaned in and kissed her and she didn't hesitate taking a taste of herself on his lips, licking at her own flavor before her tongue dove into his mouth and swept against his. He pulled her into a tight embrace, knowing there wasn't a chance in hell he'd be able to use the restraint he had the other night—he wanted her too much. His balls were in a knot after the show she'd put on with Den earlier. He felt like he'd been waiting forever to be inside her and control was already nonexistent.

A quick glance around the room and he knew exactly what he wanted. He took her hand and led her toward her towering windows, the view of Las Vegas spectacular and bright. He pulled her in front of him and wrapped his arm around her. "You like looking out these windows, don't you?"

"Yes."

He moved his hand along her ribcage, letting his palm rest just below her breasts. "I'll bet lots of guys have fucked you right here."

"I wouldn't say lots."

"You like being on display?" He pulled the straps of her dress down, then the bodice, baring her breasts. He cupped them, using his thumbs to roll over her nipples, taking in her reaction to his touch.

"Sometimes." Her head fell against his chest, her breathing short and rapid.

His erection pressed hard against his jeans. He moved it against her ass, wanting her to know what she did to him. She reached between them and palmed him, rubbing her hand along his length.

"That feels good."

"I want you inside me, Mike."

He smiled. He wanted that, too. More than he could tell her. But this play was too much fun to stop, her body too beautiful bathed in the lights to end it. "Soon. Touch your pussy for me."

She let out a little gasp—excitement, he hoped—and raised her dress, fingering her pussy.

"It's so wet," she whispered. "You made me come hard."

"I'm going to make you come again. Next time it'll be all over my cock."

She squeezed his cock and he wished he were naked. She had such soft hands. So different than when he touched himself. He liked her touching him.

Her nipples were hard little pebbles that he rolled between his fingers. He plucked them, testing her to see how hard she liked it. When he pinched lightly, she gasped, but arched against him, giving him more. He pulled them, elongating them, wanting to flip her around and cover the buds with his mouth, his teeth. But oh, he liked having her sweet, firm ass nestled against his crotch, so he was just going to have to suffer and satisfy himself with fondling her breasts.

Her hair was pinned up tonight, a silver clip holding it together. He removed it and let the raven waves cascade down her back, burying his nose in the fragrant softness, then sweeping the tendrils over her shoulder so he could have access to the nape of her neck. He kissed her, then nibbled, taking a soft bite. She shuddered and let out a low moan.

That was it. He couldn't take any more. With a harsh oath he unzipped his pants and pushed Grace forward. She planted her hands on the window glass and spread her legs. While he prepared for her, he took a step back and admired the picture she presented. Her legs spread wide, the dress pulled up over her hips, exposing her swollen pussy lips to his view, her small breasts dangling down just waiting for his hands.

She turned her head and shot him a look so filled with hunger and need that he wished he could take a picture of her posing just like that. He'd never seen a woman look so beautiful before.

Cock in hand, he approached, smoothing his hand over her back, down over her hips and buttocks, giving her a light smack.

"Yes," she said. "Please."

He fit his cock between her legs, finding the warm, wet center, and drove home, this time not gentle, not taking his time, but plunging inside her with force, taking what he felt was his and making her accept it.

She did, crying out his name and pushing her ass back against him. She took it, all of him, and wanted more. That meant something to him. He growled and pulled her against him.

A raging beast had taken him over. He gripped her hips and reared back, only to power forward again, burying his cock deep inside her. She gripped him in a tight vise of supple, wet silk, the hottest rain imaginable pouring over his balls.

He reached between her legs and rubbed her clit as he pumped inside her. "Come for me, Grace." He pulled her ass against him, tightening his hold around her with one hand while rubbing the hard bud with the other. "Come on my cock."

With every stroke he felt the walls closing in around him. He pulled partway out, then in, keeping his strokes shallow, gliding along her G-spot, wanting her to explode around him. "Do it. I want to feel your pussy squeezing me."

"Oh God, Mike," she whimpered, then let go, rocking back against him as the waves of her climax crashed over them both. He went with her, pushing into her with a final deep thrust and staying there, wrapping both arms around her and holding her as he emptied over and over again. With a final shudder, he pulled out and turned Grace around, kissing her and pushing her hair away from her face so he could see her eyes.

Purple, luminous, like the dark sky outside. So incredibly beautiful with her lips parted as she caught her breath. She laid her head against his chest and wrapped her arms around his back.

He might just be content to hold her like this . . .

He'd almost thought "forever," but a word like that wasn't in Mike Nottingham's vocabulary.

So maybe just all night. He'd be content to hold her like this all night long.

NINE

After Mike spent the night—again—Grace wondered how she had let it happen—again—but didn't allow herself to dwell on it.

They were having great sex and a good time together, but he lived in Oklahoma and would be going home in a day and half, so after that she wouldn't have to be angst-ridden over it anymore. Why not simply enjoy what they had right now?

Right now. They had discussed those two words last night and the phrase seemed to fit, made her more comfortable, eased her mind. With the pressure off, she had settled into whatever it was they had together and just let go.

Wow, had she ever let go. Exploring her sexuality with the same man over and over again was definitely fun. Tiring, since she once again hadn't gotten much sleep, but definitely enjoyable.

Mike had risen before dawn, kissed her on the forehead and told her he'd check in with her later. She'd rolled over, smiled, mumbled a brief good-bye and passed right out again.

That had been four hours ago. Wild Nights was closed today, so she had an entire day off to do whatever she wanted. She made it a point to take at least one day a week completely and totally away from the club, and that meant mentally, too. Not even paperwork. She was free to lie around relaxing, read a good book or get out and do some shopping.

After she took a shower and slipped on jeans and a sweater, she sat at the table with her cup of coffee and a bagel, trying to decide how to spend the day. Her mind refused to cooperate. It was filled with thoughts of Mike. Mike's hands on her, his head between her legs, his thick, hot cock inside her.

Yeah, she knew exactly what she wanted to do today. And when the outside elevator monitor buzzed and Mike's voice came through, she was shocked at the giddy excitement coursing through her.

For the love of God, she wasn't sixteen. Yet she did run into the bathroom and check her hair while he was coming up the elevator.

Brainless twit. She really had to get over this infatuation she had with him. Grace Wylde did *not* moon over men, dammit!

Okay, maybe she did, because when the elevator door opened and he walked out, she tried swallowing and it didn't work. Her throat had gone dry. Because he was rolling toward her wearing tight jeans, cowboy boots, a button-down shirt and a cowboy hat.

Oh. My. God. The hat was tipped down low over his brow, shading his forehead and lending him that movie-star dark-and-dangerous look. He hadn't shaved, and the dark stubble across his jaw only added to the sexy allure.

Holy cow. She'd seen her share of cowboys belly up to the bar at Wild Nights, but Mike was a natural, born and bred to the jeans, the boots and the cowboy hat. All he needed was a holster loaded with two six-shooters and some spurs and she'd probably have an orgasm on the spot.

He stopped in front of her, swept his hat off and pulled her into his arms. No, he dragged her into his arms, planting a long, slow kiss on her lips that left her bone-meltingly drugged.

Dayum.

"Mornin'," he said when he released her, laying his hat on her kitchen table.

She was speechless. It took a couple swallows past the dry desert in her throat to find her voice. "Good morning. You look . . . Wow."

He grinned. "I'll take that as a compliment."

"Would you like some coffee?" Tea? Her, naked and spread-eagled just about anywhere?

"No, I'm fine. Actually, I'm here to take you on an adventure, if you don't have plans today."

"I have no plans. What did you have in mind?" Her, naked and spread-eagled somewhere she hoped. *Way to go with the one-track mind, Grace.*

"It's a surprise."

"Uh, okay. Should I change?"

He looked at her. "No, you're perfect. Put on some socks and boots and bring a jacket."

She had a date. Holy shit, she had a date. She never dated. This was kind of exciting.

An hour later she wasn't sure if she was more excited or terrified as she faced down her very first horse. Probably equal parts of both. Mike had driven them outside Las Vegas to a ranch that catered to private horseback riding tours. They were in the mountains, an area she'd never seen. Actually it was a rocky canyon surrounded by red-colored hills, peppered with brush and tall cactus. The sun warmed the area and kept the early morning chill away.

The ranch was huge, filled with horses and cattle and fenced farther than her eyes could follow. Mike told her it was thousands of acres. She felt like a little kid, turning her head from side to side after they'd parked and got out. She didn't know which way to look. A working ranch, it was owned by one of the veterinarians Mike'd met at the conference, who agreed to let them saddle up a couple of the horses and ride the property.

She was about to mount and ride her very first horse.

"They sure look a lot bigger in real life than they do in the movies," she said, sizing up the horse in front of her. A chestnut mare, Mike had told her. The horse looked skittish and about as nervous as she was.

"You grew up in Kentucky. How can you not know horses?" Mike asked, a teasing glint in his eyes as he smiled down at her.

She looked up at him and rolled her eyes. "City girl. Never been around them in my life. Never went to the Derby, either, because I know that's your next question."

He laughed. "Don't be scared. These horses are well trained. She won't buck or run off with you. All you have to do is get up on there and learn a few simple commands."

Not being one to back away from a challenge, Grace was game, and pretty excited about having the chance to do something she'd never tried before.

So she stared up at the giant beast and the stirrup that was as high as her chest, trying to figure out how to do this without falling on her ass and making a complete fool of herself.

"Let me help you. Grab the saddle horn while I lift you. Slide your left foot into the stirrup, then swing your other leg over," Mike said, putting his hands around her waist. He lifted and she grabbed and swung just as he told her. She was on! The horse hadn't even budged, either. Once settled, she smoothed her hands over the horse's coat, loving the warm, rough texture against her hands.

Mike adjusted the stirrups for the length of her legs, showed her how to hold the reins and what signals to give to make the horse move forward, left and right, and stop. He explained those were pretty much the only commands she'd need to know. Easy enough. This, she could handle.

If seeing Mike walking into her house dressed like a cowboy was devastating to her female senses, seeing him on a horse was nearly fatal. When he mounted and pulled up alongside her, a grin showcasing his dazzling white teeth against his tanned face, her heart took a fast tumble.

Wow, the man was truly a specimen of rugged beauty, just like the backdrop of the Mojave Desert.

They took off down a well-worn trail, away from the hustling activity of the main ranch and toward the towering canyon walls. The day was beautiful, the scenery incredibly gorgeous. Crisp, clean air, not a glittering light or another person in sight. Only Joshua trees, cactus, brush and birds overhead. It was breathtaking.

They must have ridden for about an hour when Mike stopped, dismounted and helped her off her horse.

"I don't want to ride you too long. You'll get sore."

She'd lost all track of time and could have ridden the rest of the day. The morning chill was gone and she was warming considerably. They'd stopped on the other side of the canyon, the towering, smooth, red-rocked sides surrounding them.

Mike tethered their horses to a nearby tree and reached into his saddle bag for a couple bottles of water. "Not wine, but it'll have to do. Drink?"

"I'd love one."

He laid out a blanket on a smooth patch of thin grass, a fast-moving stream flowing alongside them. They sat and Grace drank while listening to the sounds of rushing water and birds overhead.

It was amazing. She'd never felt more relaxed or had a better time on her day off. "I've never been out here. In fact, I didn't even know places like this existed."

"They do. Most of us never see what's in our own backyards."

She laughed. "True enough. We get too busy, wrap ourselves around our own little world and stay within our comfort zone. Thank you for bringing me out here."

"You're welcome. I'm glad I did. You look beautiful in sunlight."

"Thank you." She warmed under his scrutiny, realizing that while she was extremely knowledgeable about sex, she had very little dating experience. Outside her element, she didn't know how to handle men. Or at least she hadn't yet figured out how to handle Mike.

Maybe she should stop trying. Maybe she should just touch him, kiss him and make love to him for whatever time they had together and stop trying to figure him out. She screwed the top back on the water bottle and laid it down, then leaned across the blanket, rubbing her palm across his jaw.

"I love that unshaven look you're sporting today. It's very sexy."

He arched a brow and rubbed his cheek against her hand. "Really. I'll keep that in mind."

"Yes, really. Makes you look very rugged and outdoorsy."

"Does that make you hot?"

She laughed. "I think we've determined that pretty much everything about you makes me hot."

In a second she was dragged across the blanket and onto his lap, his arms around her. "I make you hot, huh?"

God, he really was gorgeous. Even without the dark stubble and the sunglasses and the cowboy hat, he'd still make her wet. But the whole package was incredibly stimulating. "Want me to show you how hot?"

The wicked upward turn of his lips was her answer. "Go right ahead."

"Just how . . . remote, are we?" she asked, squeezing the muscles of his upper arm, loving the feel of being caged within them.

"Remote enough for you to do whatever you want. I told Carl where we were headed. He said his hands were working up north today. We're south. Completely alone."

She rubbed his face again, the sensation across her palm sending little shocks between her legs. "Alone, huh? So I can do anything I want to you?"

"Anything you want, babe."

She slid off his lap. "Lean back and stretch out your legs."

Mike didn't know what Grace planned, but he was more than willing to put his body in her hands. Her eyes sparkled with devilish delight and he forced back a laugh at the eager way she licked her lips.

He rested his upper body on his elbows and slid his legs out straight. She maneuvered herself to his side and flipped over onto her stomach, her head at his hip. When she began toying with his belt buckle, he had a pretty good idea what she had in mind.

So did his cock. A rush of heat flooded there, hardening him. Her eyes widened as the bulge grew against the denim.

"I haven't even touched you yet." Her gaze flitted from his crotch to his face.

"You don't need to touch me. My mind is already there."

"Hmph," she said, her mouth affecting a cute little pout. "I might simply intend to lay my head in your lap and quote Shakespeare's sonnets."

"Baby, if you lay your head in my lap your mouth is going to be too full to talk."

She snorted. "You're rather sure of yourself, aren't you?"

"Are you saying I'm wrong about your intent?"

She shrugged, undoing his belt buckle. "Maybe. Maybe not."

She didn't say another word, just popped the button open and drew the zipper down. When her knuckles brushed his erection, he sucked in a breath. Christ, she wasn't even touching bare skin yet and heat burned through his jeans. Good thing there was a cool breeze to go with the warm sun, because Grace was burning him alive and his cock wasn't even free of his jeans.

"Lift," she commanded. He did, and she jerked his jeans down, freeing his erection. It sprang up, hard and ready. Her hands were on him before he'd even settled back down. She wrapped her palms around his shaft and stroked upward, then down, seemingly fascinated with watching the skin move over the head of his cock.

He, on the other hand, was trying to maintain control and not erupt all over her in seconds. She had magical hands and knew just how to stroke him, squeezing as she reached the head, rolling her thumb over the soft crest and eliciting drops of fluid that she swirled around with the pad of her thumb.

Though he'd always enjoyed having a woman touch him, this was different. Grace was different. At the moment, he couldn't stop to examine why. And her touch was a sweet balm across his tortured flesh, her warm breath a teasing caress that nearly shattered his control. He gritted his teeth and dug his fingers into the blanket as she bent low and licked his balls, the sensation so overpowering he shuddered.

He jerked in response, his hips rising, giving her access as her hands glided along his flesh, her tongue doing a magical dance with the sac below. She murmured against him, a vibration that made him weak in the knees. He was glad he wasn't standing or he'd have embarrassed himself.

She looked up at him, her braided hair falling over her shoulder. He reached for the band holding it and pulled it off, unwinding the strands so her hair blew free in the wind, falling against her face. He wrapped it around his hand and fisted it, jerking her toward his swollen cock head.

He'd never needed a woman's mouth on him more than he needed Grace's. He needed it and now.

"Suck me, Grace. Wrap those sweet lips around my cock and suck me."

TEN

The musky scent of Mike's arousal encompassed Grace's senses, his hands in her hair telling her how much he needed her.

So hot. So incredibly erotic, her mouth just a fraction of an inch from the wide, swollen head of his cock. She shot him a sidelong glance; his jaw was set, his chest heaving as he panted and she knew she had him right where she wanted him.

But who was the victor here? Her body was on fire, her nipples hard and tingling as they pressed against the soft fabric of her sweater. Her pussy was damp with desire and the denim rubbing against her was only stoking the flame. She wanted to fling off her clothes and impale herself on his cock, pinch her nipples and ride him to a quick, satisfying orgasm.

Not yet. Not until she teased him a bit. And herself, too. The buildup would be so worth it.

"Grace."

Mike's tone was a warning, a message that if she didn't do it voluntarily, he was going to push. She thrilled to his dominance, wondering how far she was willing to press it. She moved against his hand to lift her head so he could see her face.

Then she licked her lips.

"Goddammit." He tugged at her hair and the sweet pain made her clit tingle. Taking control, he jerked his hips upward and pushed her mouth over his cock. She smiled as she took the head between her lips, her tongue snaking out to wrap around the crest and lap at the drops of pearly fluid gathered there.

He tasted hot and spicy. She covered the head with her tongue, feeling it pulse, so alive with a soft strength and a maddening allure. She engulfed him then, taking him deep, as far as she could, swirling her tongue around him as she swallowed him.

"Christ, Grace," he murmured, tangling his hands in her hair now, holding onto the sides of her head to pump his cock into her mouth with rhythmic strokes. She raised up on her knees to bob up and down over his shaft, using her hands to stroke the base while she sucked him, wanting to pleasure him like no woman ever had. She cupped his balls, feeling them tighten within her grasp.

She wanted him to come in her mouth, needed to have that part of him inside her. With relentless pursuit she went after what she sought, stroking and squeezing, loving the power she held within her hands and mouth, the way he jerked underneath her, rising up to meet her as she tightened her grip and massaged the soft head with her tongue and mouth.

"Oh yeah, baby. Just like that," he murmured, jabbing his cock upward, driving with hard thrusts into the back of her throat. She felt the hot, salty burst as he let go with a hard groan, erupting, flooding her mouth with his come. She swallowed, the taste of him making her hot, wet and desperate to be fucked.

She held on to him until he stopped shuddering, but he still stroked her hair. A damp sheen of sweat coated the skin of his thighs and stomach as she let go of his shaft and glanced up at him.

"Damn," was all he said before dragging her across his chest to plant a hot, long kiss on her mouth. He slid his tongue inside and licked at hers, kissing her with such force she moaned and crawled into his lap, needing to be closer. Now it was her turn to latch onto his hair, rocking her pelvis against his quickly rehardening cock. Because as much as she could kiss him all day out here in the breezy sunshine, she wanted more. And he had to know that.

He pulled his mouth from hers. "You want me, Grace?"

"You know I do." She reached between them to stroke his cock. "Give it to me."

He grasped her wrist and pulled it behind her, latching onto her mouth again and driving her crazy with a kiss that was filled with passion, with promise. It was meant to torment, to seduce, but she was well past the point of foreplay. She needed him inside her. Having his cock in her mouth, swallowing his taste—such an incredibly intimate act, it made her yearn to get closer to him—closer than even this. And he was keeping her from it.

She whimpered against his mouth, tried to pull away, but he wouldn't let her go. Passion erupted as a violent force. A new game—one of force and take—one she was more than willing to play. She tore her mouth away. "Let me go."

He didn't. Instead, he rolled her onto her back, pinning her there with his strength. "You don't really want me to let you go."

Arousal fired her nerve endings. She searched for a vulnerable spot, finding his hand near her head, and bit down on it. He growled, but didn't release her, instead pulled her arms above her head and lifted her sweater, exposing her bra. Without preamble he bent down and captured the peak of one breast between his teeth, nipping at the quickly responding nipple through the thin fabric. It hardened, an exquisite sensation shooting between her legs and dampening her further.

But she struggled, trying to throw him off—a senseless effort, but fun nonetheless. Who knew that trying to fight against him could be so incredibly arousing? She tried not to laugh, but it was difficult, especially considering how easily he held her down. With any other man she'd be scared to death. With Mike, she knew it was just a game. If she got serious about it and asked him to stop, she knew he would.

She sure as hell didn't want him to stop. She was stimulated beyond the ability to think rationally. Instead, she bucked up against him, inflaming her senses and, apparently, his. He tore at the button and zipper of her jeans, jerking the denim down her thighs and to her ankles. He dragged her to a sitting position, with one hand holding both her wrists together, and pulled her boots off, then her jeans, pushing her to the ground again. She continued to struggle against him to no avail. He was really strong.

Once he had her pinned, he palmed her sex through her silk panties. "You're wet."

"I am not," she protested.

"You need to be fucked. Hell, you *want* to be fucked."

She refused to answer, though she knew it to be true.

"You need a hard cock inside you, ramming hard against that sweet pussy of yours until you come."

"Fuck you. Get off me."

His low laughter infuriated and excited her.

"I *am* going to fuck you." With a quick jerk, her panties were history.

Oh well. The cool breeze wafted over her naked sex and she longed to spread her legs wide, but this game wasn't over. She was supposed to fight this for a while longer.

Mike shoved his jeans aside and he was on her again, his hips against hers, his cock sliding along her the top of her pussy.

Oh God, yes. Right where she wanted and needed him. But she fought it, keeping her thighs together. His teeth gleamed as he smiled, his knee insinuating between hers as he dropped down fully on top of her, pushing her thighs apart.

"Open for me, Grace."

"No," she said, gritting her teeth, loving this. Her pussy was flooded with moisture now. Excitement pulsed through her blood-stream. She was throbbing, aching, desperate to scream the words, to beg him to fuck her. She was hanging on by a thread and if he didn't take her soon, she was going to give in.

"This isn't going to be gentle."

Good. She hoped not. She wanted it hard, forceful, violent, needed him to plunge inside her with a desperation she couldn't fathom.

With a final push, he opened her thighs and moved between them, positioning his cock at the entrance to her pussy. He bent his head and took her mouth in a punishing kiss at the same time he drove inside her.

He was right. It wasn't gentle. She screamed against his mouth as he thrust his cock all the way inside. She was so wet he slid in easily, his balls slapping her ass as he immersed himself to the hilt.

He stilled then, panting against her, and she was afraid he was going to gentle his movements, but he didn't. He reared up and powered inside her again, this time deeper, harder, this thrust with more force than the first. Her walls closed in around him, gripping him tight and firm. Now that her legs were open, she acquiesced, wrapping them around his waist, lifting her ass to give him more. Anything he wanted was his for the taking.

"Fuck, you're tight," he murmured against her mouth, only to slide his tongue inside again, pulling out to nibble at her lips, then her jaw, sliding down to capture her earlobe with his teeth. He bit down on the tender spot between her neck and shoulder as he rocked his shaft against her with punishing thrusts.

She cried out as she tightened around him, spilling her juices as she climaxed. He growled and continued to fuck her, refusing to stop until she was climbing again. She was exhausted from the fight and still he wouldn't let up, dragging his shaft against her clit. And she was going to go over again. The rush of her orgasm brought tears to her eyes as hot splashes of ecstasy spilled from her. With a harsh oath he went with her this time, grinding against her and then stilling, shuddering, clasping her tight against him and kissing her in the way only Mike could.

He rolled to the side, taking her with him, stroking her hair, her face, pressing light kisses to her bruised lips.

"I hurt you, didn't I?" he whispered.

"I'm tougher than you think." She smiled at him, stroked his hair.

"You're an amazing woman, Grace."

"You're an equally amazing man."

"I hope there were no low-flying aircraft going over when we were having sex."

She laughed. They cleaned up and Mike rolled the blanket, tucking everything into his saddlebag. Sweetly sore and spent, then rode quietly back to the ranch and turned in the horses.

When they got back home, Mike ordered her to undress. He pushed her onto the bed on her belly, but instead of sex, he grabbed some lotion and rubbed her back, butt and legs, massaging out the kinks from the ride. Then he curled up against her and they napped. Napped! She never napped. But it was so easy to fall asleep in the middle of day, wrapped up in his arms.

She fixed him dinner at her place that night. Steak and potatoes, figuring that was a "real man" kind of meal. They had wine and great conversation, and Grace realized how much she was going to miss having him around.

She hated the idea of missing anyone. For years she'd lived alone and liked it that way. She had friends whom she hung out with when she wanted company. Otherwise, she had always been content with her life, with her solitude.

Mike refilled her wineglass.

"I've really enjoyed the time we spent together, Grace."

Her stomach knotted. She smiled and reached for her glass, taking a long swallow of wine before answering. "I have, too. Thank you again for the ride today."

"You're welcome."

"What time is your flight tomorrow?"

"Early. I have to be at work the next day."

She studied her wineglass, feeling stupid for the tears that stung her eyes.

"I'm going to miss you, Grace."

Don't say it. She couldn't bear the emotion stabbing at her heart. "I've . . . really enjoyed spending time with you." Didn't she say that already?

He grinned. "I think we both agreed that we enjoyed our time together."

Shit.

"It's okay, Grace. Neither of us is going to handle this very well. It's not like we've had what you would call a relationship. We've had fun. Let's leave it at that."

Yes. Let's do that. Before she started feeling any worse than she already did. Her stomach hurt.

He stood and walked around the table, reaching for her hand. "I want to make love to you."

She laid her glass on the table and slipped her hand in his, letting him lift her. He led her to the bedroom and he undressed her slowly, kissing every inch of her skin that he revealed. She sighed at every touch of his lips, a hot, melting sensation that made her shiver.

"On your knees."

Her skin broke out in chills. She crawled onto the bed and he got behind her, pressing his lips to her back. He kissed every vertebra, from her neck all the way down to her tailbone and farther, his hands all over her. He parted her legs and licked the length of her pussy, drawing out a long, low moan that she couldn't hold in. She was already wet, quivering with the need to join with him. She bent forward, her head hitting the mattress, spreading her legs farther to give him better access as his tongue snaked out to flick at her clit. When he parted her buttocks and licked her anus, she cried out at the exquisite sensation of having his mouth there, circling the sensitive nerve endings with his hot tongue.

"I want to fuck your ass, Grace."

"Yes." She'd allow him any intimacy, wanting him close to her, inside her in every way possible.

He licked her there again, his tongue probing inside the tight hole. She nearly came off the bed at the hot, stabbing motion of his tongue invading her anus. Dear God, that was erotic as hell. He moved behind her, positioning, then reached around to stroke her clit while he parted her pussy lips and slid inside her cunt, fucking her with long, slow strokes until she was writhing against him, needing the orgasm that was so close.

"Make me come," she begged, pushing back against his cock, trying to get closer to the hand massaging her clit.

And then she was there, tightening around him as she climaxed in a rush of hot, spiraling pleasure. He wrapped one arm around her middle and pulled her against his cock while she spasmed, rocking back and forth as the sensations rushed along her nerve endings.

Panting, she barely had time to catch her breath before he pulled out and coated her anus with lube. He kept his hand on her clit, massaging gently now but keeping her in a state of heightened arousal. She wanted his cock again, dammit, needed him inside her.

"Mike."

"Easy, baby," he said, sliding his finger against her anus. He pushed, entered her, the burning sensation subsiding quickly as he finger-fucked her ass. The pleasure rocketed her. His finger inside her tight hole, his other hand rubbing her swollen clit, and her mind somewhere lost in the stratosphere.

He moved his finger in and out until she grew accustomed to the sensation, then withdrew.

"My dick is going to be a lot bigger, baby. Push out when you feel me enter. That'll make it easier to take."

She nodded. He coated her with more lube, then she felt the wide crest of his cock against her anus.

"Push, Grace."

He was so gentle as he entered her. She relaxed her muscles and pushed and he breached the tight muscle. The burn was intense and she breathed through it. Mike didn't move, just let her settle into the sensation, her body adjusting to the invasion of his thick cock. It only took a minute, and he slid in farther.

He was so easy with her, stopping when necessary, never ceasing his movements along her clit, making sure she was okay. That alone was such a turn-on—his care of her.

And when she was adjusted to his invasion, it finally started feeling good—oh Lord, was it good. Thick, filling her, sliding in and out of her while his hand drove her insane. He strummed her clit in slow, easy, maddening motions. She was going to come and it was going to happen in a hurry.

"You have the best ass, Grace," he said, his voice tight with strain.

He wasn't going to last either. She liked knowing that she could take him to the edge so fast. She moved, fucking back against his cock. His loud groan was incredibly arousing, making her tighten even more around him.

"Goddamn!" He pushed forward, not as easily as he had before.

She was ready for it, pushing back, taking it all in. Her body was on fire, her skin covered in moisture. She grabbed the bed sheets and pushed again, listening to the rasping sound of his breathing, feeling the way his movements along her clit intensified.

Her orgasm rocketed her and she tensed, then screamed. She felt the pulses of her orgasm in her anus, and knew Mike would, too. He groaned and yelled out her name, pushing with relentless force as he came, then becoming still against her while she shuddered out the last ounce of energy she possessed.

Spent, she fell forward on the mattress. Mike retreated, lifting her and carrying her to the shower. He washed them both and dried her off, carrying her back to bed and pulling the covers over them.

She wouldn't think about this being the last night she'd fall asleep nestled in his arms. She just slumbered while she could, content to have his heartbeat against her.

When he woke her before dawn, she rose and went through the motions, dressing and making coffee. They drank a cup together in silence.

"I need to go," he said, his voice low, his expression grim.

"I know."

He pulled her into his arms and kissed her. She fought back tears she had no right to shed.

"Thank you, Grace."

"Good-bye, Mike."

She walked him to the elevator and kissed him again, smiling at him as the elevator door closed.

When he was gone, she went back to the bedroom, sat on the bed and smoothed her hands over the sheets, touching the pillow where he'd slept. It was still warm.

Only then did she allow herself the luxury of dissolving into the heart-wrenching sobs she'd held back for so long.

ELEVEN

Mike had held it together on the plane ride back, then threw himself into work for the next week. Fortunately, he was busy as hell and didn't have time to dwell on how much he missed Grace.

Much. Other than every free second he had. He thought he'd done a pretty good job being stoic and acting like he didn't care. That's what Grace wanted, right? To keep things between them unemotional and low key. No strings.

That's what he wanted, wasn't it?

So how come he felt like shit? How come every woman who called, every woman at the country club who'd approached him in the past week and tried to capture his attention, did absolutely nothing for him? Not a spark, not even a twitch of his cock. He was totally and completely uninterested. It was as if he'd come back from Las Vegas a eunuch.

Because those women didn't have beguiling violet eyes. Those women didn't have a slender body with small breasts and perky nipples. Those women didn't have a laugh that made his dick stand up and take notice. Those women didn't have a pioneering spirit, a feisty independence and the guts to make it on their own with virtually nothing. None of them had a warm vulnerability underneath a tough exterior that had melted the icy wall around his cold heart.

None of those women were Grace.

He'd never missed a woman he'd spent time with. Not once. He fucked them and promptly forgot about them, moved on to the next one.

Now he wasn't the slightest bit interested in the next one. Or the one after that.

"You sure are moping around a lot this week."

Mike looked up from his desk at his partner, Seth Jacobs. "I'm busy. And I never mope."

"Uh-huh." Seth sat in one of the chairs across from Mike's desk. "If you say so. But you've snapped the head off everyone in here this week. I thought vacation was supposed to relax you."

"It was relaxing." He opened the file on his desk and decided to ignore Seth.

"So what happened in Las Vegas?"

"Nothing. The conference was good, then I hung out for a few extra days. Had a great time."

"You're full of shit. This is me, remember? I know you better than anyone. Start talking."

That much was true. He and Seth had been buddies since they were kids. Seth knew him inside and out and Mike could never hope to hide anything from him. He closed the file and dragged his hands through his hair. "I met a woman."

Seth leaned back in the chair. "Oh, there's a shocker."

Mike laughed. "She's different. There was a . . . connection."

"Really?"

"Yeah. Really. I can't stop thinking about her."

"So why don't you do something about it?"

"Like what? She has a life and a career back there. Mine is here. She's independent. Owns a sex club. She doesn't want a relationship or any kind of entanglements in her life."

Seth laughed. "She sounds a lot like you."

Leave it to Seth to state the obvious. "Yeah, she does. We're similar in many ways."

"Which is probably why you're attracted to her." Seth shook his head. "So the mighty Nottingham has finally fallen."

Mike frowned. "This is *not* funny."

"I think it is. I think it's fucking hysterical. Wait 'til I tell Abby."

Abby was Seth's fiancée and a fellow veterinarian. She had worked as an intern in their offices last year, and Seth and Mike had actually had a ménage with Abby one weekend. But Abby had chosen Seth over Mike. Smart girl. Mike hadn't wanted to settle down and Abby had made a strong bond with Seth. They were good together. Seth was a lucky guy. Abby was golden.

"I'm sure Abby will laugh her ass off, too."

Seth leaned forward. "Abby loves you and you know that. She wants to see you happy. Mike, all kidding aside, if you care about this woman, don't let her slip out of your hands. Make it work."

"I don't see how it can."

Seth rolled his eyes. "Then you're not looking hard enough. Love doesn't come around all that often, especially for people like you."

Mike snorted. "Gee, thanks."

"You know what I mean. You've been playing games your whole life. You've closed yourself off to every woman you've ever met. Now one has finally reached you. That means something. Don't let her go."

He looked at Seth and smiled. "I have a practice here. A life."

"Man, I love you like a brother. You know that." He swept his hand around the room. "But you can do this anywhere."

Mike stared at Seth. He couldn't believe what Seth had said. But dammit, he was right. "You're a really good friend."

Seth grinned. "Yeah, I know. Now put that brilliant brain of yours to work and think with something besides your dick for a change. And go figure out how to make it work with the woman who's managed to do what no other ever has."

"What's that?"

"Make Mike Nottingham fall in love."

Grace looked around at the club and frowned. This sucked.

Once again Wild Nights was filled to capacity. Based on preliminary figures, she was probably going to have her best month ever. Liquor sales were up, attendance was up, new membership was up. The club was flying high.

And she was absolutely miserable.

Which was all Mike Nottingham's fault, because he'd made her fall in love with him. The sneaky bastard. How could he do this to her? She felt sick to her stomach and all she wanted to do was run to her apartment, curl up in a ball and cry her eyes out.

She'd pondered tracking him down in Oklahoma, calling him, seeing if maybe they could get together again. She'd gone as far as looking up his number. And every damn night she'd picked up the phone, her fingers hovering on the buttons, wavering for a few seconds. Then she'd slam the phone down, feeling ridiculous for the attempt.

It was over. They'd agreed. It had been a fling and nothing more, right?

She scrunched up her nose and shook her head. Disgusting. She couldn't stand emotional, weepy women, and she'd become one. A week had gone by already, for the love of God. One would think the aches and pains would be gone by now.

But they weren't. In fact, they were getting worse. She didn't think it possible, but she missed Mike more now than she had the day he left. She couldn't stop thinking about him and it was interfering with her work.

She wasn't having fun anymore. And she had always had fun at Wild Nights. Coming to work was the high point of her day. But for the last week she'd dreaded it, knowing Mike wouldn't be here. She'd gone through the motions, played hostess as normal and chatted up her guests, but her heart hadn't been in it. And still she found herself loitering by the door.

Looking for who? Mike? As if by some miracle he'd show up? That he'd be so miserable without her he'd fly back from Oklahoma, swing her into his arms and tell her he couldn't live without her, that they'd find some way to make this work?

Ha! She'd long ago stopped believing in fairy tales. The harsh reality of her childhood had cured those fantasies.

It was damn time she snapped out of it and got back to her life and her club. That was her real love. Her forever love. The one that would always be there for her. The one that would never cause her pain. This was her choice and she damn well better get back to loving it.

But how was she going to erase Mike? How was she going to forget the wild nights spent in his arms, the taste of his lips, the feel of his hands on her body? How was she going to forget what it felt like to sleep tucked up against him? How was she going to forget how she felt when they were together, the kind of person she was when she was with him? She'd laughed more, she'd relaxed more, she'd felt safe and comforted when he was with her. For the first time in her life, she'd felt as if she could be who she really was with a man. Without games, without just sex being involved. She could talk to Mike about anything and everything and he never once judged her for what she was and the paths she'd chosen.

How was she going to forget loving him?

Dammit, she had no experience with this. She didn't know how to handle it. She moved to the bar and asked the bartender for a glass of wine, smiling and visiting with the clients there.

But soon they moved off to the playrooms, the night grew late and she found herself alone.

Loneliness wrapped itself around her like a cold blanket. She shivered as the front door opened. It was cold out tonight. Her bouncers had probably moved inside to get away from the chilled wind.

"Need some warming, babe?"

She almost knocked her drink over as she twirled around on the bar stool, convinced the voice she heard had to be her imagination.

It wasn't.

"Mike!" For a split second she'd thought about acting cool, but then threw that right out the window. She flew off the barstool and launched herself into his arms. He caught her, his mouth meeting hers in a hot, bone-melting kiss.

This time she didn't care about the tears. She let them come. They spilled down her cheeks as his lips moved over hers, his tongue sliding inside her mouth. She shuddered in his embrace, wrapping her arms so tightly around his neck she was certain she cut off his circulation. She didn't care. He was here!

When she finally let go, he set her down on her feet, smiling at her. "God, I missed you, Grace."

She blinked away the tears. "I missed you, too." She grabbed his hand and signaled to the floor manager. "I'm gone for the night."

The manager grinned and nodded, waving her off.

The ride up the elevator was excruciatingly long. She latched onto Mike's hand, refusing to let go. "Why are you here?"

"I told you. I missed you." He pulled her against him again, kissing her long and hard and by the time he broke the kiss, she had no doubt how much he had in fact missed her. The rigid length of his cock pressed against her hip as he palmed her lower back to push her closer to him.

The elevator opened and Mike picked her up in his arms. They didn't make it very far, though. She'd thought about this moment the entire week—reuniting with him, his desperation to see her, her own need drilling her into a frenzied anticipation. She wanted it so badly her body thrummed with anxious expectation. She wasn't going to be denied, and thank God he wasn't going to be either.

He slammed her up against the living room wall and lifted her dress. She was already wet when he pulled her panties to the side, jerking down his zipper and freeing his cock. His gaze was so intense it was shocking, thrilling her, making her wet with anticipation and need.

She was sobbing when he entered her, lifting her with one hand on her ass. She wrapped her legs around his hips and slid down on his shaft, her pussy pulsing. With a hard thrust he drove into her again and again, his strokes long and deep. He was telling her without words how much he needed her. He was claiming her, making her his, and she was accepting it all, claiming him right back.

God yes, she needed him, needed him inside her, a part of her. She held on, reveling in his possession of her, raining kisses all over his lips, his jaw, murmuring to him the entire time. She couldn't get enough of him, wanting him to crawl as deeply inside of her as possible. Arching against him, she gave him full access and he took it, slamming against her until she splintered.

She came hard, crying out and raking her nails down his shoulders. He dug his fingers into her ass as he emptied into her, burying his face into the crook of her neck and groaning as he rode out a long orgasm, his body pressed full-length against hers.

It was possible she'd be content to be held like this forever. But he let her down, held her against him while she found her footing on very shaky legs.

"Welcome back," she said, pressing a light kiss to his lips.

"I'm glad to be back."

After they readjusted their clothing, she sat on the sofa and he went with her, pulling her across his lap. She dragged her fingers through his hair, still not quite believing he was here.

"I'm never going to forgive you for this, you know," she said, resting her hand on his chest.

He arched a quizzical brow. "For what?"

"For turning a sexually confident woman of the world into a quivering, weepy mass of feminine hormones. I've been a mess."

He tilted his head back and laughed. "Well it's only justice, babe. You turned an arrogant, alpha, don't-give-a-shit male into an emotional, caring wreck of contradictions."

She cast him a smug smile. "Good. Then we're perfectly suited for each other."

Then he went serious on her, cupping her cheek with the palm of his hand. "We have to make this work, Grace. It was hell last week without you."

Her heart swelled, broke a little, and the tears came again. "How? You live across the country."

"Right now I do. I've been doing this a long time. I've invested well. I can have a veterinary practice anywhere. Carl was talking at the conference about how he wanted to retire over a year ago, but he wants to sell his practice since he doesn't have kids to hand it down to. He's leery of just anyone taking it over. He wants a vet he knows and trusts."

"Carl? The vet who owns the ranch where we went riding?"

"Yeah. He has a practice in Las Vegas."

"You would consider buying his practice here?"

He smiled, swept his hand across her hair. "I would."

"What about ties to your home? Your family?"

"My life is my own. I can live it wherever I want. I want to live it where you are, Grace. I'm in love with you."

Oh. Wow. Damn. That was a big admission. Her heart thudded against her chest and a wave of nausea hit her. She swung her legs around and bent over, shoving her head between her knees.

"Uh, Grace?"

"Yes." The blood rushed to head, but she was clearing a bit now.

"Are you going to be sick?"

"I'm considering it."

"So, me telling you that I love you makes you want to throw up?"

She giggled. She really couldn't help it. Raising her head, she swept her hair away from her face. "I'm sorry. No one ever told me that before. I wasn't prepared for it."

God, she was handling this badly.

"I see."

She felt awful about the confused look on his face and knew she needed to set him straight right away. She sat upright and faced him.

"Mike, I love you, too. I've been sick all week. My heart hurt. It's never hurt before. I've never been so unhappy. I hated feeling this miserable."

"Really?"

She laughed at the hopeful expression on his face. "Yeah. Really. I've never been in love before. I don't know how to handle it."

"Neither do I." He took her hands. "I know you value your independence, Grace. I would never want to take that away from you. I love what you do for a living. I love Wild Nights. It's what makes you who you are and I'd be damned angry if you gave that up for anyone or any reason."

Could she possibly love this man even more? He was everything she wanted but never thought existed. A man who would let her be herself, a man who loved her and didn't feel the need to change her.

"So what do we do now?"

"Now we realize that we love each other and take it a day at a time. Build on that, and see what happens. I'm going to buy Carl out, take a leave of absence from the clinic in Oklahoma, and take over his practice here."

"You'll really do it. You'll move out here just to be with me?"

"If you want that."

"Yes, I want that!" She kissed him, pouring out her emotions, holding nothing back. When she pulled away she said, "You know, I'm long overdue for a vacation. This place runs itself. I might want to check out the wild life in Oklahoma, see where you live. Maybe enjoy sex outside with the wind whipping through my hair."

He tugged on her ponytail. "I seem to recall you enjoying that."

"I did."

"Just like I enjoy that sexy club you run. Be prepared for me to spend a lot of my nights there."

She affected a heavy sigh. "Okay, if you must. As long as you don't mind having sex in dark corners of the club, or engaging in voyeurism, a little mutual masturbation, maybe playing in the kink room, or any of the other wonders Wild Nights has to offer. With just me as your partner, of course."

"That works both ways, darlin'. I might have enjoyed watching you put on that show with Den, but we're exclusive now. I don't share what's mine."

She thrilled to his possession of her, something she never thought possible. But he was right. There was no other man for her but Mike. "I'm all yours. And you're all mine."

Mike smoothed his hand over her hip, his gaze filled with sensual promise. "I think I might have just found the woman of my dreams."

And Grace had discovered that fairy-tale princes did exist, after all.

PURPLE MAGIC

LISA RENEE JONES

Thanks to my agent, Natasha Kern. She knows why this one is special. Also thanks to Kate Seaver for sparking great ideas.

ONE

Manhattan's "invitation only" underground clubs held the answers Jolene Morrison sought.

Filled with sins of the flesh and vampire sex games, these clubs represented danger. A smart female, even one like herself—half-vampire, half-human—knew entering such a place held extreme risks. Regardless, Jolene Morrison had no option but to take her chances. Her best friend and roommate, Carrie Wright—the closest thing she knew to family—had disappeared, lured into the sensual world of the underground.

The police wanted Jolene to believe Carrie had run off with her rich vampire boyfriend. She'd believe that the day she believed in the super heroes she marketed for her employer, BK Comics. Carrie wouldn't leave without telling Jolene. She just wouldn't do it.

To find Carrie, Jolene needed entry into the clubs and to find the man her friend had been dating. *Alex*. If she found Alex, she'd find Carrie. For a painful two hundred dollars, the bartender on

Eighty-eighth had directed her to a man he'd said could get her where she needed to go and that was good enough for her.

Walking past a line of men standing outside Howard Stern's favorite high-end, topless bar, Scores, Jolene endured whistles and blatant head-to-toe inspections from hopefuls who wanted into the club. Limousines lined the side street, the transportation for the rich and famous who were allowed automatic entry into the hotspot. She stared straight ahead, ignoring the attention, determined to reach her destination. Nothing mattered but finding the address written on the torn paper balled in her hand.

A block later, the scenery changed, the crowd thinning to near nothing, the sidewalks empty but for a few pedestrians. Though Bloomingdales and a cluster of high-end shops were a mere four streets away, this area wasn't the best of the best. But then, in New York City, things changed in the blink of an eye. One minute you had high society. The next, high crime.

Jolene stopped in front of an eight-story white building. She blew a long, auburn-brown curl from her eyes. Her feet hurt from the high heels she wore, and the black silk of her blouse clung to her body like a second skin, a product of the humid night air. She was thankful for her bare legs and knee-length skirt. Mid-August brought humidity that seemed to thicken and swell between the buildings. Being Friday, the day before the weekly trash pick up for millions, overflowing barrels lined the walls and street, oozing stench. She thought of the name scribbled on the paper. *Drago.* Just Drago. Nothing more. The name sounded like something out of the comics she marketed. But it wasn't. Her stomach fluttered with apprehension. It was an ancient vampire warrior's name she was certain she'd heard before. A name that both rattled her nerves and delivered a bit of hope. If anyone could help her, it would be one of the warriors. The "Slayers," as they were called by the vampire council, were deadly warriors cloaked in secrecy. Many of their people feared what they didn't understand, and bedtime stories of vampires regarding ancient "mya," or in human language, "monsters," were often associated with Slayers.

But Jolene knew much about these warriors, especially their shielded identities, and they were not monsters. She knew, because her father was one of them. She couldn't even call him if she needed him; when he was undercover, working a job, no one contacted him. Lord only knew, she'd tried. Now and in the past. Seven years before, Jolene had celebrated her eighteenth birthday by burying her mother, unable to reach her father.

Jolene drew a breath, her resolve thickened with the distaste of her thoughts. She'd lost her mother. She wasn't going to lose Carrie, too.

Eying the mailboxes on the side of the building, the gold-painted numbers confirmed that Jolene had found her destiny. Now, she hoped she'd found her man. Going to a stranger's apartment didn't seem like a smart move, yet her options were limited. Apprehension tightened her chest. In her sales job, she talked to people she didn't know all the time, but this was different. This was a man's home—a vampire's home. Someone she didn't know and certainly couldn't trust. But she *had* to do this. Like her, Carrie had no family.

A tall, bosomy woman exited the controlled entrance into the building and Jolene darted forward. "Hold that door."

The woman tossed her long, blonde hair over her shoulders and eyed Jolene, looking as if she might deny her entry. "Enjoy, sweetheart," she finally said, and sidestepped to allow Jolene to grab the door.

Jolene murmured a thank you, watching as the woman strutted away, her hips moving in a seductive sway. The comment made her wonder if the woman had just come from Drago's apartment. Considering his involvement with the underground sex clubs, she didn't know *what* to expect inside this building.

Jolene moved through the tiny hallway and made her way to the long, narrow stairs. Great. Her feet wouldn't take much more torture.

Glancing upward, she silently cursed Drago's seventh-floor location. If she needed to make a quick departure, there wasn't one available. Not allowing herself time to think, she took the first step.

By the time she knocked on Drago's door, the steepness of the stairs had her breathless, despite a regular gym routine. Barely a second passed when the door flew open, exposing a man as broad as he was tall, as sexy as he looked dangerous. Jolene was more than breathless. She was downright speechless.

Long dark hair tied at the back of his neck exposed a strong jaw and eyes as black as a starless night. Eyes that narrowed before sliding downward in a long, far too hot, perusal of her body. Her job in sales had conditioned her to ignore such blatant inspection. But this man's sizzling attention warmed her inside out. How could it not? Everything about him screamed sex. No. Not *just sex*. Hot sex. Wild sex. Burning hot nights filled with acts from the most forbidden fantasies.

Forcing her voice from her suddenly dry throat, she said, "Drago?"

His gaze narrowed on hers. "Depends who's asking." He spoke in a deep, sensual voice laced with a hint of an accent she couldn't quite place.

"My name is Jolene." She left off her last name, not willing to give this man any more information than she had to. "I'm . . . looking for someone. I heard you might be able to point me in the right direction."

One dark brow inched upward. "Who might that be?"

"Are you Drago?" Jolene asked, not willing to play games with this man or anyone. She had to find Carrie. There wasn't room for mistakes.

His boots scraped the wooden floor, drawing her gaze downward, as he eased farther into the apartment. The door creaked as he expanded the opening, and her eyes slid across his faded jeans, which hugged long, muscular legs. She swallowed and forced her gaze back to his. With a wave of his hand, he motioned her inside.

She shook her head. "I'd rather not."

Drago—or whoever he was—gave her a probing look. "Who is it you seek?"

"Seek?" she asked, confused at first but then realizing what he meant. "Oh. A man. A man named Alex." Vampires were born into clans of numbers, not names. She narrowed her gaze on his. "No last name." In other words, she knew Alex was a vampire.

A stormy expression filled his rugged features. An expression that said he knew the name. "Who sent you here?"

"A bartender. He told me you could help me get into the clubs Alex favors. One in particular—Purple Magic."

A pregnant silence. "What do you want with him?"

Though a vampire could invade a human mind, Jolene's vampire side gave her the ability to shield her thoughts. But an ancient warrior, a Slayer, had powers beyond the average vampire. Lying to him could get her in more trouble than the truth might. Besides, the bartender might have already told him to expect her and that she'd been asking about Carrie.

She had to go with the flow now and shoot straight. "Alex was the last person to see my roommate before she disappeared two weeks ago."

For what felt like an eternity, he studied her, his reaction to her words indiscernible. Finally, he said, "Come inside." His voice was low, terse.

Instinct told her that refusal to enter would be as good as refusing his help. If he even planned to help. Her hesitation drew a frustrated sound from him. "You come here wanting something of me, yet you cower in the hall?"

Jolene knew a challenge when she heard one, and this was that and more. Without another word, she stepped forward beyond the entrance, inside his home.

A quick inspection of her surroundings told Jolene she stood in the center of one of the ultrasmall, one-room apartments that were typical of Manhattan. The furnishings consisted of a bed, a student-sized corner desk and a leather rolling chair. No table. No television. And nothing but pull-down plastic shades covered the windows.

She felt Drago move behind her, his woodsy male scent insinuating its way into her nostrils, making her aware of the intimacy of occupying such a small space together. The door shut behind her and she turned to face the man who still had no name. Their eyes caught and held midair, locking in a heat-filled stare that stole her breath away. She didn't understand the reaction. Human females found themselves susceptible to vampire seductions and mind controls. But Jolene had never found that she reacted in such a way. Her half-vampire side had given her a shield. Or it had in the past. Why did this man—this vampire—have her feeling flushed with awareness when no other had before?

"You shouldn't have come here," he said, finally, breaking the spell that had held them entranced.

His voice held a sensual quality and she barely suppressed a shiver. Good Lord, what was wrong with her? "I had no choice. I have to find my friend."

One dark brow inched upward. "And what of you? Who will find you?"

Her throat went dry at his words, a bit of fear churning in her gut. He was testing her. She was sure of it. For what? That was the question. Resolve? True desire to find her friend? Or was he taunting her? Perhaps trying to make her question her decision to come inside his apartment?

"I'm not stupid," Jolene managed in a strong voice. "People know I'm here."

He took a step toward her. "I don't think so." She forced herself to keep her feet solidly planted. Not to back away. "I think you're desperate to find your friend. Someone gave you my name, and you rushed over here without considering the consequences."

"You're right about my friend," she said as he stopped directly in front of her. The man was huge. He towered over her a good foot. With her height at five foot five, she had to tilt her chin upward to make eye contact. "I *am* desperate to find her. She was dating Alex. He . . . made her act out of character. She started going to . . . places she normally wouldn't."

His response was immediate. "Sex clubs."

She nodded. "Right. And now she's gone."

He stared at her. One second. Two. Three. Then he moved away, putting distance between himself and Jolene. She cast him a slanted look, watching him stop in the kitchen area of the rectangular-shaped room. His actions seemed to indicate less aggression. Less intention to cause harm. Relief slid across her body, though her heart still beat like a drum against her chest.

"How about a drink?" he asked, as he pulled two glasses and a bottle of bourbon out of the cabinet.

She turned to face him. "No . . . thank you." She swallowed. "So . . . you know Alex?"

He poured amber-colored liquid into a glass and took a sip. "I know him."

Hope filled her thoughts. She widened her eyes and took a tentative step forward. "Then you can tell me how to find him?"

He leaned against the counter crossing one booted leg over the other. "Nope."

Disappointment ripped through her gut. "Why?" she demanded, desperation taking hold. "Please. I have to find my friend."

"You have no idea what you are dealing with here. Let the police handle this."

Frustration roared inside, and her fists balled by her sides. He had to know the police were no help. "You think I haven't tried that route? The police do nothing. We all know vampires like Alex pay them off. I *need* to find my friend. Get me an invitation into Purple Magic and

I'll pay you." But she had no more money, and she knew it. She'd find it though. Somehow. For Carrie. For her "sister." "I know you can get me inside." She swallowed, debating her next words. "I know what you are. I've heard my father speak your name. And I know your duty to help me."

Seconds that felt like hours ticked by and she didn't dare breathe. "Who is your father?"

"Riker."

Before she could breathe, let alone think, Drago had set his glass down and closed the distance between them. His movements agile and lightning fast—those of a tiger after his prey. He pinned her against the wall, his muscular legs framing hers, pressing against her thighs. That woodsy male scent of his surrounded her, drugging her. And to her disbelief, rather than fear, she felt fire. Her limbs were heavy with desire, her nipples tight with uncontrollable arousal.

"Do you know what would happen to you in Alex's world if you said your father's name?"

She swallowed. "I wouldn't do that."

"You spoke it to me."

"Because I know you're one of them. One of . . . the Slayers."

"*Was*, sweetheart. Why didn't you go to Riker?"

"I tried. Carrie could be dead before he surfaces again."

He glared at her, his eyes half-veiled, something remotely like anger glinting in the depths of his stare. "You think you have what it takes to enter Alex's world?" he demanded.

Jolene forced herself to meet his hard gaze, not allowing him to see any fear in her. "I know I do," she said, meaning it. "I'm only half human. I'm not prey for Alex or any other vampire male." He was trying to scare her, and if he succeeded, she knew she'd leave here with no more information than she'd had before coming. "I'll do whatever it takes to find my friend. If you refuse your duty and won't help me, then get me inside Purple Magic and I'll do the rest myself."

If Jolene didn't get inside that club, she'd never find her friend. She could feel it with every ounce of her being. And she'd do what it took to save Carrie. No matter what the price.

Even bargain with the devil. And Drago might just be that. She didn't know if he was friend or foe, but then, it didn't matter. Nothing mattered but finding Carrie.

Was Alex using Carrie to get to Jolene?

Drago would bet blood and money that was the case. Months of working undercover, pretending to be a traitor to his council had taught him much about Alex. And without question, Alex would relish the opportunity to claim a Slayer's daughter. He'd need a way to control a vampire female of ancient blood beyond his own mental abilities though. In this case, perhaps Alex was using Jolene's friend as both bait and leverage.

Drago stared at the gorgeous woman who'd taken over more than his temporary apartment—she'd overtaken him. If he didn't know better, and if she wasn't half human, he'd have sworn she was his mate. Which was the last damn thing he needed. A mate meant distraction, and distraction meant death. He'd be sending her on her way and doing it fast. But not until he ensured she wouldn't be visiting Alex. The foolish woman was going to get herself killed—or worse, turned into one of Alex's pool of sex slaves. Alex would relish the chance to claim a Slayer's daughter as his own.

If her friend lived, Drago would find her. Most likely, Carrie had been placed inside the private sex pool Alex kept to sate his appetites for both blood and play. The same one for which Drago had gone undercover trying to locate.

Drago stared into Jolene's emerald green eyes and saw the fear she tried to hide behind a mental shield—to no avail. Ancient powers and a unique connection with this woman had him feeling her inside and out. The front of his pants pulled tight against his hips. He could almost taste her emotions. Just as he could smell her desire, her ripe readiness for him to take her. Whatever this roar she'd evoked inside him was, she felt it, too. Their attraction was real. Her bravado was not. Which meant an erotic preview of the sexual appetites of a male vampire would scare the hell out of her.

He grabbed her leg, lifting it to his hip, shoving her skirt up her thigh in the process, and cupped her ass. He fit his cock to her core, making damn sure she knew this wasn't a game. Not even a dangerous one. Alex was nothing shy of lethal. Drago had a good mind to take Jolene, here and now, to teach her a much-needed lesson in the real world.

His mouth lowered to her ear. "You sure you're willing to do anything? Are you willing to fuck me to find your friend?" He inched backward enough to fix her in a hot stare. In her eyes, he saw her confusion mingled with sensual heat. She was scared shitless, yet she could not help wanting him. His cock thickened with the knowledge. Mates or not, they had that kind of chemistry that no two beings could run from. He pressed past the burn in his body, reaching for duty and honor.

This wasn't about how much he wanted to bury himself deep inside this woman, though he sure as hell did. His actions were meant to scare the hell out of her. But it didn't change the satisfaction he felt at feeling her soften beneath his hold, of feeling her melting with his touch. "You want me," he whispered, his voice thick with desire. "Don't you, little one?"

Her palms pressed against his chest, and one of his hands covered them. With the other hand, he continued to explore her lush backside, his fingers brushing her parted cheeks. She was wearing a thong and he found himself burning to know the color. Better yet, burning to yank it away and discard it. He didn't give a damn what color it was.

"Yes," he murmured, being crass on purpose. This was about scaring her. About sending her home to be a good girl. "You'd fuck me and pretend you did it to find your friend. But we'd both know better. We'd both know you did it because you want to feel my cock buried deep inside you."

Her lashes fluttered, her hands moving to his arms, squeezing with force, clinging to him rather than pushing him away. "Stop," she whispered, her words contrasting her actions. "Please stop."

"Who are you talking to, Jolene?" he asked, pressing her with the truth. "Me? Or you?" He didn't give her time to respond, leaning forward and claiming her mouth, feeling the softness of her lips beneath his, tempting him with their sweetness. So much so that he pulled back, not daring to fully taste her, fearful of where it might lead him. Yet he couldn't back away either. He was still close, too close, their breath mingling, teasing, arousing. The thought of Alex touching her, of anyone inside those clubs having her, drew an odd feeling of protectiveness. One of possessiveness. It angered him. Angered him because it tested his well-guarded control. The control that made him the mighty Slayer he'd always been.

He slid one hand into her hair, a bit rougher now, and forced her to look at him. With the other, he squeezed her ass and pulled her tight against his raging cock. "Are you prepared to fuck Alex? And what of his friends? Will you fuck them?"

Drago stared down at her, waiting for her answer, his gut tight. If she didn't answer the way he wanted her to, he'd damn sure do whatever it took to make sure she did.

TWO

Jolene knew she should push Drago away, but for some reason she couldn't. Being in this man's arms, his hard, perfect body pressed close, overwhelmed her with desire. With passion. With some sort of blind yearning to feel more of what he could offer. To give herself to him.

Staring up at Drago, barely able to breathe, his words replayed in her head. *Will you fuck Alex?*

Drago's impact on Jolene was nothing shy of molten. His body set hers on fire. But his words . . . his words hit her the hardest, scorching her with their impact, setting her emotions into overdrive. Fear. Anger. Even embarrassment over her out-of-character willingness to be taken by this man. Good Lord, she was losing it because she could barely think straight. She wanted Drago in a bad way. She wanted . . . him inside her.

She bit her bottom lip, fighting her desire to lean into him, to press her mouth to his again. Drago was right. This urge, this need, the molten heat pulsing through her veins, had nothing to do with Carrie. No matter how much she wanted to claim her actions were to protect her friend, that wasn't the truth. What she felt right now, with Drago, was purely primitive. Lust in a lethal dose.

Whatever the reason she wanted Drago, her desire for him, at least, made what had to be done easier. Jolene had already decided she would sleep with Drago, or anyone else she had to, if it would save Carrie. Sex for the life of the only person she considered family was a small price to pay. With that conclusion, she charged forward, meeting Drago's challenge head on. He wouldn't scare her off.

She drew a breath. "I meant what I said." It pleased her to realize how strong her voice sounded. "I'll do whatever it takes to save my friend."

Drago's fingers brushed the strip of damp silk between her legs, sending darts of pleasure through her body from head to toe. His breath fanned her neck. Her ear. Her mouth. "Anything?" he prodded.

She swallowed against the dryness in her throat. "I told you," she said, her tone sharper, tired of his persistence and of her own lack of control with this man. "Whatever it takes."

A low growl escaped his throat, and she could almost feel his anger at her declaration. She steeled herself for whatever came next, but nothing could have prepared her for the onslaught of heat that followed.

One of his palms slid up her side, his hand cupping her breast, her skin warm everywhere he touched—and everywhere he hadn't but she wished he would. Through the thin silk of her blouse, he pinched her nipple and, despite her best efforts not to, she moaned with pleasure. He covered her mouth with his, swallowing the sound with a kiss. No. More than a kiss. His tongue slid along hers, deep and probing, stroking her into submission.

Lost to the moment, consumed by primal heat, her arms slid around his neck, her body melting against his. She couldn't get enough of his taste, his smell, his arms. It wasn't just *him* being aggressive anymore, just him taking what he wanted. She took. She wanted. She burned.

Even as she silently asked for more, her hands gliding over his shoulders, he pulled away, distancing himself. Stealing the fantasy and slapping her with a hard dose of reality.

Jolene gasped at the loss of contact, shocked at how cold she felt, how lost. Hugging herself, she shivered, surprised at how intense her reaction was to this man. She could still taste him on her tongue, still feel his hands on her body.

Her gaze lifted to his, and she found him several steps away. He watched her with turbulent, dark eyes that said he, too, was shocked by what had transpired between them.

The longer their contact remained broken, the more reality seeped into her mind. With it, a wave of confusion took hold. No man, or vampire, had ever driven her to such passion as this one, and it rattled her to the core. Needing support, Jolene inched backward, leaning against the wall so that her knees wouldn't buckle.

"That was a little taste of what Alex's world will do to you," Drago promised. "It'll take and take until you don't know who you are anymore. Until there's nothing left."

Jolene tore her eyes from his and focused on the floor, needing a full disconnect from Drago to pull herself together. She didn't know why Drago affected her as he did, but it hadn't been by manipulating her mind. But Carrie could easily be controlled by a vampire.

Heat flooded her cheeks and her head spun. She'd never felt so out of control in her life. Never felt so lost. Well, not since the day her mother had died. Not since that terrible day when she'd had nowhere to turn. Her father always seemed to be out of reach right when she needed him.

"Alex tends to send his women *away*," Drago said, not elaborating beyond the implication of the words. "Your friend could be long gone. You could risk yourself for nothing."

Jolene's gaze jerked upward at his words, his intentions now clear. He was simply playing a game of cat and mouse, trying to scare her. It wasn't going to work. "Carrie isn't gone."

His brow lifted in challenge, but he said nothing. But then, he didn't have to. His actions, his facial expression, said it all and she could read between the lines. He either knew or suspected Carrie was . . . dead. Maybe he was even involved. He might be a Slayer, but that didn't mean he played for the right team.

Anger formed like a spot of expanding blackness, growing bigger by the second. At herself. At this man. At what she'd almost done with a man who could very well be responsible for hurting Carrie. Maybe he wanted to scare her off because he had something to hide.

She pushed off the wall, hoping he wouldn't notice the way her hands began to shake. Not that it mattered. He was an ancient vampire, without a doubt able sense her emotions. Well, let him. Hers were raging for sure.

Part of Jolene wanted to charge at him. To hit him. Another part feared what he might do if she did. Somehow her voice came out steady, though low and tense. "Where is Carrie? What have you done with her?"

He walked to the door and yanked it open. "You can't save her by sacrificing yourself." His eyes bore into her. "Now, go home where you belong. You're way over your head here."

Jolene didn't know what to do. This man knew how to find Carrie. If she left with no answers, she was back to square one. Anger turned to desperation. She couldn't lose Carrie. She couldn't. "Help me. Please."

"I am," he said without hesitation. "I'm giving you the best advice of your life. Go home. If Carrie's alive, she'll come home to you."

With those words, hope filled her. "You'll find her?"

"I said no such thing."

Her hands balled into fists by her sides. "I can't leave without answers."

He gave her a hot perusal, his eyes raking her body with blatant admiration and lust. When his gaze returned to hers, he said, "Alex is no gentleman. Leave now or I'll stop pretending to be one myself."

She drew a breath at the glint of danger lurking in the depths of his stare, yet she sensed he was scaring her on purpose. And she sensed she'd pushed his buttons. Pushed beyond a place she should be and she knew it. She didn't understand how or why, but she had.

She walked toward the door. Toward him. He tracked her steps with a watchful gaze, a hunger in the way he looked at her, the air charged with electricity, with menace. Something had changed in him. He had become more distant. More threatening. And she feared him all right, but not for the reasons she should. She feared him because he stole her control with his presence, with his touch and taste.

She brushed past him, fighting a moan as her arm touched his, her nipples pebbling into tight knots of pleasure and pain. This man infuriated her, yet still she wanted him.

Pausing at the doorway, Jolene eased around to face Drago. Her chin tilted upward in defiance as she opened her mouth to declare her determination, to promise she'd find a way into Purple Magic. But as she started to speak, she decided against it. For some reason, she felt Drago might actually try to stop her from following through with her search for Carrie. Without another word, she left the apartment and entered the hall.

And as she found the stairs, beginning her descent, she could feel Drago watching her, feel him willing her to stay away from Purple Magic. The subtle mental push didn't go unnoticed, nor did it sit well. She wanted to shove back but fought the urge, reminding herself that he wouldn't help her, but he might do the opposite. He might become an obstacle. She didn't know what to make of Drago. Was he one of the mighty Slayers fighting for good over evil, or a Slayer turned dark, fighting against those he'd once served?

Jolene didn't know, but it didn't really matter. At this point, Drago was best left behind her. Carrie was another story. She would *not* leave Carrie behind. She was going to find her best friend and bring her home.

Drago walked to the railing and watched Jolene's departure, cursing because he knew damn well she wasn't going to leave this thing with Alex alone. Which was exactly why he'd gotten downright foul with her before her departure.

For almost two years now, he'd worked inside Alex's operation, an elaborate cover woven by the council, painting him as a Slayer who'd turned against them.

Alex had created an underground city filled with his army, all well fed and pleasured. All loyal enough to help Alex challenge the council. Drago's job was to break into Alex's sex-club operation and take it down. And he was close. Damn close. Seeing Alex crumble would be sweet reward for months of acting a traitor to his people.

That bartender, a paid servant of Alex, reported to Drago, because he looked at Drago as Alex's right-hand man. And though Alex hadn't mentioned Jolene to Drago, that didn't mean he didn't know about her. Alex kept secrets even from those close to him.

If Alex knew of Jolene, he damn sure had a plan to get to her. Jolene would most likely be getting that invitation to Purple Magic she wanted, and getting it from Alex. He wouldn't hesitate to trade Carrie's return for Jolene's submission.

"Damn it," Drago murmured under his breath. There was too much at risk for him to allow one woman to get in the way, but then, she wasn't just any woman. She was a Slayer's daughter. And Lord help him, not just any Slayer. A missing Slayer. No one had heard from Riker in months, and the worst was feared.

Even as he heard the warnings in his head, aware he was risking his mission, Drago reached for the door and pulled it shut behind him. Knowing he was going to follow Jolene. At the very least, he needed her address. He couldn't push aside his need to know more about her. At least until he confirmed she was Riker's daughter. Yes. He had to follow her for Riker. He ground his teeth. Right. That was a damn good load of crap and he knew it.

Drago took his time descending the stairs, forcing himself to go slow, to fight the urgency pulsing through his veins, driving him to charge forward hard and fast. An urgency he wasn't accustomed to feeling nor understanding. Women were pleasure. They were to be protected. But he wasn't a man to be close to anyone. His job was his life, and his life was deadly.

Drago took the final step to ground level, and Jolene was nowhere in sight. But it didn't matter. Her scent was embedded in his senses now. To find her, to track her, at least at short distances, wouldn't be difficult, which was why the urgency he felt made no sense.

The woman had gotten under his skin and his body still pulsed with arousal. He'd find her just fine. Forgetting her would be the task. She'd be a babe in a forest full of hungry beasts in one of Alex's clubs, no matter how strong her vampire side. The vampire males would team up on her, break her down mentally. Then they'd ravish her body, her very existence.

And there would be nothing anyone, not even he, could do about it. The thought of Jolene being possessed by the underground flared fire in his veins. Possessiveness that screamed that she was his mate was quickly shoved aside.

But as adamantly as he rejected the idea that Jolene could be his mate, he also made a vow. Alex would touch her over his dead body.

THREE

Jolene walked through her apartment entrance and tossed her keys and purse on the hall table. She ignored the lights and avoided the mirror decorating the wall—she didn't want to see herself right now. Didn't want to see the woman who had let down her best friend.

She'd handled the meeting with Drago horribly and left his apartment no closer to finding Carrie than she'd been before the encounter. And though she had no intention of giving up, she couldn't help but kick herself for foiling what could have been her ticket inside Purple Magic.

Flipping her locks into place, she reached for any measure of control. For the comfort of knowing, at least in her own home, she had security. But lately, no matter how hard she tried to keep life under her thumb, it seemed to steal her breath away. She squeezed her eyes shut and leaned against the door.

"Where are you, Carrie?" she whispered into the darkness, pressing her hand to her face.

Her thoughts went to Drago, and to her behavior with him. What had she been thinking back there in that man's apartment? She'd let a complete stranger touch her, and worse, she'd done it with Carrie's life on the line. What kind of person was she to do such a thing?

Drago.

God. He hadn't actually confirmed his name, yet somehow he'd managed to get his hand up her skirt. She'd completely lost herself in those minutes with him. So much so that it downright frightened her.

She knew vampires were sexual beings, and she was, in fact, half vampire. Until now, she'd simply assumed her sex drive was a human drive. She was raised a human and lived as one. That meant dating human males. To some men, her being half vampire rated as the equivalent to a fantasy ménage with two women. To others, it was as good as saying she was a leper. Often it was simply more than she wanted to deal with.

But tonight, she'd felt every bit the ravenous sexual being of her vampire self. Perhaps her behavior had been a product of her emotional state of mind. The possibility of losing Carrie, as she had lost her mother, scared the hell out of her.

Okay, think. Jolene dropped her hands to her side. She'd blown one opportunity and that was it. *One.* She'd find another way to do this.

And with that thought, she went into action, reaching for the light and kicking off her shoes. Determination burned in her gut as she headed toward Carrie's room. She didn't need the police. She didn't need Drago or whoever he was. Jolene knew about Purple Magic, and she knew entry required a VIP pass. But she'd find a way through that door.

Hell, maybe she'd just walk in and ask for Alex. She'd tried by phone and gotten nowhere, but maybe if she showed up, dressed to kill, she'd get attention.

At this point, Jolene would do whatever it took to find Carrie.

Thirty minutes later, Jolene stood in the center of her best friend's room and ran a rough hand through her hair, feeling the frustration of no success. Somewhere in this room was a journal that Carrie had written in every single night. Inside it might be answers to where Carrie was now and to where she'd been in the past. Carrie hadn't taken any of her things. Nothing. That journal was here. It had to be. A thought flashed in her mind. The bathroom. She hadn't searched there. Carrie loved long, hot baths. A few moments later, Jolene dug through cabinets. In the back of the towels, she found what she hunted for: a red velvet journal . . . a little piece of hope.

Jolene carried it with her to the bed and propped pillows against the wooden headboard before settling against them. With her feet curled to the side, she let out a shaky breath and opened the cover of her friend's private world. Though she knew this was necessary, she couldn't help feeling that she was betraying Carrie by invading her privacy. Thumbing through the pages, Jolene focused on the last few entries and started reading.

Tonight I graduated from the Blue Room to the Purple Room. Over the next week I will face my final tests. I will become the dream. The sexual creature that Alex promises will be rewarded. The one he will make his, forever.

But I'm scared. So very scared. What if I am not good enough? What if I can't please him, or the others, the way he wants me to? What if I can't make them feel the heat and intensity I do when they touch me?

I stood in front of the mirror tonight and searched for the woman I once was. The one afraid to touch a man. To be touched. With relief, I couldn't find her. Gone was the self-conscious girl who didn't know how to please herself, let alone a man. She doesn't exist anymore. And for that, I am thankful. I don't want to be her anymore.

When I stare at my reflection now, I see a confident, sexy creature who knows her purpose. As Alex says, women are meant to pleasure and to be pleasured. I realize this now. I know what must be done. I close my eyes now and simply imagine the touch of his hand on my body, and I shiver. To conjure a fantasy of his mouth exploring my skin is all it takes to get me wet and wanting. The pleasure I feel with Alex makes everything else so . . . unimportant. I can hardly remember existing before now. How did I do it? How did I make it through the days? I need this. I need Alex.

Jolene felt the hot tears on her cheeks without even realizing she'd been crying. Emotion had taken hold the minute she'd started reading. She swiped at her cheeks with shaky hands and set the journal on the bed. The person who'd written those words was not her friend. Carrie had loved her job as a chef for the Sweet Bakery. *Loved* it. Her dream had been to open her own restaurant. Guilt tightened Jolene's stomach. She should have noticed how different Carrie had become. Deep down, Jolene knew she *had* noticed and simply failed to act. That realization only served to dig the knife of her guilt deeper.

She'd even known Carrie was going to sex clubs, because Carrie had invited her to go with her. Jolene had refused and even tried to talk Carrie out of going. One night not long before Carrie's disappearance, they'd fought, Jolene warning her friend about the underground, trying to get her to see the light. But clearly, Jolene hadn't tried hard enough. After that, Carrie had pulled away from her. To complicate matters, Jolene had been away from home a lot, spending long hours preparing for a comic-book convention. Jolene squeezed her eyes shut, disgusted at her excuse-making. That's all those long hours were: An excuse. She shouldn't have let this happen.

Pushing to her feet, she knew she had to act. She charged toward her room, determined to dress in her most seductive outfit. The

Purple Room was surely inside Purple Magic. She saw no option but to seduce her way inside the club.

Even if it meant seducing Alex.

Drago stood in the security booth of Purple Magic watching the many cameras. Each held images of naked bodies. Of erotic explorations made of fantasies and of bold, hold-nothing-back desire. Drago understood this world. He'd lived it now for damn near a year. And he knew of five of the six clubs Alex ran. It had taken time to become a trusted part of Alex's world. Time to establish himself as someone to be included in the inner circle. To do this, he'd watched far too many human women become pawns in Alex's games. But Drago had been forced to sacrifice a few to save many. He had to shut down Alex completely.

Skyler, one of his security guards, sat in front of the control panel. Drago had never quite figured out Skyler. The vampire kept to himself, rarely speaking to anyone. He took Alex's orders, but Drago had sensed hesitation in him on more than one occasion. As if Skyler didn't completely support Alex's ways.

Skyler let out a low whistle. "Check out the entrance camera."

Drago eyed the woman displayed by the camera, talking to the doorman, and everything inside him stilled. Jolene. *Damn it!* His efforts to scare her away hadn't worked. And now . . . now, he could only hope she didn't get inside the club.

He watched her on the monitor, his eyes ravished by the erotic vision she made in a short black skirt, long, pale legs that elicited images of having one of them raised to his hip. His zipper tightened uncomfortably as he thought of how close he'd come to ripping away her panties and sliding inside her. He wondered if she wore any now.

And her blouse was meant to do nothing more than tease a man's cock. Sheer and white, it left nothing to the imagination, her nipples puckering against the thin silk as they had against his fingers.

He'd done some checking on her, and she was indeed Riker's daughter. What she didn't know, and he'd been appointed to tell her, was that Riker was dead—ironically, killed by a group of vampires suspected to be Alex's. He would have gone to see her tomorrow had she not shown up here tonight.

He watched as she smiled at the doorman, hoping like hell she turned on her heels and walked away. Watched as she tossed her dark hair to the side, *flirting* as she tried to get inside the club. Drago inhaled, his memory filling his senses with the soft rose scent of her hair, an aroma forever engraved in his mind. A scent, he realized he wanted to smell again. Hair he wanted against his cheek, his chest, his fingers.

Women and men lined the exterior of the building, all wanting the same thing she did. Purple Magic had a reputation for fantasy and pleasure reserved for only a few. People wanted what they couldn't have. Entrance came only with a referral, something that should have deterred Jolene, but it didn't. Drago ground his teeth as he watched her disappear inside the club and reappear on a different camera.

He moved forward, stepping close to Skyler and pushing a button to talk to the doorman. "Who gave you authority to let that woman in?"

The six-foot-six doorman eyed the camera. "Alex."

"Something tells me Alex is going to be in a good mood later tonight," Skyler commented.

Drago let go of the intercom button. "She's mine," he said, and didn't give the man a chance to respond.

He could feel Skyler's surprise. Drago had never claimed anyone as his own. As one of Alex's inner circle, and his right-hand man, he could claim whomever he wished. Alex wouldn't deny him. Not a woman. Not even if Alex knew she was Riker's daughter. Riker might not be alive to protect Jolene, but Drago was, and he'd damn sure do it for his dead brother in arms. Alex would not touch Jolene. Not tonight and not ever.

But if he didn't get to Jolene and fast, to state his claim openly, it would be too late. Jolene had the power to protect herself from one vampire's mind meld, but not several at once. If anyone was taking Jolene tonight, it was him.

He sped down the winding stairs to the bottom floor of the club and found his way to the entrance room. The place everyone started their night. It was here that they mingled and played, deciding which flavor or delight would be theirs for the night. Every sin of the skin could be found inside Purple Magic. Every form of lust and desire satisfied. But only the very best, the most daring, made it to the level of ultimate satisfaction. To the Purple Room. To a place they thought held passion and play. In truth, it held destruction. It was a place you never returned from. It was there that Alex claimed those who would be seduced and turned into his personal slaves.

He found Jolene standing near the doorway, looking both sexy and innocent. And lost. So very lost. She didn't belong here. Yet her body, ripe with curves, begged for the attention she would surely find here. Her eyes were locked on a threesome, two women and a man, naked and entwined. While she stared at them, seemingly mesmerized, two female vampires from Alex's harem approached with a mission. Women who had once been pure humans, now they were something else, something not quite human, lost in their servitude to Alex. Lost in their mission to convert others into what they had become.

The two female servants settled on either side of Jolene, pressing their bare skin against her. Drago sensed her discomfort even before she stiffened beneath their touch. The woman on the right, a redhead, had large, full bare breasts, one of which pressed against Jolene's arm. She reached out and lightly stroked Jolene's nipple, plucking at it through the sheer silk. The other caressed Jolene's shoulder, then her hair. Petting her like one would an animal, which is how Alex viewed his servants.

Drago could feel Jolene's desire to push them away. He couldn't close the distance between them fast enough. One second. Two. It felt like forever before he was there, standing in front of her.

For an instant, their eyes locked and he saw her register both shock and relief. Though he knew deep down she didn't trust him, she felt safer with him than alone.

"She's mine," he told the two servants, his gaze moving from one to the other, making his intent clear. He was claiming Jolene.

"What?" said the servant he knew as Catherine. "Yours? You've never shown interest in the . . . guests."

She meant humans. Drago had managed to convince Alex he preferred only vampires. Catherine had always been one of his first choices when it came to appeasing his sexual hunger. With long blonde hair and voluptuous breasts, she sported a willingness to do anything and everything many times over. But now, with Jolene beside her, Catherine did nothing for Drago. Jolene had a quality that touched him well beyond the sensual. It made him protective and, yes, possessive.

Drago reached forward and gently grasped Jolene's wrist, pulling her tight against his body. His palm slid down her waist and across her ass, molding her against him. She settled her hands on his chest, and their eyes locked. He gave her a warning look, telling her without words to do as he bade her. For a moment she remained stiff, and then slowly, she melted.

Cupping her backside, Drago fit her hips against his raging hard-on. The scent of her, of roses, all womanly and sweet, invaded his senses. He laced his fingers through soft, silky hair and angled her mouth to his. With nothing for motivation but pure lust, he claimed her lips, sliding his tongue past her teeth and tasting her, long and deep.

When he raised his head, he found jealousy in Catherine's dark eyes. "Alex wants this one," she said. "You can't have her."

Drago narrowed his gaze on Catherine and then smiled. "We'll see about that. Let's go visit Alex."

Catherine stared at him and then made a frustrated sound before starting to walk away, clearly expecting him to follow. The other woman laughed and fell into step with Catherine.

Drago pressed his mouth close to Jolene's ear. "You're a fool for coming here. Do everything I say without question."

He leaned back to look into her face to ensure she understood.

"And if I don't?" she whispered, but there was no defiance in her voice. She was scared. He saw it in her eyes.

"Then you won't survive the night." His harsh whisper declared the hard reality of her situation. He didn't wait for her response. He grabbed her hand and started walking.

Jolene was his, if only for this night.

His lust would be her salvation.

FOUR

Alex's private room was like a vault, well guarded on the outside and packed with luxuries on the inside. Double oak doors opened to allow entry with discreet, well-armed guards on either side. Both guards reported to Drago and he knew them well. Knew their complete and total loyalty to Alex. Of course, they saw Drago as sharing their philosophies and beliefs—that he, too, believed they had a right to claim human women as their own. A philosophy he planned to ram down their throats in the not-so-distant future.

Both guards gave Drago a respectful nod. He returned their gesture, grinding his teeth together as he thought of the charade he played, detesting it more with each passing day. Beneath well-tailored suit jackets, each of the men wore a shoulder holster, a Colt semiautomatic tucked inside. Only one of several weapons they carried in preparation for human intruders. Vampires were another story. Bullets only slowed them down, but not for long.

Just as sunlight had no effect on vampires, killing them wasn't as mythology told, either. Despite decades of the two races living together, most humans still believed as much. Sure, a stake in the heart would hurt, but it wouldn't bring death. No. To kill a vampire, its heart had to be shredded to bits. That or the vampire had to be decapitated. Both methods were nasty tasks few humans had the stomach for.

Thus, the reason why Alex feared nothing from humans.

Though Alex had well-trained guards on staff, none of them were a match for Drago or any of his brothers in combat. Drago tracked the two female servants as they entered Alex's chambers. Catherine, who was actually half vampire, held her head high, defiance crackling in the air around her. He chose her to sate his desires because unlike the human servants, she operated of her own free will, her morals ranking at about the same low level as Alex's. And right now, she was putting her nasty side to work, clearly on a mission. The mission of a jealous female who wanted revenge. A complication he didn't need right now.

With Jolene tucked beneath his arm, pulled tight against his side, Drago felt the rise of protectiveness. Of all the innocents he'd encountered, none had made him feel this way. He knew war, and this battle with Alex was that and more. There had to be casualties. The human women in the clubs, farmed for slavery, were sacrifices that he hoped he could recover later. The last step toward taking down Alex was getting inside his slavery camps. Drago knew where two of the camps were but he needed the third before they moved forward for the take-down. Though he had allowed humans to be taken to those slave camps, vowing to save them later, he wouldn't sacrifice Jolene that way. She wasn't going to one of those camps. He told himself it was because she was Riker's daughter, but deep down he knew it was far more personal.

Holding her close, he could feel the tension in her body. She might have come here willing to do whatever was necessary, but saying and doing were different things. She was ready to bolt at any moment; he could sense it. But it was too late for that now. Once she'd walked inside the club, once she'd entered Purple Magic, she'd set herself up to face Alex.

He reached for her mind, attempting to communicate with her, attempting to get her to drop her shields and let him talk to her. When she didn't immediately budge, Drago knew he could push past her guard, but didn't dare. It would take concentration he needed to extend other places. Especially considering they'd now entered Alex's private chambers, the guards shutting the doors behind them, the sound of heavy locks bolting them shut sounding in the air.

Directly in front of them, a pair of black velvet couches framed the doorway. Alex sat in the center of one of them, a naked woman straddled him, her breasts in his hands. He suckled her nipples and she moaned. Catherine and the other female moved to stand behind the couch, each silently waiting until Alex acknowledged their presence. Even in her pursuit of vengeance, Catherine knew to keep silent until spoken to. Alex liked control. Complete, utter control.

In the corners of the massive room were black satin drapes, each covering what Alex called "pleasure zones." It's where he tested his pupils for the different rooms they might enter; each woman had to satisfy his desires in order to graduate to the next level of the process, the ultimate reward being to achieve "Purple Magic." Once she was there, the pupil thought she'd find some hidden reward. What she found was herself shipped off to one of the slave camps. By that time, Alex had mixed their blood with his enough times to own their minds. The process wouldn't convert a human into a vampire, but it damn sure promoted servitude.

The woman straddling Alex cried out as he pinched both nipples at once. A soft gasp escaped Jolene's lips and she tried to move away from Drago. He tightened his grip on her, and fixed her with a warning look. She wasn't deterred, tugging at his hold on her hand, her struggle beginning to become a scene. He'd hoped she would simply play the role of willing submissive who wanted her friend back.

Since that wasn't the case, Drago had no option but to act, to treat Jolene as a captive. Alex knew she was Carrie's friend. The chance that the bartender had told Alex she'd seen him was even a possibility. He'd simply let her resistance become a show. To keep her alive, he would have to be her captor, determined to make her submissive.

If he didn't get her under his thumb, Alex would.

Drago yanked Jolene hard against his body. "Be still," he ordered in a low voice, his mouth close to hers. "Believe me. It's for your own good."

Alex shoved the woman from his lap, his attention now on Drago and Jolene. "Ah, yes. The lovely Jolene." He ran a hand over his short, well-groomed hair. "I knew she'd come for Carrie." His gaze stroked her skimpy attire. "And I knew she'd come ready to please."

"I just want Carrie back," Jolene whispered, and then to her credit, she took a direct approach that hinted she might submit rather than fight the physical play that had already been set in motion. "What do I have to do to make that happen?"

Alex's lips thinned slightly and then turned up at the corners, amusement in his eyes as he addressed Jolene. "If you prove you're worthy of Carrie, you will see her again. Your friend has worked hard to get where she is now. You will have to do the same."

Dressed in a shirt of the finest silk, a suit tailored to fit to perfection, Alex looked like the head of a major corporation, a man who belonged in a boardroom. His nails were manicured. His face, sleek and well shaven. His image was a facade, an image designed to lure human women into his web of desire.

"I want to see her," Jolene said, in a low, terse voice. "Show me Carrie and I will do whatever is required of me to take her home."

"She is safe and well sated," he assured her, his tone dry. "Just as you can be." His gaze slid to Drago. "She's special, this one. A Slayer's daughter."

"Riker's daughter," Drago replied, and quickly began the important task of staking his claim. With a rough tug, he flattened Jolene's soft curves against his hard muscle. "As in the Slayer who turned me in to the council. The man owes me." Alex would expect Drago to seek revenge, so he let the impact of his words hang in the air before adding, "I want her."

Drago wasted no time showing how serious he was about his claim on Jolene. His hand slid upward, along her waist, until he cupped her breast, her nipple tightening against his palm.

She sucked in a breath, but to her credit didn't pull away. "Drago," she whispered, his name on her lips a mixture of protest and pleasure.

"Carnal satisfaction is the path to your friend," Drago murmured to Jolene, holding her tight, possessiveness thickening inside him with Alex's presence, with the thought of anyone else touching her. "My carnal satisfaction."

"How do I even know she's alive?" she demanded.

"I guess you'll have to trust me," Drago commented, hoping she read between the lines and truly gave him her trust.

Alex interjected then. "You must pass our tests, Jolene. When you do, you will enter the Purple Room, which is where you will find Carrie."

Her mouth opened and shut, her head tilting to study Drago before turning her attention on Alex. "And I can take her home?"

"What makes you so sure you'll want to leave?"

Jolene inhaled a sharp breath. "If I make it to the Purple Room, can I take her home?"

Alex smiled. Evil. "If you can convince her to leave."

Catherine's hands stroked Alex's shoulders. He cut her a look. "What is it you want?" His tone was sharp.

Drago took that moment to press his cheek to Jolene's, his lips to her ear, choosing his words carefully, knowing that Alex would use his exceptional hearing to take in what he said to Jolene. "Surrender to me and you will not be sorry."

Catherine's voice filled the air. "You promised I could help you claim the Slayer's daughter," she purred, rounding the couch and joining Alex on the cushions, her body pressed tight against his side, her breasts hugging his arm.

Alex stared down at Catherine body, but he didn't touch. And Drago knew it was because she wanted him to. Alex did nothing on anyone else's terms. He'd touch only when he wished it. Not a moment sooner. "Drago asks for little," Alex told her. "If he wants this woman, he shall have her. Besides," he added, turning his attention to Jolene. "I'm quite looking forward to the show."

"Please, Alex," Catherine said, brushing her lips across his cheek. "You promised."

Catherine, like all the vampire women at Purple Magic, enjoyed dominating her own kind. But that wasn't what this was about. Catherine wanted Drago. What she didn't seem to understand was that Alex knew this as well.

Alex gently stroked Catherine's cheek, studying her as he did. Then, abruptly, he moved his hand and grabbed a huge handful of her hair. He pulled her mouth to his. Jolene wilted against Drago, and he fought the urge to comfort her.

"Jealousy does not become you, little one," Alex said to Catherine, his lips lingering above hers. "Control it or I will. In fact, I expect you to watch Drago fuck her because fuck her he will. And you know what else?" he demanded, not expecting an answer from his whimpering captive. "He'll enjoy every last minute of it." He pressed his mouth to hers in a hard, punishment of a kiss before shoving her away.

Pushing to his feet, he smoothed his shirt, seemingly irritated to find a wrinkle on his upper shoulder. Then, attention back on Jolene, he smiled. The sharp angles of his square jaw and straight nose seemed to enhance the predatory gleam in his eyes.

Alex walked toward them, stopping only a few steps from Jolene, ravishing her with his stare. Drago squeezed her waist in warning. If she angered Alex, they could end up with trouble better avoided. Any sign of aggression toward Alex could escalate into danger. Fighting Alex was lethal. That was a job for Drago . . . when the time was right.

And now *was not* that time.

Jolene watched Alex approach and fought the urge to run. It was true, she'd come here telling herself she could fuck that man to get to Carrie. She knew now, she didn't want to. Wasn't sure she could. And the only thing standing between her and Alex was Drago. The closer Alex came, the more she melted into Drago, trying not to be too obvious. She trusted Drago, she realized. She didn't know why, but she did. Perhaps because he was a Slayer. The more she thought about his duty, the more certain she became that he hadn't turned against his own kind. Her mother and father had been clear about how deep the Slayer's blood ran, how deep their commitment to the council. No. Drago wasn't dirty. Drago was a Slayer undercover, trying to take down Alex. She felt it in her gut.

If she had to pay the price of pleasing, she wanted it to be with Drago. She'd wanted him, before this club and this night. And right now, she wanted him to take her someplace private, away from Alex.

Alex had now stopped in front of her, his eyes all but raping her with their blatant inspection. "She has a hot body," Alex commented to Drago. "Beautiful breasts. Nice, ripe hips. Carrie tried to talk her into coming in before now." Alex fixed Jolene in a challenging stare. "Your friend assured me I would enjoy you."

Anger burned inside of Jolene, dark and furious, out of control, darkness borne of weeks of worry, weeks of guilt. Tears pinched the back of her eyes. Gone were rational thoughts. Emotion prevailed. "Liar," she yelled at him. "Carrie would never say such a thing." Drago tightened his grip around her waist, and she sensed his uneasiness, but she didn't care. "Where is she? Where is Carrie?!"

Alex tilted his head back and laughed. "She's a spitfire. I can't wait to see you take this one down a notch." His face went serious. "I have a good mind to do it for you." He eyed Drago. "I'll let you have her, but I get to set the stage."

He snapped his fingers, and before she could blink, two men dressed in nothing but loincloths appeared. My God, was she in some sort of bad dream? Who wore freaking loincloths?

The next thing she knew, they grabbed her. "No," she shouted, wanting to call for Drago. But instinct made her refrain, fearful that Alex would take him from her if he knew she found him a comfort. But the men were pulling her forward, toward a doorway in the corner. She wanted to call for Drago. He wasn't supposed to let this happen. Slayers saved innocents.

"No!" she shouted at the men, kicking and fighting. "Let me go. Let go." She eyed one of the men, frantic now, wild with desperation to get her feet planted solidly back on the ground and next to the Slayer. "Where are you taking me? Where?"

But there was no control to be found. In fact, she lost more of it as someone threw something over her head. Darkness enveloped her. Her chest tightened as she tried to reach for her face, but her arms were held by the men. The next thing she knew, she was lifted in the air and then thrown over someone's shoulder.

Jolene forgot the bag over her face and the fact that she could barely catch her breath. She reached for something to hold on to, anything that might stop the movement forward. Her fingers grazed walls on either side of her. Close walls. She was in some sort of tunnel. *Oh God.* Who knew where it led? Her stomach tightened into knots and blood rushed to her head. She stopped fighting, somehow managing logical thought. Conserving her energy for a time when a struggle might offer results seemed her best option. But she wasn't sure there was any hope for her now. *I'm going to die. This must be what happened to Carrie.*

But before the thought could take root, Jolene was on her feet, and her hands were stretched far to her sides. Cold metal closed around her wrists, and then the bag was ripped from her head. She blinked into a dimly lit room. Red silk draped a massive bed and lined windows that led nowhere.

And before her stood a man.

Drago.

FIVE

Jolene stared at Drago. She'd been willing to do what was necessary to save Carrie, but she'd hoped it wouldn't have to come to what it had. "The chains aren't necessary," she whispered, jerking against the restraints because she couldn't help herself.

His brow lifted, arms crossing in front of his broad chest and she could feel him pressing into her mind, trying to enter. She rejected his attempt, blocking him with all her energy. Only one other had ever entered her mind, and that had been her father. He'd spoken to her in her mind, and taught her how to shield herself from intruders. She used those skills now. Somehow, giving that part of herself away felt like the ultimate invasion, and chained to a wall, she simply couldn't bear it.

Drago's teeth ground together. "*Trust me*, little one. You must submit. Give yourself to it. Don't fight what you can't change."

He didn't give her time to answer. With a wave of his hand, he motioned the men in loincloths forward. Suddenly, her clothes were being cut from her body, knives ripping away the silk and cloth with perfect precision. She could feel the hot breath of one of the men on her neck and shoulder. Feel their lusty stares as they pulled her shirt away and left her bare breasted.

Jolene squeezed her eyes shut, mortified. This couldn't be happening. It had to be a bad dream. A nightmare. She braced herself for their hands only a moment before she felt their exploration. Rough hands kneaded her breasts and pinched her nipples. Fingers slid between her thighs and across her clit.

Worse, she felt arousal take hold. It made her ashamed. Embarrassed. Part of her wished for the drugs they'd mentioned. Anything to allow her an escape from—not just these men—but herself. She wanted to scream, but she couldn't find her voice. It was frozen somewhere inside the trauma of what was happening.

In the midst of the rage in her mind, Jolene heard Drago's voice. Abruptly, the men moved away, but she didn't dare open her eyes. Not immediately. She didn't want to see these strangers looking at her. So she waited . . . expecting their return.

After several seconds, when they didn't come, she forced her lashes upward and found the hot stare of Drago. She swallowed against the heat in his gaze, her eyes darting from one side of the room to the other, looking for the men. They stood at the door, their loincloths gone, their bodies naked. Only remotely did she take in their shaved heads and broad shoulders. What she did notice were their cocks. Exposed and hard. And their eyes filled with lust. Telling her what they wanted. Her. They wanted her. She shivered beneath their scrutiny.

"You said you would do whatever it took to find Carrie," Drago said, drawing her attention, his voice low.

She studied his face, looking for his intentions beneath an indecipherable mask. He still wore his clothes. Black slacks and a black, well-tailored button-up shirt, yet still he oozed pure sensuality. But it was more than that. He had an air of darkness. Jolene wasn't sure what to expect from him. Nor could she figure out why, chained to a wall, stripped of her blouse and skirt, she wanted to trust him.

Her throat felt so dry, she barely managed to speak. "I . . . I know what I said."

"You must pay for entry into the club. To give satisfaction and pleasure." He paused, his eyelids lowering as he started at her feet and moved upward, giving her a thorough perusal. When his eyes once again met hers, he said, "If I send them away, you must agree to do anything and everything I say. When and *if* you leave this club, it will be because I allow it."

As his words lingered in the air, he walked toward her and there was more than fear inside her as he approached. More than apprehension. She felt . . . hot. Aroused. Like she had back in his apartment. It was as if her body responded without her consent. In fact, the fear of injury slipped away, replaced by the frightening feeling of losing herself to this man. To the here and now. She tracked his progress, feeling the warmth of anticipation in her body despite the fear that laced her mind. She swallowed. His state of dress made her feel, in her own undressed state, all the more . . . exposed.

Only a few steps separated them when he stopped. "Do they stay or go, Jolene?" he asked.

She swallowed against the nerves that made her heart leap to her throat. It felt as if Drago stalked her, though he now stood in one place. Like she was the prey and he the beast. Yes. That was it. There was an animal-like quality to Drago. Dangerous. And male. God, he was so masculine. So . . . sexual. A man like this would take a woman and leave her with nothing but desire. He'd take all she was and all she might ever be. And in that moment, she knew once Drago claimed her body, she would never, ever, be the same. Just as Carrie hadn't been the same after that first date with Alex.

"I grow impatient. Make your choice. Me," he paused. "Or them?" He raised his hands, indicating the men behind and at either side of him.

Her stomach did a somersault. "Y-you," she managed hoarsely.

"Louder," he demanded. "I can't hear you."

She jumped at the sharpness of his tone and responded instinctively, this time louder. "You."

Drago seemed to consider her a moment, as if he questioned her commitment to her choice. Then he snapped his fingers. "Leave us," he demanded.

Jolene stared at him, unable to take her eyes from his. Mesmerized. Terrified. Excited. The doors opened and shut. A shifting of metal told, once again, of locks being bolted into place. Complete, utter silence followed.

Then, and only then, did Drago move. A step. Another. He stopped in front of her. So close he could reach out and touch her. So close she could smell the spicy maleness of him. The same scent that had scorched her with arousal during their first meeting.

"It's just you and me now," he said, in a low, sensual voice that promised intimacy beyond the simple words he spoke.

He leaned forward, pressing his fists against the wall, a mere whisper between their bodies, his mouth lowering near her ear. The warmth of his breath caressed her skin, and goosebumps spread across her body, her nipples tightening. With every ounce of her being, she wanted to arch her back and press them against his chest. He whispered in her ear, so low she barely heard what he said. "We're alone. Just us and a room of cameras."

The implications of what he'd shared darted through her mind. People were watching them. *Alex* was watching. That Drago shared this information in a secretive way confused her. Was he trying to warn her or simply playing with her mind? She didn't know. Nor did she have time to give it much thought.

He leaned back enough to fix her with a hot stare. Then, slowly, his gaze dropped to her breasts. For long moments he stared at her, making her skin tingle with the need for his touch. Finally, his eyes lifted. "You know what I'm going to do to you, don't you?"

She swallowed. "Force me to have sex with you."

"Force?" His sensual mouth hinted at a smile. "Am I forcing you, Jolene? Did you not agree to do what was necessary to find Carrie?"

"Yes," she admitted. "I agreed." His eyes narrowed and she corrected herself. "Agree."

Apparently satisfied, he said, "You want me." He dipped his head and inhaled. "I can smell your arousal, Jolene." His cheek pressed against hers. "You've wanted me since the moment you laid eyes on me."

Which was true, but she wasn't about to admit it. She didn't want to feel this . . . need. The yearning. This heat he evoked. Not here. Not under these circumstances. Giving up her body and admitting her personal desires were different things.

"Believe what you want," she managed in a shaky voice, challenging him on purpose and praying her strategy worked. He was pressing at her mind again, trying to reach inside. She shoved him out of her head and reached for more control, needing to be free of the chains. "Why tie me up? Because Alex willed it? Or because you don't really believe I want you?"

"It is true this amuses Alex, but I didn't argue his choice, for reasons of my own." He leaned back and fixed her in another sizzling stare. "You do want me. You simply think it's wrong, and unless I take away your excuses, you will never submit. And submission, Jolene, is the only way I can help you get what you want." The words danced in the air with the distinction of truth, with underlying meaning.

One of his index fingers just barely brushed her nipple. Jolene sucked in a breath, as pleasure rocketed through her body and exploded between her thighs. She could feel the moisture there. The heat. The burning need.

"By the time I take off those cuffs," Drago promised. "I'll have slain your conscience for you. All that will be left is pure lust."

His voice was deep. Resonant. Compelling. It made her want to forget this place. The watchers. The world. To be lost in him. The thoughts scared her and she mentally shook herself. Had she been drugged? Or perhaps he really slipped past her mental barriers and she didn't know it. What else explained how easily she turned from ice to fire with this man? But then, she'd felt the same back at his apartment, and she most certainly hadn't been drugged there.

"Never," she proclaimed, fighting with her mind if not her body. Giving in completely meant forgetting her reason for being here. What she did now with Drago wasn't about her own lust and desire. It was about Carrie. She couldn't forget Carrie.

As if proving his ability to devour her with lust, he tweaked her nipple. Jolene bit back a moan as he repeated the act. "Does it turn you on to know we have an audience? That Alex watches with lust in his eyes. And there are others. Men. Women." He continued to tease her nipple. "They're watching. Perhaps fucking as they watch. Some of them are thinking about what they will do to you if I let them have you."

"No," she whispered, but already his other hand went into play, delivering more erotic sensations. He tugged on both hardened peaks at once, and then rolled them between his fingertips. Despite her best efforts to bite it back, she moaned again. "Please." The hoarse word was a plea.

"Please don't stop?" He rolled her nipples and palmed her breasts. "Or please don't let them have you?"

Her eyes went to his. "Just let me leave."

"I can't do that." He leaned close, his mouth brushing hers. Against her lips, he murmured. He still held her breasts in his hands, possessiveness in the touch. "You know I can't. Besides, you said you wanted to find Carrie."

Accusation laced her voice. "You know where she is." It wasn't a question.

"Carrie, as you knew her, is no more. Now she is a part of this world. Now she helps others join this world."

"I don't believe you," Jolene rasped through clenched teeth.

"It's true." His hand slid down her to her hip, leaving a trail of goosebumps behind. A satisfied smile played on his lips. "She enjoys the pleasure we bring her." He paused. "Just as you do."

"No. I . . . I don't believe that."

"Yes, you do," he said, slipping his fingers into the dark triangle between her legs. "You aren't ready to admit it, but you like it here, too." Drago flicked her clit and she gasped. "You like it a lot."

"I want to see Carrie." The words came out with effort, as Drago teased her body, assaulting her senses.

"The path to seeing Carrie is an erotic one, Jolene. One you must travel freely." His voice dropped low. A whisper. "Forget everything but you and me. Just get lost in the desire we share."

She squeezed her eyes shut. Carrie. She wanted to find Carrie. But what Drago asked was too much. Jolene had thought she could do this but she couldn't. Coming here was one thing. Getting lost in it was another, much more frightening thing. Because if she did, she had the most horrible feeling she might never come back.

"I can't," she said. "I can't."

Cupping her face with his hands, Drago forced her to look at him, gentleness in the action. "You can, and you will."

She swallowed and closed her eyes. "No." Jolene shook her head, ever aware of her arms at her side, her nipples jutting forward, begging for more of his touch.

A slow smile turned up the corners of Drago's mouth. "I'll make you forget."

Her lashes lifted abruptly. "By drugging me?"

For several seconds he held her stare. "I don't want you drugged. I want your surrender." He paused. Then his hands slid down her sides, over her hips. When his fingers found her thighs, her breath caught in her throat. Suddenly, he was on his knees and her legs were being pressed apart. He looked up at her as his finger slid along the silky wet proof of her arousal. "And I don't like to be kept waiting."

SIX

Drago slid to the floor, between Jolene's legs. He desired her as he had never before desired a woman. Arousal pulsed through his limbs, heat flooded his cock, which pressed uncomfortably against his zipper. He didn't dare undress. Not yet. He felt as though he might snap at any moment.

Though there was no logic to his need, he ached for Jolene to offer herself to him freely. To know he hadn't forced her submission. Yet saving her life could well mean demanding submission from her. With the intensity of the attraction they shared, he knew it was possible to entice her physical response. But he would have to have more. He'd have to have her complete, utter submission . . . her trust.

Again and again, he had tried to enter her mind, tried to tell her he had to behave in certain ways, had to say and do things Alex would expect of him. But each time, she shoved him away. Each time, he resisted forcing his presence in her mind. He had to take so much from her tonight. He would offer her the free will he could, for as long as he could safely allow.

His fingers slid into the tangle of dark curls between her legs, touching the silky wet folds of her core. The desire to take her called to him with a deep hunger, demanding to be fed, threatening to fog all thinking. She was beautiful. A carnal roar screamed in his body, in his cock; his urgency to claim her was overshadowed by only one feeling . . . *possessiveness*. A thought formed in his mind. *Mate*. It rang in his head over and over, screaming to be noticed. The implications of such a thing were many. He shoved aside the complicated thought, focusing on the here and now, on Jolene's pleasure, on her submission.

Drago drew a line up and down her core, and a soft, sexy whimper escaped her lips. He smiled at the sound, loving how responsive she was to him. He could only imagine what she would be like in a different setting. Alone with him. Feeling safe and secure, free to explore her wants and needs.

The word *mate* screamed in his head again, refusing to be dismissed. *Holy hell*. Who was he kidding? He knew it was true, knew she belonged to him. The idea of Alex touching Jolene brought near fury. Watching the other males fondle her had damn near burned a hole in his gut. A necessary evil to ensure he didn't arouse suspicions, but damn near poison to his nerves.

There was no room for anything like duty in his life but still Jolene had taken him by storm. *Duty*, he reminded himself. And right now, fucking Jolene was part of that duty and possibly a life or death equation.

He slid a finger inside her and felt her tense. But he didn't try to calm her or ease her, didn't try to offer comfort as he had before. Instead, he demanded her submission, slipping another finger inside her and starting a pumping action. To get her out of this place, he had to have her complete trust. Had to. Understanding this, he pressed her forward, mimicking sex with his movements, demanding she give him all she had, all she could be.

When she began rocking against him, he blew on her clit, his cock thickening with the anticipation of her sweetness on his tongue. With the anticipation of spreading her wide and burying himself deeply.

With a lap of his tongue he teased her nub and felt her shiver in response. Oh yeah, she wanted him all right. She was practically dripping, she was so wet. And this pleased him. No matter how he tried to make this about work. To justify taking her, he could not shake the desire to please her. It remained important she not look back on this and feel he'd done anything but offer her satisfaction. It really shouldn't matter. He was saving her from Alex, from the rest of this place. Saving her from a life as a slave. He reached for the anger of only seconds ago, but already that emotion had faded, lost in other unfamiliar feelings only Jolene evoked.

He suckled her nub, his tongue working with delicate strokes that slowly built into a frenzy of faster licks. When he felt her knees begin to buckle, Drago slid his hand around her perfect, round ass and offered support.

He lapped at her, drinking in the essence of her arousal and lifting her leg over his shoulder to allow himself better access. Pleased she wasn't fighting him, he drove onward, his tongue sliding inside her, imitating what he soon would do with his cock.

She moaned and panted more loudly now. Sounds that drove him wild with their soft, sensual play along his nerve endings. With a low growl he lost himself in her, licking her up and down, side to side. Faster. Harder. His tongue thrusting deeper. His fingers playing along with the motion. In. Out. All around.

She cried out and then stiffened, signaling the moment before release. With one last roll of her clit, he drew her orgasm from her. Her body tightened around his fingers, and he sunk them deeper inside her, massaging and pleasuring. Fast at first, giving her as much intensity as possible, and then slowly easing . . . easing . . . bringing her down.

With a deep breath, he eased her leg to the ground and willed his raging body to calm. He wanted to take her now, wanted to take her in a way he'd never wanted another female. Screw Alex. He'd give him a show, but he was going to enjoy this his way.

Drago's mouth pressed against Jolene's flat stomach and she shivered in response, his nostrils flaring with her sweet feminine scent. He kissed the spot again, silently vowing that before this night was over, he'd kiss every inch of her lush body. And she'd be begging for more. He'd make sure of it. He wanted all of her. What that meant exactly, he didn't know right now. He'd figure it out later. Right now, he simply wanted every last moan of pleasure she had in her.

Jolene couldn't believe she had just come with such intensity. For God's sake, people were watching. And she was chained to a wall. Part of her had begun to actually feel relief over the shackles. Those pieces of metal wrapping her wrists were all that had kept her from completely losing herself in Drago. It was hard enough to know this man took her places within herself she didn't even know existed, but to go there with an audience unnerved her. The craziness of her desire for this man had her aching to touch him. No doubt, if she were free of restraints, she'd forget Alex and his people and be doing that and more.

Even now, as Drago's lips brushed her stomach, the unmistakable rise of desire roared to life again. Desire that made no sense. She'd just had the most intense orgasm of her life. How could she want more? How could she even have allowed herself to be turned on under such circumstances?

Was this part of being a vampire? Had her mother sheltered her from this, raising her as a human for that reason?

The flicker of Drago's tongue in her navel, gentle, enticing, sent a rush of molten heat through her limbs. Drago drove her wild.

Drago did. No one else. This couldn't be about this place or about her vampire side. This was about him. About her. About something unique they shared, and it confused her.

Her gaze dropped to his dark head, wishing she could slide her fingers through his hair, watching as he trailed kisses along her skin. Gentle kisses. Tender kisses. Kisses that held the promise of more than sex. When she'd expected Drago to take from her, he seemed determined to give. Ah, but he *had* taken. He'd taken her orgasm, her pleasure, and damn near brought her to submission, despite her best efforts to avoid giving it.

Her eyes darted around the room, looking for cameras. She couldn't stop thinking about the people watching. Lord help her, it didn't change how aroused she felt. How hot. Sizzling hot. So on fire, she could do nothing but moan at the rough caress of Drago's tongue, biting back the plea that almost escaped her lips, feeling as if it would be the final demise of her will.

But in her mind, she begged for her freedom. "Drago," she murmured, his lips trailing her hip now. *Drago.* In her mind, she pleaded to have him inside her.

As if he heard her thoughts, he stepped away, leaving her cold without his touch, without his mouth. His eyes met hers; the look in his, the fire and desire, could have scorched her skin.

Slowly, he reached upward and began unbuttoning his shirt. With a flutter of her stomach, heat darted up her thighs. She wanted to do it for him, she realized. To undress him. To explore his body. Her thoughts were free of guilt, free of reprimand. Full of anticipation.

Her eyes followed his fingers, savoring every inch of skin as it appeared. Dark hair covered his tawny skin. He was the rich color of warm brown. European maybe. The color of milk chocolate, creamy and rich. Addictive even. She gobbled up the sight of him. She'd never been this attracted to a man. Never. It frightened her to desire a man who was holding her prisoner, but at the same time it thrilled and enticed.

He toed off his shoes and kicked them away. Then he reached for his belt. Only moments later, he stood before her naked. Perfect. Erect. Big. She swallowed then, as the ache between her legs intensified to near unbearable intensity. She was beyond want. She needed him inside her, on top of her. She just needed . . . him. Her captor. She should be thinking of ways to fight. Instead, all she could think about was giving herself to him.

With a hungry stare, she traveled his body; biting her lip, she took in his long, powerful legs. Thighs like steel. Abs rippling with deliciously defined muscle. And as her gaze slid back to his cock, she felt the fire of urgency. She was locked in this room with Drago, a man she had wanted before this night.

She wanted him. He wanted her. The sex already in play and inevitable. Alex expected nothing less. She *wanted* nothing less. He was her only hope of getting out of this place. To trust Drago might be dangerous, but she had to. Not trusting him left her alone, and without hope. Something she desperately needed. Reaching deep, she studied her instincts and the connection she felt to this man—to this vampire.

And she found her answer. She had to gamble on Drago.

She fixed him in a stare, searching his eyes for the truth. For a reason to believe that her next words, her next actions were the right ones.

"Take off the chains," she said, her voice strong as she gave what he'd demanded, what Alex would expect before Drago freed her. "I surrender."

Then, she dared to let down her mental barrier, reaching for Drago's mind, not completely sure she even remembered how to do such a thing. It had been years since her father had spoken to her in such a way or her to him.

She repeated her words in her mind, relaying them for Drago alone to hear. *I surrender.*

SEVEN

The sweetness of Jolene's arousal still flavored his tongue; the scent of her lust floated in the air, calling to him like a soft whisper. He wanted to fuck her. No. *Needed*. He needed to fuck her. Perhaps that would destroy the hunger gnawing at his gut. A quick release would give him back control.

The reality of just how on edge he was, how near losing control, agitated him. Her words repeated in his head, as if she thought he hadn't heard them.

I surrender.

He'd heard them, all right. Finally, he was in her head, past her barriers and he couldn't think of anything but burying himself inside her body. Her surrender sent flames licking at his body. Set his blood on fire. Worse, it had roused his hunger for her. He could feel his cuspids elongating, feel the depths of his turbulent need. To claim her. To claim his mate. He could not longer deny she belonged to him, and him to her. The depth of his thirst, his desire to taste her and claim her, persuasive in its demand for satisfaction, stole all doubt.

Which meant he had a problem beyond the many others he was juggling. If he drank of Jolene, their bonding would be one step closer to permanent, one step closer to an eternal seal. He wasn't prepared to do that without some serious soul searching, not to mention Jolene's consent. A Slayer led a dangerous life, and every step she took with him would put her in harm's way.

Lord help him, though, because Alex would expect him to drink of Jolene. A female vampire had mental control a human did not. Alex would never allow Jolene to leave without absolute confidence that Drago could contain her.

Drago drew a deep, calming breath and spoke to Jolene through their mental connection. *I must show complete dominance this night, Jolene, or Alex will not allow you to leave. He must feel I own your mind and body.*

Her eyes flashed with concern. *How do you know he will let me leave at all?*

Jolene didn't hide their conversation well, her expression far too readable. *No more talk. Trust me if you want to live. I'll explain everything later. I promise.*

Drago firmly cut off their mental path. If he didn't leave her somewhat unsettled, if there wasn't the appearance of a true battle to submission, Alex would know something was wrong. He strode forward, intentionally appearing to stalk her.

Jolene bit her bottom lip at his approach, her eyes sliding down his body, fixing on his arousal, heat flaring in her eyes. Her gaze jerked upward, as if she realized her distraction and reprimanded herself.

He stopped in front of her now, his body raging beyond their words, lust pulsing through his body like hot lava. He stood close. So close that another step would allow him the sweet bliss of sliding his rock-hard cock along her slick folds.

To admit his role as a Slayer broke a code of silence, but this woman was his mate. She would have to know about his world, and they would have to discuss the implications of being together or turning away from each other.

"Are you willing to prove your surrender?" he challenged.

"Yes," she whispered. "Please. Just set my hands free."

His gaze dropped to her breasts, watched her nipples tightening beneath his stare. She had beautiful breasts. Full and high, and incredibly sensitive. He wondered if he could make her come just by stimulating them. The thought intrigued him and he decided to explore it. Just not now. Later. Once he'd spilled himself in her and regained his composure.

His eyes lifted to hers. "And if I do? How will you prove yourself worthy of that freedom?"

A flash of uncertainty passed through her eyes. He leaned forward, his nostrils flaring with the sweet scent of woman and roses. Unable to stop himself, he took another step and pressed his body against hers and slid his cock between her thighs. The wet heat of her core brought both a feeling of relief and urgency. He took a moment to simply enjoy the feel of skin against skin.

His lips pressed close to her ear, but he knew Alex could hear. "What will you do?"

"Anything you want," she said, so low he barely heard her words, but there was no hesitation in her voice. In fact, she seemed to melt against him as she spoke, her hips grinding ever so slightly against his.

The wet heat of her arousal surrounded him, pressing him over the edge. A low growl slid from his lips as he reached behind her and filled his hand with her ass, lifting her. In a matter of seconds, he'd positioned her for access and slid inside the tight, warm heat of her body and thrust deep. She gasped and then cried out his name. The sound rocketed fire through his veins.

Blinded by pure lust, by physical demand, he began to pump his hips, hands still wrapped around that sweet ass for leverage. While Drago moved in and out of Jolene's lush body, her breasts bounced, her muscles grabbed and squeezed. He ground his teeth and pumped harder, faster. Jolene arched into him, moaning and panting, and then cried out. A second later, she tensed, spasms milking his cock, squeezing him with so much pleasure he could barely catch his breath.

She arched hard against him and he felt his body shudder and shake. He reared back, driving into her with all the force he owned, hitting her core with an explosion that rocked him from head to toe.

He took only a moment to recover, burying his head in her neck. Vampire males had dry releases, which fed the intensity and hunger of their sexual need. He was still hard. Still ready to take her again. One release only began the process of complete satisfaction.

Inhaling, Drago forced himself to back away from her, and somehow managed to retract his cuspids. He turned away from her and walked to the corner. He felt the heat of her gaze follow him as he shoved a piece of red silk aside to display a small compartment. Grabbing the key he needed, he returned to Jolene's side, avoiding eye contact. Afraid she might see the hunger he felt, the blood lust. He removed the first cuff, intent on finishing his task before he lost himself again to desire. When he unlatched the second cuff, he pulled her hard against his body, fighting the primal part of himself that simply wanted to take her again.

At the same time, an unfamiliar desire to comfort slid into his mind. It was a dangerous feeling that could get them both killed. If Alex suspected Drago wanted anything more than sex and submission, they'd be in the ground. That thought brought a needed dose of reality. There could be no comfort offered this night. Jolene had walked into Purple Magic knowing what to expect. He could save her from the others. But he couldn't save her from the game she'd set in motion.

Drago stared down at Jolene, no compassion in his voice, only command. "It's time to prove your surrender." He paused and set her free. With a nod of his head, he motioned to the silk-covered king-size bed. "Knees on the mattress."

She stared at him, eyes wide. There was no more time for comfort. *We won't leave this room until he's satisfied that I completely dominate you, Jolene. Alex expects no mercy so I have none to give.*

EIGHT

Jolene's legs trembled as she eased her knees to the mattress, her back to Drago. She felt uncertain and exposed, her body displayed for any who wished to see. Being free to touch Drago, to be with him, was one thing. To expose herself to all those watching felt quite different.

She squeezed her eyes shut, fighting the wild array of emotions filling her. Hating that she actually felt a bit aroused by this. Telling herself the burn of desire came from Drago, not from knowing they were being watched. Her stomach fluttered as she faced what felt like some darker side of herself. The part that seemed to revel in the erotic nature of her exposure. Was this what had happened to Carrie? Had she gotten lost in the erotic high and couldn't find her way back home?

"Bend over. Palms in front of you."

Drago's voice, deep and commanding, came from closer than she'd expected. She started to turn, and his hand pressed in between her shoulder blades. His touch felt like an electric charge. She shivered with reaction.

Suddenly, his body pressed against hers, hips fit to her backside. "You shouldn't have come here."

"I—"

"Don't speak," he said, planting a firm hand on her ass. "You're here now and you have to pay."

"I—"

Drago cut her off by palming her ass again. Hard. Not so much that it caused pain, but she damn sure knew it was meant as a warning. "Don't speak," he said.

She swallowed the words of explanation she wanted to speak, biting her bottom lip as she waited for what came next. For whatever "pay" meant. Why did he suddenly seem so angry with her? She reached for him with her mind and found he'd shut her out.

Before she could consider reasons, he was gone. It was the last thing she'd expected, and she didn't know how to react. With a sideways glance, she saw him moving to the end of the bed.

"Get in the center of the mattress," he ordered, pointing.

She scooted forward, doing as he said. A mixture of sexual heat and dark menace radiated from him like a second skin. Electric. Potent. He wanted to take her. Jolene felt it. Knew it. Hell, she wanted it. Yet, there was more to his mood than lust. Drago had an animalistic quality, primal and not quite human or vampire. The ancient Slayer in him brought an element of danger and command. She'd felt it before, but now it oozed from his presence, filling the room with its dark quality. And as crazy as she knew it to be, this quality turned her on.

Drago stood at the foot of the king-size bed. Tall, broad, gorgeous, his long hair a bit wild, he looked more sex warrior than Slayer right now. And Lord help her, as her eyes slid over that broad chest and rock-hard cock, she wanted to be claimed. She swallowed, thinking of what it would feel like to have him touch her again. To touch him.

When her eyes lifted to his, she found him looking at her with a narrowed gaze. For long moments, they simply stared at each other. And though he said nothing, the anger from before was gone. Instead, she found warmth. Heat. A silent promise . . . of what, she wasn't sure. Though his mixed signals were confusing, Drago made her feel she could get through this.

He broke the silence, his voice holding authority. Cold almost. Not at all matching the warmth in his eyes. "If you truly mean to surrender, I need proof."

"O . . . kay." Jolene swallowed against the dryness in her throat. Then in a stronger voice. "How?"

"Spread your legs," he ordered. "Let me see you."

Jolene didn't move. Surely, he didn't want her to just open up and give him a view. It had been hard enough sticking her ass in the air. To do this . . .

When she didn't immediately respond, Drago seemed to lose patience. "Spread you legs." The words were abrupt. Sharp. "Now."

Jolene jumped at the harshness in his tone. With her heart pounding in her chest at double time, she inched her knees apart. But he wasn't happy with the small spread she offered. "Wider," he said.

With a deep breath, Jolene inched her knees as far apart as they would go. Drago reached down and circled his erection, his eyes catching on hers and holding. His deep, dark stare smoldering with passion, with the promise of satisfaction.

"Touch yourself," he said, sliding his hand up and down the length of his cock.

She registered the significance of his hand wrapped around his erection. Registered the symbolic give and take it represented. Even without speaking to her in her mind, he'd told her he wasn't asking what he wouldn't give.

Recognizing this offering from Drago didn't stop the wild beating of her heart. She wanted *him* to touch her. She'd never gotten off in front of someone before. Certainly she'd had sexual encounters. Often she had even found herself the aggressor. Never, ever, had those encounters included her pleasuring herself for a man, let alone an audience. At this point, she ached with the need to feel Drago inside her, ached to touch him as he now did himself. She needed relief. Having his cock between her legs and then suddenly gone had left her throbbing with a need for fulfillment.

Easing her hand between her thighs and past the dark triangle to her sensitive core, her fingers slid into the slick proof of her arousal and a moan rose in her throat. He had her so aroused, so hot, that the need for release called to her, easing the embarrassment and pushing her into a lusty fog.

She squeezed her eyes shut, allowing that fog to take hold, working her swollen nub. Imagining him touching her as she was touching herself. Amazingly, she felt herself grow bolder, the aching in her nipples begging for her hands—even better, his mouth. She palmed her breast and pinched her nipple imagining his tongue lapping at the hardened tip. Still, it wasn't enough. A spasm tightened her core, the pain of needing Drago inside her almost unbearable.

As if he knew what she felt, suddenly, he was there, his fingers replacing hers, his hard body pressing hers against the mattress. She gasped as he stroked her sensitive core and sunk a finger deep, preparing her for his entry. She sighed as his mouth came down on hers, his tongue sliding past her lips, tender yet passionate. A reward for her show that quickly deepened into primal demand.

Drago.

He pressed her knees farther apart and then, in one deep thrust, he buried himself deep in her core. Before she could even let out a breath, he rolled and pulled her on top of him. She straddled him, on show for him and everyone else. For several seconds, it paralyzed her. Why, she didn't know. She'd done plenty this night. The fear was fleeting, and then he grabbed her hips and anchored her as he gave a mighty thrust.

Sensations rocked her body, darting through her limbs, and leaving her no option but to move. To ride him with a frenzied bucking of her hips. She slid back and forth, side to side, her breast bouncing with each grind of their hips. His gaze was intimate. Hot.

He ground his teeth and reached forward, plucking at her nipples. His head turned, his teeth scraping her arm, and she sensed the tension coiled inside him. Sensed him fighting, tumbling into complete erotic bliss. Knowing this ignited liquid heat in her core. She cried out, arching her back and thrusting her chest into the air. He sat up, covering her breasts with his hands, and then suckling one nipple and then the next.

Her fingers laced into the silky strands of his hair and their eyes locked and held. The connection she felt to him in that instant rocked her world, touching her soul-deep, tightening her chest. When his mouth found hers, she melted into him. He tasted like cinnamon and spice and masculine perfection. Like everything she wasn't but needed to be a part of her.

He kissed her deeply, passionately, the ache in her core spreading, building. His mouth trailed along her chin, her jaw, then to the sensitive area behind her ear. She tilted her head to the side, shivering with the scrape of teeth on her neck, the sensation darkly erotic. Again, his teeth scraped her neck, but this time they sunk into her skin.

Jolene stiffened, shocked by the sensation, a hint of pain spiking and then disappearing, replaced by warmth spreading through her limbs. Sensual warmth. She eased into his bite, letting his hands behind her back hold her weight, her fingers sliding into his hair. The warmth in her body began to turn to heat, then to fire. Goosebumps raised on her skin as if she were cold. But she wasn't cold. She was hot. Burning up hot.

"Oh God, Drago." She wasn't sure if she spoke out loud or in her head. "I need . . . I need," she didn't know what. She didn't know but she needed whatever it was in a bad way. Her mouth watered and she realized what that something was. She wanted to taste him as he had her. "I need you."

But she couldn't explore that thought, couldn't try to understand. Her body exploded in release, muscles clenching around Drago's hard length buried deep inside her. In some faraway part of her mind, Jolene knew Drago eased her onto the mattress and that he shuddered in climax. She even knew when he sealed the holes in her neck. But she couldn't react. Couldn't move. Her body still shivering with the overwhelming release Drago had delivered her to. The all-consuming pleasure.

Something had just happened between her and Drago. She didn't know what. Only that it felt more than necessary. More than part of a show. Before she could analyze that thought, she felt Drago enter her mind, willing her to sleep. Sated and drained, she couldn't find the will to fight him.

Her lashes fluttered, her thoughts on Drago, on the unique way he drew her trust and enticed her desires. If they made it through this night, saying good-bye wouldn't be easy. But it was inevitable and she knew it. Good-byes were part of a Slayer's world.

NINE

Beneath Drago, Jolene's soft curves warmed his body. Just as the sweetness of her blood now filled him. He told himself he'd tasted her for Alex, because it was expected. But he'd been lost in Jolene when he'd sunk his teeth into her neck. Alex's expectations had been nowhere in his mind.

He stared down at her pale face, her lashes resting on her cheeks. He'd ordered her to sleep with a mental push. Achievable because her blood now ran thick in his veins. Their unique connection added to his ability to influence her. Of course, she could fight him, but she wouldn't. Not now, at least. He felt her surrender, her trust. And though she knew nothing of their mating bond, he did, and her body and soul did. As did his. He admired what she had done tonight. Admired her bravery to come here to save her friend. As a Slayer, he understood what that took. She had been willing to sacrifice herself to save her friend.

Drago let a slow breath trickle from his lips. She'd put on a good show for the camera. Now it was his turn to do the same. It was time to convince Alex that Jolene was under his control enough to leave and still return of her own free will.

Grinding his teeth, Drago thought of the cameras. He yanked at the silk covering and pulled it over their naked bodies. Then, and only then, he moved away, to the edge of the bed.

His mind raced as he solidified his plan to get her out of the club. To convince Alex that Jolene wasn't a risk. From there, he'd hide her until Alex forgot about her. Then, he'd come back and get Carrie. He'd save Carrie for Jolene.

The sound of the locks popping open drew Drago's attention. Catherine appeared in the doorway. She wore nothing but red thigh-highs and a tiny slip of silk between her thighs. Drago wasn't blind to Catherine's beauty. He'd chosen her as his frequent bedmate for that reason. He wasn't blind to her pure evil either. She enjoyed this world as much as Alex did and not because of blood exchanges or mind control. She embraced it willingly. She wasn't at the slave camps for a reason. Catherine enjoyed breaking the innocent humans. She lived for it.

So taking Catherine, fucking her, had never felt wrong. Nor had making her submit despite her best efforts not to. For all the pain she caused so many others, it was the least he could do.

"What do you want?" Drago demanded.

Her dark eyes glistened with anger. "Alex wants you."

"Why?"

She rolled her eyes. "I don't ask Alex questions."

Drago bit back another remark. She knew what Alex wanted; they both knew it. He shoved aside the blankets, ignoring his nudity and walking to where his clothes lay on the floor. Catherine leaned against the wall and watched him dress. Though Drago gave her his back, he felt the lust within her. She wanted him. She *always* wanted him. It was as if she needed the self-torture of desiring what she couldn't have.

Once he was dressed, Drago started toward the door, stopping shoulder to shoulder with Catherine. "Let's go."

She shook her head, her breasts jiggling with the action. Drago expected she knew as much. "Alex wants me to stay and watch over her."

"What?" Drago asked. "There are cameras and locks." He grabbed her arm. "You're coming with me."

She smiled. Evil. "You afraid she might want me more than you?"

Drago snatched the key from the wall and then grabbed Catherine's arm, moving her away from the room. Once she was in the hall, he reached for the keychain around her neck and yanked it free, ignoring her objections. Next he slammed the door shut and locked it. He held the only keys that allowed entry to where Jolene rested.

"I will have her, Drago," Catherine hissed.

He fixed her in a steely look. "Only in your dreams, sweetheart."

Drago started walking, giving her his back. She spat nasty words at him but he tuned her out, eager to talk to Alex and get Jolene the hell out of here.

He'd die before he'd allow anyone to take Jolene but him.

Drago entered the boxlike theater booth where he'd been told Alex awaited, knowing what to expect. Yet, as he closed the door and took in the images on the big screen directly in front of him, he wasn't prepared for his reaction. The vision of Jolene sleeping took him by storm, the thought of how close up and personal Alex had viewed their intimacy tearing at his gut.

On either side of Drago similar scenarios played out, sensual scenes on smaller screens. He told himself to look at them. To divert his attention from Jolene for fear he'd show his attachment. But he couldn't stop staring at her. She looked innocent and pure. Too pure to be here, a part of Alex's dirty world.

Drago stood, legs spread wide, arms crossed. "I ordered her to sleep."

Alex glanced at Drago over his shoulder. "So you've opened a mental path and control her will?"

"Completely."

Alex's expression registered approval a second before he eyed the screen to inspect Jolene a bit closer. "Such a lush piece of ass, that one." He swiveled his rolling chair around to fully face Drago. "You've done well with her, but we must be careful. Ancient blood runs within her. She will be harder to win than the others."

A smile touched Drago's lips. "You forget that same ancient blood runs within me. Jolene isn't a problem. She will come to us willingly."

"Yes, well, she might be more of a problem than expected. As you know, I rarely choose women with family ties. I'd taken care to ensure Riker was dealt with in advance."

Drago gave a short nod, careful to keep his expression guarded. "Meaning?"

"He was supposed to be dead and gone."

Alex picked his recruits carefully, always ensuring they had no family to miss them. "And he's not?" Drago asked, his brow inching upward.

"Wounded, not dead." He cut an irritated hand through the air.

"I assume the men who failed you have been dealt with."

"I took pleasure in taking their heads," Alex said, evil lacing his tone. His eyes narrowed on Drago. "You'll need to deal with Riker before he comes for Jolene. He could easily expose our ways to the council through her."

Drago said a silent thank-you. He'd been handed a gift. Jolene's father not only lived, but now Drago had a reason to get her out of here. "Easy enough. She'll make damn good bait."

"Meaning what?"

"She's been trying to reach him over Carrie. I'll make sure she does. When he comes to aid her, I'll be waiting."

Alex studied him a moment, his dark eyes indecipherable. "Very well," he said. "You have one week." Alex studied Drago, uneasiness radiating off of him. "Don't betray me, Drago. You might be a Slayer, but I have an army of men who outnumber you."

Drago feared nothing from Alex's men or anything else in this world. Realization washed over him then, tightening his chest. Oh, but he did have fear. He feared for Jolene.

"I have no reason to betray you," he said, his voice steady despite how rattled these new emotions regarding Jolene had him.

Soon Drago would make Alex pay for what he'd put Jolene and so many others through. He'd make Alex pay for his sins.

TEN

Hours later, Drago shoved open the door to Jolene's apartment with her in his arms. He'd kept her in a deep sleep, determined to wake her in familiar surroundings, hoping it would lessen the blow of all she'd endured at Purple Magic.

He froze inside the entrance, ignoring the lights, his vision as clear in darkness as light. The room took him by storm, overwhelming him with its homey feeling. Though the furnishings weren't immense, they were warm. An overstuffed couch and chair. A fireplace. A square coffee table. A blanket over the back of the chair with a book sitting on the arm. Knickknacks and pictures peppered the room with family flavor. The compact kitchen overlooked the main room by way of a tiny open bar that served as a tabletop with a flower arrangement in the center.

Carrie had been ripped from a home, not just an apartment. And if fate hadn't brought Jolene to Drago, she might have told the same story.

Tightness pressed against his chest and he kicked the door shut, noting two rooms off the main one. He stepped into one of the entryways and surveyed the cluster of stuffed animals on the bed. Carrie's room, he decided.

The instant he entered the second room, he knew it belonged to Jolene, both from the strong, sexy scent of roses lacing the air, and the neat, perfectly organized décor. A smile touched his lips. He knew her well, had touched her mind, her soul. She liked order and control, just as he did. For the first time in his life, he wondered about sharing it.

Jolene murmured and buried her head in his chest. A rush of tenderness overtook him. He'd never felt such a thing. His family had been killed when he'd been but a baby. He knew nothing of love, nothing of caring for others. Most considered him a cold-hearted bastard, at least in human terms, for his ruthless approach to his job.

He settled Jolene on the mattress, easing back the blankets and then maneuvering her beneath them. His brows dipped as he considered her attire, a skimpy dress Catherine had given him to take her home in. She'd be asleep a few more hours. Better she rest comfortably in different clothes. He ground his teeth. Damn it to hell, he shouldn't care about her comfort. He'd seen males find softness from their mates and end up dead for their stupidity.

But even knowing this, he found himself eying the room, and walking toward a small dresser. Chaotic emotions hammered at his mind. What the hell was wrong with him? This woman had him acting like . . . well, like, a mated vampire. And nothing good could come of it. Nothing but trouble. Her own mother had been killed because of her connection to a Slayer. His parents, too.

He ran a rough hand through his hair and leaned on the wooden dresser, tension thick in his body. He'd have to contact the council and demand to speak to Riker. He needed to know about his daughter and the threats from Alex so they could decide how to move forward—a phone call he dreaded.

Slayers were dominant males, protectors of those who they held dear. Wrestling the mating question between him and Jolene before Riker became involved would be desirable. Unfortunately, Drago didn't have the luxury of time. Not with Alex breathing down his throat.

He damn sure wasn't going to tell Riker all that had transpired at Purple Magic. Selective information is all the Slayer father would hear. Enough to save Jolene's life.

"No," Jolene murmured, clinging to the darkness of peaceful sleep. "I . . . no. I don't want to wake up."

"It's time," a male voice said. A familiar voice, both soft and seductive. It slipped inside her dream state and become a part of it. For a moment . . . then reality hit.

Jolene rocketed to a sitting position, her eyes catching midair with the deep, dark stare of Drago. "Where am I?" Her gaze traveled the room, frantic. She reached for memories and struggled. Shadowy images were all she could make out. Her gaze darted around the room. Her room. She was in her bedroom. At least a familiar place. Only, Drago being in her bedroom—this she didn't understand.

She looked down to find herself wearing a T-shirt and boxers. "I don't even remember putting this on."

"The longer you're awake, the more you will remember." He stared at her, his eyes like dark coals. Lonely eyes, she realized. So damn lonely. "I brought you home last night."

She shook her head, trying to get rid of the clouds cloaking her memories. "See, this is insane. I don't even remember telling you where I live. Nothing. I remember nothing." But a flash of their naked bodies pressed close made her breath catch in her throat. She diverted her gaze from his and clenched the sheet. "Oh God." She couldn't quite fully bring the details to mind, but they'd done things together. Intimate, erotic things. "Okay. I remember a little."

"The safest way to get you out of Purple Magic was to put you in a deep sleep. Almost like a coma. I didn't want to risk anyone getting into your head and deciding that your leaving the club was a risk." He pushed to his feet. "Coffee is a stimulant. I'll make some. That'll help you clear the cobwebs."

If his making coffee would give her a moment alone to gather her wits, then so be it. "Coffee sounds like a good idea."

Drago gave her a curt nod. "Coffee coming up."

He turned to leave, and Jolene followed his movement. A blue T-shirt clung to broad shoulders and a muscular back. Faded jeans molded strong legs and hugged a tight, incredibly nice ass. Boots scraped her hardwood floor as he exited the room. Good gosh, the man was gloriously hot.

She pressed two fingers to her forehead and forced herself to think, to pierce through the haze that filled her mind, but found it difficult. Patience not being her strength, Jolene decided to follow Drago and ask questions.

Shoving aside the blanket, she darted toward the closet, yanking a robe from the hook inside the door. She shoved her arms inside it and tied the knot around her waist.

At that moment, Drago walked back into the room, his big body filling the doorway, his head almost touching the top. She'd only known one man that big and that was her father.

He raised the cup. "I forgot to ask if you wanted cream or sugar?"

How crazy was this? A Slayer, a "monster" to many in the vampire world, was asking what she wanted in her coffee—the coffee he was making for her in her very own kitchen.

"Cream," she said, touched by the willingness of this warrior male to tend to her needs. Her first meeting with him, he'd come off uncaring and brutal. Now, she knew why she'd been drawn to him despite the hard shell. Because that shell covered a softer, sweeter one. "I like cream."

His gaze dropped, sliding over her body and taking in her robe. She felt all warm and aware, like she could melt at any moment. When his eyes lifted, he turned to leave, but not before she noted the hint of amusement in his face.

"What's so funny?" she demanded, following in his footsteps, images playing in her head, becoming clearer by the minute. Images that warmed her cheeks, and then her body. Flashes of her naked body pressed intimately to Drago's, of her crying out his name in pleasure. No wonder the man was amused over her covering herself. He'd already done a personal inspection of what the robe covered.

She took a minute inside the entryway of her tiny kitchen to gather her wits and consider the intensity of her attraction to Drago. There was more than sex between them. Watching him open a cabinet and search around a bit, she felt he belonged here, a part of her world. Felt a familiarity to him that expanded beyond their short time together. Is this how her father had made her mother feel?

Drago abandoned the cabinet and opened the fridge. "Is this where I would find cream?" he asked, not looking at her, but clearly knowing she was there.

"Yes. Sorry. I should have mentioned that. In the door." Shoving her hair behind her ear, she realized her hand trembled ever so slightly. Even her knees felt a bit wobbly. Maybe she needed food. "Drago?"

Cutting her a sideways glance and setting the creamer on the counter, he turned to give her his full attention. And then he did the most remarkable thing. He answered the question she hadn't even asked, and she knew he hadn't entered her mind. She would have felt him there.

"Your memories are intact," he said softly. "I promise. You'll remember everything."

If only she could be certain. "I've lost hours of my life, and I still don't have Carrie home with me."

Drago stared at her a moment, his expression indecipherable, but she felt his concern. And it mattered. It mattered in a big way. She didn't want it to matter. He was a Slayer. A vampire who'd be gone in the blink of an eye.

He filled her cup, added cream and brought it to her, taking her hand in his and sliding the mug inside it. "If you will sit down, drink your coffee and give yourself some time to think, it'll come back to you."

His touch was like rocket fuel in her blood. Awareness rushed through her body just as memories flooded her mind with dangerously sexy images. Of his taste. His touch. The perfect feel of his body pressed to hers. Reeling from it all, she took a step backward and his hand, thankfully, fell away. Needing something to do, anything, she brought the cup to her lips. The coffee was warm. She was hot. She gulped it, praying the caffeine would help her clear her fuzzy thoughts. Drago brought the pot to her and she held the mug out for a refill.

"Thank you," she murmured.

"Why don't we go sit?" he urged, his voice too calming, too gentle for his dark, almost menacing exterior.

Her heart beat like a drum in her chest as Jolene turned in silent agreement, wondering again, why she felt so close to Drago. Regardless of what might have happened at Purple Magic, they had only met a short time ago.

Settling onto the single chair in the living room, she intentionally put space between herself and Drago, concluding her potent attraction to him indicated distance to be wise.

Drago claimed a spot on the couch, still close to her, giving her space, but with limits. He could still reach out and touch her, still lean his leg a bit and brush it against hers. She found herself wishing for that contact. She damn near ached for it.

"You saved me from Alex, didn't you?" she asked, thinking back to the prior night.

His eyes flashed, his response fast and hard. "I wasn't about to allow Alex to touch you."

The hint of possessiveness in his words surprised her, and shockingly, warmed her inside out. She'd never wanted a man to try to stake a claim on her, always valued her independence. But his words, his demeanor, didn't offend her as they would with another. They seduced and soothed.

"Thank you," she said. "I went there prepared to do anything to save Carrie, but when it came down to it, I didn't want Alex, or any of those people to touch me." Emotion welled inside. "I feel I failed her. I couldn't have let Alex touch me."

"You shouldn't have gone there," he said, reprimand in his voice.

She cut him a hard look. "Someone had to save Carrie. I didn't see you volunteering."

"I would have saved Carrie."

"Would have?"

"Will. I always planned to save her. I was undercover. I couldn't tell you what was going on, and I damn sure wasn't encouraging you to go to Purple Magic."

Relief flooded her at his declaration. "Carrie's alive then?"

He gave a quick nod. "Alex won't kill her unless she becomes a problem. He uses the women for pleasure. Part of my assignment is to locate the slave camps Alex keeps and rescue the women."

Slave camps. Sex slave camps. What a horrible place to be. Her heart hammered against her chest, fear taking hold. "How do we know Carrie isn't a problem and in danger?"

"He considers Carrie leverage."

Somehow, she knew she wouldn't like what came next. "Leverage?"

"A Slayer's daughter is the ultimate conquest to Alex. He wants you, Jolene. And once he decides he wants someone he doesn't give up. He even tried to have your father killed to ensure he couldn't come after you."

Jolene could barely breathe at the thought of her father being dead. Her hands gripped the arms of the chair. She needed reassurance. "My father is okay, right?"

Drago gently eased one of her hands free of the chair. "He's not only okay, he's on his way here."

Jolene's gaze dropped to their joined hands. "I haven't seen my father in years," she murmured, her eyes lifting to his. "After my mother died, he stopped visiting."

"I'm sure he has reasons."

"Reasons?" Anger stirred, a product of years of hurt. "What reason could there be to avoid your own daughter?" She tried to jerk her hand away, but he didn't allow her escape. One second she was in the chair, the next she was sprawled across his lap.

"Let go of me," she demanded, trying to get up.

He held her with ease. "I can't do that."

She struggled. "Drago! Stop!"

His fingers laced into her hair, angling her mouth to his. He kissed her then, and try as she might to resist, she felt her body ease of its own accord, melting with each stroke of his tongue. Tender strokes. Gentle strokes. A kiss meant to calm, to make love. And right now, unsettled and confused as she felt, he was the calm in the middle of a storm. A storm she feared had only just begun to show its fury.

And with that kiss, she found the events of the night before clearly spelled out in her mind. When she found herself resting forehead to forehead with Drago, she admitted as much.

"I remember now," she whispered, leaning back to look at him, searching his face, trying to understand the meaning of it all. Some things didn't add up. "You spoke to me through a mental path. I thought vampires could only do that if they were blood relations."

"Vampires influence humans through a mental path, but communication isn't possible. With a blood relative, a mental path exists."

"But you talked to me. I know you talked to me."

He hesitated. "There is one other bond that allows this communication." A knock sounded on the door. "That will be your father. Before you answer the door, Jolene—He was distraught when I talked with him. I know it upsets you that he doesn't visit, but he blames himself for your mother's death and now he blames himself for Alex targeting you." The knock sounded again. "You better get it."

Jolene drew a calming breath. "This is crazy. I'm nervous about seeing my own father."

Drago kissed her forehead. "That'll be gone the instant you see him."

He was right, of course. The knock sounded again, and her father's voice filled the air. "Jolene!"

"Coming!" she called, and forced herself into action, finding the entranceway in seconds.

She yanked open the door to reveal her father. Tall with dark auburn hair, he looked every bit the mighty Slayer, authority oozing from him as readily as did danger. His attitude of "move or be moved" was as much a part of him as his standard leather pants and leather jacket.

He stepped forward, barely glancing in Drago's direction, his attention on his daughter. Riker shut the door behind him and then pulled Jolene close, embracing her with the force of a man who'd felt pain. She could barely breathe, her feet dangling off the ground, but Jolene didn't complain. She'd missed him so much that tears welled in her eyes; she realized how lonely she'd been since the death of her mother, how empty.

"I can't believe how close I came to losing you," he whispered in her ear before settling her back and releasing her.

"I'm fine, thanks to Drago," she said, eyeing Drago, who now stood watching them, tension in his body, in his face, and she wondered why. "I guess Drago explained what's going on. About my roommate disappearing and all."

Riker gave Drago a nod. "He did and he told me Alex is after you. Which is exactly why you're packing a bag and coming with me."

Jolene shook her head. "I have to get Carrie back."

"This isn't a discussion," Riker countered. "Pack a bag. You've got ten minutes."

Suddenly, Drago stood behind her, and before he even spoke a word, his possessiveness claimed the room. "I'm afraid I can't let her leave."

Riker stiffened and Jolene stared at Drago in shock. "You dare to challenge her father?" Riker half growled.

Jolene looked from one Slayer to the other, the room crackling with testosterone, both men trying to make her choices for her. Well, they were both about to learn a lesson. No one decided the who, where, what and when of her life but her.

Not her father. And not Drago.

ELEVEN

Drago stood toe-to-toe with Riker, his stomach coiled in a tight knot. The minute he'd heard Riker demand Jolene's departure, Drago knew he could never let that happen. Knew he would never be able to walk away from Jolene. Half human or not, she was his mate.

"She's not going anywhere," Drago ground out between his teeth.

Riker spoke with steely words. "I won't have my daughter used as bait."

"I won't leave Carrie, or any of the other women for that matter," Jolene insisted. "I won't do it."

Drago took the opening Jolene gave him, directing the situation away from their mating. He'd prefer to discuss the mating with Jolene before announcing it to her father.

"I've spent two years working undercover with Alex," Drago inserted. "Dozens of women could be lost forever if my cover is blown. Jolene has become a part of that cover."

Riker's arms crossed in front of his chest. "Find another way." His tone held a command.

Drago shackled the heated words he wanted to say. This was Jolene's father, he reminded himself. "Alex found you once. What makes you think he can't get to you again?"

Riker ignored the question. "You called me. I'm here now so you can back the hell off. I'll take care of my daughter."

"Why should I believe that?" Drago challenged, the threat of Jolene leaving firing his temper again. "She can't even reach you when she needs you."

Riker's eyes turned black as midnight, the air crackling with the depth of his anger. His hands dropped to his sides as if he prepared to put them to use. "Who the *hell* are you to judge me, Slayer?" He didn't give him time to respond. "*Nobody.* Nobody is who you are. I'm taking my daughter with me."

"I can't leave without Carrie!" Jolene declared loudly.

Riker cast his daughter a frustrated look and took a step toward her. Drago cut him off. "She stays."

"Move your ass, Slayer," Riker hissed. "Or I'll move it for you."

Drago threw caution to the wind. Caution would not keep Jolene by his side or calm Riker. "I have the right to protect her." He hesitated only a split second and then dropped his bomb. "I'm her mate."

A pregnant silence and then, *"Mate?"* Riker and Jolene spoke the word at the same time.

"That's right," Drago said, pinning Riker in a direct stare, letting Jolene's father see the truth in his eyes. "And she isn't going anywhere without me."

"I don't understand," Jolene murmured. "What does that mean?"

"A mate wouldn't put his other half in jeopardy," Riker argued. "Involving her with Alex is putting her in jeopardy."

Drago was losing his temper. "I know how to protect her, Riker. You, on the other hand, can't seem to protect yourself, let alone her."

A growl escaped Riker's lips, and Drago knew Riker was ready to fight. At this point, so was he. Before they could charge each other, Jolene pushed between them.

One hand on each man's chest, she ensured their separation, her attention shifting from one to the other. "For your information," Jolene proclaimed. "I am going to do whatever *I* feel is necessary to get Carrie back. I decide what I do. Period. The end. And both of you, stop talking about me as if I am not here." She cast Drago a demanding look. "What haven't you told me about you and me that I need to know?"

Riker tried to reason with her, his voice completely different from the one he'd used with Drago. "Sweetheart—"

She cut him off, turning a warning look on him. "Father, I need to hear from Drago."

Her father hesitated and then nodded, a fierce Slayer brought to his knees by the wrath of his daughter. Drago didn't miss this fact, nor did he miss the concern in Riker's eyes. Riker loved his daughter, and this realization began to calm Drago. He and Riker wanted the same thing: Jolene's safety.

Jolene turned her attention on Drago, demand glinting in her eyes. "Well?"

"I wanted to tell you," Drago began. "In fact, I started to—"

Riker chimed in then. "I'm not even convinced it's true, Jolene."

Drago ignored Riker, restarting where he was interrupted. "The conversation we began about sharing a mental communication path."

Her brows dipped. "That's because we're . . . mates?"

"That's right," Drago said.

Jolene looked at her father, whose entire demeanor had changed, all signs of hostility gone. "I'm half human. Is what he says possible?"

Riker looked uncomfortable. "Maybe we should sit down and talk."

"Just answer my question, Father. Is what he says possible?"

"Your mother wasn't fully human," Riker admitted, obviously uncomfortable with the announcement. "She was half vampire." His eyes lifted and locked with Drago's. "So yes, I believe what he says is valid." He shifted his attention back to Jolene. "A mental path would only be shared with a blood relative or mate. Drago most certainly is *not* a blood relative."

Jolene's face had turned pale, her expression confused. Drago reached out and rested his hand on her shoulder, unable to stop himself. He'd never offered comfort to another living soul, yet he couldn't seem to help doing so with Jolene.

"Maybe we should sit down and talk," he offered softly.

She nodded, her gaze probing his for several seconds. "Yes," she agreed. "We most definitely need to talk."

Jolene sat in the chair she'd occupied earlier, reeling from the information she'd just received. Her father stood by the fireplace, Drago behind the couch; both men appeared to be as on edge as she felt.

"I don't understand," Jolene said. "Why would I not know this about my mother?"

She watched emotion flash across her father's features. "It's complicated," he said. "Not telling you was a choice your mother felt strongly about. At least not until you were older."

"I still don't get it," Jolene said, frustrated. "Why in the world would something like that be kept from me?"

Riker scrubbed his jaw. "You have to understand the history to understand the reasons for your mother's choice. I knew the minute I met her that she was my mate." He drew a breath. "But she was half human. There are doctors within our race who believe that represents a risk. That to complete the mating process, to seal our bond forever, might even have killed your mother. The longer I was with your mother though, the more certain I was they were wrong. She was my mate. I felt it with every breath I drew. I wanted to move forward and seal our bond."

"But that would risk her life," Jolene argued. "How could you want that?"

"Sealing our bond would have given her the life span of a vampire and none of the physical weakness of a human. And Jolene, if you are indeed Drago's mate, you know it. You feel it. A true mate isn't going to die sealing that bond. The doctors had simply never seen two mates who were not wholly vampire. Make no mistake. Your mother was my mate, and I will never forgive myself for not fully claiming her. She might be alive today had I pressed harder."

Jolene digested her father's words, her gaze shifting to Drago. Their eyes locked and held, and she felt that contact clear to her toes. In human terms, she barely knew Drago, yet she knew him as well as she did herself. She didn't know what that meant about her future, but she knew she couldn't ignore what existed between them.

"I had almost convinced your mother to follow through with our mating, but she became pregnant," her father said, drawing her attention back to him. "Mating would have risked your safety."

"What about after I was born?"

"She wouldn't even consider leaving you alone and her death would have done that." He corrected himself. "*Did* do that." His gaze took on a turbulent look.

Jolene's chest tightened as she thought of her mother's sacrifice for her. And of her father's actions since. "You shut me out," she whispered. "You weren't even here for me when she died."

He dropped his head for several seconds, and then fixed her in a tormented stare. "She lived as a human. I was afraid to be around her, to draw danger to her." He shook his head, his lips forming a grim line. "I tried as hard as I could to protect her, and still she ended up dead. Now you're in danger, too."

His words swept over her and then sank deep, cutting like a knife. "You're telling me that it's not your duties as a Slayer that keep you away?" Jolene demanded. "You chose to stay away from both of us?"

"I was trying to protect you."

She pushed to her feet, anger and hurt churning inside and growing with each passing second. "Do me a favor," Jolene spat at Riker. "Spare me the protection. It's painful." With that, she rushed from the room, needing space to think it all through. Afraid if she said more she'd regret it later.

She slammed her door shut and curled up on the bed. Tears came and she let them for the first time in years. Tears to cleanse what she couldn't change. To allow her to face her future, whatever that might be. Her mother was gone. Her father absent. Carrie was lost and in danger. Everything she'd known to be true in her life had been a façade. The future felt uncertain and full of unsettling change— change that involved Drago now.

And she had to deal with the implications of his presence. He would come for her soon, and he would try to claim her as his mate. The question was—what would she do when he did?

TWELVE

Drago watched Jolene's departure and fought the urge to follow. He and Riker had business to attend to that directly related to Jolene's safety.

"Alex found Jolene by accident, through her roommate," Drago offered quietly, sensing Riker's needed to get past some of his self-blame and think about the battle ahead.

"Regardless," Riker said. "The danger comes from her connection to me."

"To wish that connection away is to wish she was never born."

Riker gave Drago an unblinking stare. One second. Two. His shoulders slumped slightly and he gave a short nod. "Point taken." He hesitated. "I lost her mother. I don't want the same to happen to her."

"You've lost her already, but she's alive and well. You can still get her back. Help me save Carrie. It will mean a lot to her."

His response came slowly. "You have a plan?"

"You were right about Jolene being bait. Bait to get to you. Alex wants you dead."

Riker snorted. "No surprise there. He made a damn good first attempt."

"And he'll keep coming at you until we shut him down," Drago commented. "I'll tell Alex you were already here when I brought Jolene home, responding to messages Jolene had left for you. I'll detail a battle with your retreat and Jolene still in my possession. He'll be furious, of course. One of Alex's biggest fears is the council charging in and shutting down his operation. He'll fear you can make that happen."

"What's keeping the council from taking him down, anyway?"

"Alex has human women held as slaves. Three camps, all well guarded by a female army that Alex controls. I know where two of them are but not the third. That's the one he visits frequently. I've earned Alex's trust, but he lets each of his people know only so much."

Riker's lips thinned. "So where does that leave us?"

Drago sat down on the couch and kicked his feet up on the coffee table, one booted foot over the other, his decision already made. "I talked with the council. Alex has to go down. It's long past due. I'll tell Alex you want to make a trade. Yourself for Jolene and Carrie, and you want them brought to you. You won't go to him."

"Why would he give up Jolene and Carrie? He'll consider them a risk, won't he? They know about his operation."

"Not if Alex believes I'll kill them," Drago said.

"It's risky," he said, his expression grim. "Surely Alex will involve his army."

"He will," Drago agreed, "but we'll have ours involved as well."

"And the third facility? What of it?"

"That's where Carrie is being held. She'll be under Alex's influence, but we can get into her head and read the location. Fast action will be critical or Alex will move the women before we get to them. The slave camps have to be hit at the same time that all of this goes down."

"And a third team on standby to go after the third camp when we get Carrie," Riker added.

"Exactly."

"It's dangerous," Riker said. "Everything has to go just right to make this work."

"We'll make it work." Drago pushed to his feet.

They discussed a few more details and agreed that once the stage was set with Alex, Riker had to leave. If his presence were known, if it looked as if Riker was anything but Drago's enemy, the plan would fail.

"Why don't you take a little time and talk to your daughter?" Drago suggested. "I'll wait until you're ready to leave to call Alex."

Riker hesitated and then agreed. "I will."

"I'll step out to grab her some food. You know. Give you some space and all."

Riker murmured a quick thank you, then, "Keep her safe, Drago."

"I plan to," he said, and walked toward the door, hopeful Riker could begin the healing process with Jolene to overcome the past.

And he could only hope her past didn't destroy their future.

Jolene stood in the kitchen, having finished a two-hour conversation with her father, a coffee mug in her hand. Her head felt clearer now, but she didn't want to lose any details of the past day that might be important to her future.

Riker appeared in the doorway. "Now that Drago's set everything up with Alex, I'm taking off."

She set her mug down and closed the distance between them, hugging him. Though it pleased her that they'd opened up communication, she was sad for the time lost, the time they couldn't get back. "Be safe," he murmured.

Jolene leaned back and looked up at him. "You too," she said, contemplating the danger of their plan to rescue Carrie, but also hopeful of the results. Alex had already agreed to a trade the next night. If all went well, Jolene would have her best friend home soon.

Riker pinned her in a warning stare. "I know how stubborn you are, but Alex is dangerous. Listen to what Drago wants you to do. One mistake could be deadly. I wish you didn't have to be involved in this at all."

"I'm well aware of what Alex is like." She gave him a soft smile, deciding now wasn't the time to let her independence flare. "Thank you for doing this for me. And for Carrie."

He kissed her forehead. "Anything for my daughter."

Fighting tears for the second time that day, Jolene watched her father depart, her breath coming out in a slow, shaky trickle.

She returned to the main room to find Drago setting several bags on the bar, amazed at how she warmed inside at his presence.

He stopped what he was doing when he saw her, simply stood there, staring at her, his dark eyes probing. "Everything go okay with you and Riker?"

"Yes." She eyed the bags. "Whatever that is smells wonderful. I'm famished." She wet her lips a bit nervously. They had a lot to talk about, and she couldn't help but feel a bit apprehensive. She'd just learned the man was her mate. "I'll get us something to drink."

Making her way to the kitchen, she found two glasses, filling them with tea, the only thing she had in the house.

Returning to the bar, she scooted onto a wooden stool next to Drago, settling a glass in front of each of them.

They busied themselves eating, falling into silence, a comfort level between them that long-time lovers might share, despite the untouched subject of their mating.

When Drago reached for his third burger, she spoke up. "Tell me you aren't eating another one?"

He shrugged. "Two more. Vampires have big appetites. Slayers, even bigger."

"I guess I have more to learn about vampires than I realized." She inclined her head a bit. "My mother talked a lot about my father, and I asked a lot of questions." She smiled. "I never thought to ask how many burgers he could eat in one sitting."

He returned her smile, his a bit sly. "Now you can ask *me* those questions."

She shoved her food away. The edge of her hunger was sated; her desire to know about Drago wasn't. "There's a lot I want to know," she commented. "I feel like I am living in some sort of alternative universe." She made a vague motion to the bar. "I mean, here we are, eating fast food, having casual conversation. Yet only a few hours ago we were in a sex club." Intimate, sensual images of her and Drago together flashed in her mind and she suppressed a shiver. "You'd think we were never there. It's like none of it was real."

Drago rotated around to face her, and she did the same, moving so her knees were aligned with his. Anticipation swirled inside Jolene, her stomach fluttering like she was a teenager about to be kissed. When his fingers brushed her bottom lip, she felt like she couldn't breathe.

"It's all real," he said, his voice low and sensual. Dark eyes lifted to hers, his hand settling on her knee. "Our bond is real."

She didn't know what to say. She knew he was right, but all of this had happened too fast. When she didn't immediately respond, his hand dropped away from her leg. She missed his touch the minute he withdrew. Missed it in some deep place inside her. Never in her life had she felt this way. Everything around her was falling apart, yet Drago felt safe. Strong. Right.

"I'm trying to digest all of this, that's all, Drago. A few days ago, I thought my mother was human. I saw how lonely she was when my father was gone, but still, she loved him. There was no other for her."

"For a vampire, there is only one mate, Jolene. I didn't realize how much truth that held until I met you. You don't know you need or want that person, until they show themselves. A week ago I would have told you I would never mate."

"And now?"

The words had barely left her lips before Drago's fingers laced into her hair, his big body moving closer, his woodsy, masculine scent taking her senses by storm. "I have every intention of claiming you, Jolene." And then his mouth slanted over hers, his tongue sliding past her lips, his kiss hungry, passionate, full of demand.

She melted into him, her hand settling on his chest, everything inside her calling out with acceptance of what this man, this vampire, meant to her. Beyond time, beyond words, he was part of her, her other half. Her soul mate.

Long moments later, Drago drew back enough to speak, their lips close, their breath mingling. "A week ago, I would have claimed no mate existed for me. Now, I can't imagine a day without you. As much as I want to press you forward, to claim you right this minute, I will wait until you are ready." His mouth brushed hers. "But I have to warn you. I've never been a patient man."

She slid off the barstool and faced him. Close. So close. Not close enough. "Nor I a patient woman." She needed assurances on a few things. "Nor will I do as my mother did, and wait by the door for a mate who is never around."

"As my mate, you have the right to live with me at the council compound in the Adirondack Mountains. And I wouldn't be working a case like Purple Magic as a mated male."

This pleased her, but there was one other thing that males of the vampire race were known for. "I've lived as a human, Drago. I won't take orders from you."

"What if those orders are meant to protect you?"

She shook her head. "No matter how you package an order, it's an order." She tilted her head to the side. "Are you willing to share control or not, Drago?"

"Well?" Jolene challenged.

Drago stared down at Jolene's delicate little hands as they settled on the top of his thighs. He'd been rock hard since she sat down next to him, struggling to contain a desire to rip her jeans off her and bury himself inside her.

"With you, I'll share all things," he finally managed, forcing his gaze to hers.

She ran her palms up his thighs. Slowly. Her tongue slid along her full bottom lip. As if she couldn't wait to taste him. Hell, he couldn't wait. Yet, for some reason, he knew he had to keep his restraint in place.

Drago held his breath, shackling the hunger burning within him. For some reason, he was afraid to move. Afraid it might make her turn him away.

Easing his legs apart, she stepped between them. They were chin to chin now, and the deep, dark green in her eyes sparked with a hint of challenge. She fingered the material of his T-shirt and her hands crawled beneath the hem to touch his skin.

"You say you want to protect me." He gave a short nod. "I imagine you justified tying me up back at Purple Magic to protect me, too."

He narrowed his gaze on her. "I did." She brushed his nipple and scraped a nail over it, and it was all he could do to keep from reaching for her.

"To save me."

"I did what I had to."

A smile played on her lips as she molded his chest with her cool, soft palms. "Will you do what you have to do now? To prove you can share the control?"

His brow lifted, and his body tingled with the need to pull her close. To feel her lush curves next to his. "How exactly do you propose I do that?"

She reached down and took one of his hands in hers. "Let *me* tie *you* up."

Drago went completely, utterly still. He'd never in all his two centuries of living given that kind of control to anyone. Not under any circumstances. But this was Jolene, his mate, and for the first time in his life, he understood the power that held. And he gave in to it.

He pushed to his feet, more than willing to let her have her way with him.

THIRTEEN

Jolene intended to test Drago. To tame him in the process.

He stood in the doorway of the bedroom, his watchful gaze potent as she removed two long scarves from a drawer. One red, one black. She'd never played dominant in the extreme way she planned to now, but anticipation of doing so sent little pulses of heat darting through her body.

Ready to begin their game, Jolene cast Drago a steely look full of command. "Get undressed and lay on the bed." She would be leaving her clothes on, just as he had in the club.

He didn't move at first, and for a moment, she thought he might refuse. But then, without words, he began doing her bidding. Jolene leaned against her dresser, enjoying the show as he exposed sinewy muscle and taut, bronzed skin. When he finally stretched out on the mattress, her mouth watered at the sight of him. Her gaze traveled the length of his delicious body, taking in the perfection, lingering on the muscular thighs she'd felt beneath her palms only minutes before.

He was hard, his cock ready for her. It pleased her to know that he was aroused, that giving away the power didn't change his desire for her.

She forced her eyes upward, taking in the tapered waist and broad chest sprinkled with just the right amount of dark hair. When she finally allowed her eyes to meet his, she allowed the depths of her desire to show. At the club, she had feared what she felt for him. Feared what she didn't understand. There was no reason to hide it now. She wanted. He wanted. It was as it should be.

Yet what she found in the depth of his stare surprised her. She saw . . . vulnerability. Oh, there was lust. Desire. Heat. But beyond all those emotions, the vulnerability lived. To give himself to her in this way was new to him.

Her stomach fluttered with excitement at this realization. She walked to the edge of the bed and trailed one of the scarves up his calf, then his thigh. And because she couldn't resist, she let it caress his shaft. It jerked in response and he began to reach for her. She took a step backward and pointed at him. "Hands to your sides."

He inhaled heavily and she felt his edginess. His lust. The tightly wound primitive desire to take her. Their eyes locked in a standoff of sorts and silently, she dared him to act. Dared him to prove he couldn't truly share the power.

The breath he'd been holding gushed from his lips, and he let his arms drop to the bed, submission in his actions. She waited a moment, cautious to ensure he was well under control. Then, and only then, she stepped forward, reaching for one of his wrists, tying a scarf around it and then tying it to the metal post above the bed. She repeated her actions with the other wrist.

Sensing his uneasiness, she sat beside him, her hand gently cupping his jaw, the roughness of his dark stubble beneath her palm. His gaze probed hers, as if trying to find some sort of malicious intent, some reason to reclaim control.

She reached for his mind, pleased to find she could connect, that her memories of their communication path were true. *Trust me.*

After a moment, his gaze softened. *It is not my trust in you that is being questioned. It's yours.*

And then the most amazing thing happened. They shared a look so tender, so intense, she could barely breathe. In that moment, she knew, without any doubt, no matter what the future held, she loved this man. It was crazy. Ridiculous even. They'd only just met. Still it was true. There were none of the insecurities of a human marriage in the vampire world. A vampire soul knew its mate.

She reached out and touched his bottom lip, so sensual and full, and shivered with the contact, amazed at how the littlest things impacted her with Drago. He had a strong face. A face full of strength and character. A face full of life, pain and darkness . . . but she knew he'd felt no love and she wanted to change that. She knew this from touching his mind, from touching his soul. And somehow, she knew she was meant to heal his wounds, to make him whole.

With that thought she stood up, no longer wanting to play a game. She wanted to make love to her man. She undressed, forcing herself to go slow when she wanted to rip her clothes off and press her body close to his.

He watched her, primal heat in his hot stare, devouring her body, ravishing her in the most intimate of ways. His eyes caressed her breasts, her thighs, the touch more sensual, more potent than most men could achieve with their hands.

Jolene climbed on top of the bed and settled between his thighs. She hungered to simply feel him inside her, and she had to remind herself of her purpose. Tying him up was a test. A way to find out if he could really allow her to be an equal before she bound herself to him for all eternity.

She settled her hands on his knees, doing a slow slide up his thighs, enjoying the flex of muscles beneath her palms. Lingering at the V of his legs, she eased her hands around his sac, teasing him, knowing what he really wanted, where he really needed her touch. He moaned in response, satisfaction filling her with the sound, urging her onward in her exploration.

Her hand wrapped around his shaft, feeling him grow beneath her grip. Her nipples ached with arousal and she leaned into him, brushing them across the soft head of his cock—one and then the other, trembling with the tiny pricks of burning pleasure the act created. She could feel her core growing wetter. Hotter. More needy. It would be so easy to just climb on top of him and ride.

Instead, she fed his hunger for her another way, teasing his cock with a soft whisper of air blown from her lips. His hips bucked, lifting. He was trying to get her to take him in her mouth.

Jolene flattened her hand on his stomach, smiling at his actions. Loving this feeling of control. "You might have to learn some patience after all."

She filled her hands with her breasts, touching herself as he seared her with his scorching stare, and then fitted his shaft between them. Instantly, he pumped his hips, sliding back and forth. She was half panting now, aroused and starting to lose control. She stroked her nipples with her thumbs, trying to end the ache that seemed only to build and grow larger, more demanding. Pressing her to take things higher and hotter.

Driven by this need, she pulled away from him, wrapping his shaft with her palm, and lapping at the head with a long stroke of her tongue. The salty proof of his arousal told her just how excited he was.

Wanting all of him, every bit of pleasure and submission he had to give, she drew him into her mouth, sucking him hard and deep. He was the one panting now, moaning. Using her hand as a guide, she pumped him, urging his hips into action. Working him over and over, with all she had. Her lips. Her tongue. Her hand.

But she didn't let him come. The minute she knew he was approaching release, she pulled back, blowing on the tip again. Taking him back down a bit. She licked him like she might an ice cream cone, from top to bottom, and then repeated the act. She wanted to continue to pleasure him, to tease him, but her body screamed for relief, for him inside her.

Caving to her need, Jolene straddled him, guiding him with her hand. Taking his cock inside her, she did a slow slide down his length until she took him all. She leaned forward, hands on his chest, ready to ride him, to feel him, to go beyond the burn of anticipation.

But her eyes locked with his and she went still.

They stared at one another, intimately joined, the sexual play of moments before falling away, replaced by something deeper, more emotional and intense. Warmth spread through her in all ways possible, through her body and soul, a feeling unlike anything she'd ever experienced in her lifetime. A feeling of pleasure and peace, sensuality and sweetness. An unexplainable sense of completeness.

"If you must leave me tied up, at least kiss me," he said softly, no demand in his voice. Only tenderness.

Suddenly, she wanted him free. Wanted the mutual touch. The feel of lovemaking. She leaned forward and tugged at the silk on one of his wrists. The instant he was free, his hand inched into her hair and pulled her mouth to his. He kissed her with such passion, such potent perfection, she couldn't even begin to think about the other scarf.

When he tore his mouth from hers, his breathing heavy, he pinned her in a sultry stare. "Did I pass your test?"

"Yes," she whispered, reaching for the wrist that remained tied. Good Lord, he passed, and then some.

His hand went to hers, stilling her action. "Don't do that unless you are prepared to become mine, Jolene. I don't trust myself not to take you."

There was no question left for her. She felt him as the other half of her soul. How could she turn away? "I want you, Drago."

He didn't give her time to respond, yanking at the scarf and proving he could have freed himself all along. Perhaps the scarves had been a mental barrier for him more so than a physical one. He'd contained himself for her, for his mate. And to Jolene, this proved more than any binding rope.

Drago pulled her tight against his body, molding her with his hand, his hips beginning to pump, his cock making an erotic slide inside her body. They became one; time didn't exist. Their kisses, their touches, their movements consuming all else. Jolene couldn't get enough of him. Couldn't get close enough. Couldn't take him deep enough.

As if answering the silent cry she screamed for more, Drago's teeth sank into her neck. The world seemed to spin around her then, perhaps because she knew this was the beginning of forever. Erotic sensations danced along her nerve endings and she melted into his body, chest to chest, her stomach pressed to his.

Amazingly, she felt her mouth water, her desire to taste him as intense as her desire to feel him move inside her. Instinctively, she knew that to drink of him, as he had of her, would seal their bond. And she wanted it. She wanted that more than life itself.

Drago. She whispered the desperate cry in his mind, and he responded, pulling back from his bite and sealing her wound.

His hands framed her face. "If I give you what you want, what you crave at this moment, there is no turning back."

She didn't have to think. "I don't want to turn back."

He studied her a moment and then brought his wrist to his mouth, biting himself and then pressing it to her lips. The first drop of coppery crimson touched her lips and she moaned, her teeth elongating. A second later, he pulled his wrist away and she knew what to do.

She leaned forward, and sunk her teeth into his neck. He moaned, erotic and deep, and she felt his cock stir inside her again, felt herself responding to his arousal in a primal, animalistic way. She drank deeper, moving with him, desperate for all he could give her, all he had to offer, all she could take. And like the bittersweet taste of the first sip of wine, she felt her release begin to form.

She tore her mouth from his neck, barely finding the control to seal his wound before kissing him. And kiss him she did. With more hunger than she'd ever felt in her life. Feeling each stroke of his tongue, each stroke of his cock, with the intensity of a firestorm. She rocked on top of him, a frenzied rush toward release until she exploded with such force it completely stole her breath.

In her mind, she called his name, but her lips could not. She felt him arch his hips, felt him shutter and shake, heard him in her mind as well. Heard him moan. Heard him call her his mate. And she wished this moment never had to end.

Drago answered her wish with a whisper and a promise. "We have forever, Jolene."

She sighed with the sweet bliss of complete, utter satisfaction. The kind she'd never felt, never known, until Drago, and she repeated his words because they sounded so perfect. *We have forever.*

FOURTEEN

A mere twenty-four hours after Jolene and Drago completed their mating ritual, plans were underway to rescue Carrie and take down Alex. Well past midnight, standing on the deserted pier that docked the Staten Island Ferry, Jolene had both her father and her mate by her side.

Gareth and Galen, the Slayers she'd met only a few minutes earlier, stood within hearing distance. Twins, both wore leather jackets that wouldn't be needed in the sixty-degree temperature, if not for their ability to conceal an arsenal of weapons. Blond with blue eyes, the two Slayers were not wholly vampire, but apparently part shape-shifter. Jolene didn't ask details as she might on another occasion. Right now, her focus was bringing Carrie home safely.

Drago glanced down at Jolene, his hands going to her shoulders, his voice and expression full of concern. "You okay?"

The truth was, she wasn't all that okay. Everyone she loved stood in harm's way this night. "Nervous," Jolene admitted. "I wish this was over."

"You shouldn't be here," he said, his expression grim. He'd tried to talk her out of coming, offering several plans that would eliminate her presence.

"We can't risk putting up red flags. It could cost lives. You know that."

Someone spoke to Drago in his headset. He listened a minute and then eyed Riker. "We're a go. All teams are in position, here and off-site." He listened a minute longer before adding, "Five hostiles in covert positions outside our immediate perimeter."

"You were right," Riker commented dryly. "Alex didn't trust you."

"He wasn't about to risk me betraying him. Alex always takes out insurance."

Jolene's nerves kicked into high gear. Five hostiles. Drago had three of his own men positioned in the shadows, prepared to deal with Alex's army. "We're outnumbered."

"A Slayer fights at a five to one ratio," Riker commented. "*They* are outnumbered."

Drago's hand went to his earpiece again, then, "Show's on. Four approaching with Carrie in their possession."

Air rushed from Jolene's lungs. "She's alive."

"And we plan to keep her that way," Riker said, running his hand down the back of his daughter's hair before giving Drago a nod and moving into position.

Riker and the twins formed a row, facing off with Drago as if he were the enemy. The four vampires who would soon appear believed Drago to be their boss, directly beneath Alex. They would join Drago to stand against Riker and the twins.

Drago yanked a rope from his pocket and Jolene held out her hands. He wound it around her wrists, but didn't tie it off. When the time was right, she'd free herself with a practiced tug.

Positioned in front of Drago, a knife at her neck, Jolene could hear her heart beating in her ears, feel each passing second like a year. The steel wall of Drago's hard body behind her offered her the only source of calmness.

I will never forgive myself for allowing you to be here for this, in harm's way, to witness the blood that will be spilled this night.

Jolene could feel Drago's edginess, the nervous tension racing through his body, charging the air. She had to be strong for him, for all those involved. She sensed her response would impact Drago's state of mind, perhaps his performance in battle, so she chose her words with care.

Then stop talking, Slayer, and kick some ass so we can go home.

Though he didn't respond, she felt warmth flood her mind. She'd helped Drago as much as she could. Instinct told her he was focused on the battle before him.

For the second time in a short window of time, she had done what she'd never allowed herself to do. She'd handed control to another. Passed the power to Drago.

She inhaled and let the rightness of that decision fill her. If they made it through this night, she would never face a challenge alone again.

Drago had never felt fear in battle before, but he felt it now. Felt it for Jolene. Correction. "Terrified" more aptly described the wrenching pain in his gut. For the first time in his life, he had something to lose. But as the wind lifted her hair, the soft scent of his woman insinuating itself into his nostrils, he realized something else. He realized what he had never understood before this moment: A Slayer wasn't weaker when mated. Drago had a reason to fight he'd never possessed before. He had Jolene.

He watched the four vampires under Alex's command approach, the ones he'd personally chosen for the mission. To them, he still worked for Alex, still ruled their actions. He watched the vampires come into view and motioned for them to join him. Dressed in a long trench coat, Carrie walked willingly with her captives, controlled by their mental connection to her.

"Carrie!" Jolene screamed out the minute she saw her friend. Carrie acted as if she hadn't heard Jolene. "Carrie, please. Are you okay?"

"Shut up," Drago growled at Jolene, putting on a show, but hating every minute of it.

Riker took a step forward. "Tie her up," he said, inclining his head at Carrie. "I know you control her mind. I don't want her trying to run off."

"Do it," Drago ordered the vampire closest to him.

Riker continued, "Jolene and Carrie will leave with my men so I know they're safe. Then, and only then, will I hand myself over."

"Not happening," Drago said. "They stay until we finish this or there's no trade."

"We both know you have no intention of letting me live," Riker argued. "I won't have my daughter be a witness to my demise."

"I'll be gracious and do it without an audience," Drago said, "but the women stay until you're secured." He let the challenge linger in the air. He had to play this out in a way that wouldn't raise suspicion. "Deal or no deal?" He pressed the blade to Jolene's throat. "Does she live or die?"

"Fine," Riker conceded reluctantly. "But hand the women over to my men."

With Drago's approval, one of Alex's men shoved Carrie forward and Gareth grabbed her. A second later, Jolene gasped as Gareth sunk his teeth into Carrie's neck. He had to take her blood in order to control of her mind, to steal it away from the other vampires. It would also allow him to read the location of the third slave camp.

Now, the moment of pain for Drago. He had to let Jolene go. *Remember what I said. Stay close to Galen.*

Stop worrying about me and focus on staying alive yourself, damn it.

He would have laughed at her fiery attitude if the situation wasn't so grave. Reluctantly, he released her, and she rushed into her father's arms, a planned event.

Riker hugged her and kissed her forehead. Following her script, she pleaded with her father. "You can't go with them. They'll kill you."

Riker didn't respond, a hard shell in place as he handed her off to Galen who shoved her behind him, shielding her with his big body. Drago and Riker stepped forward, toe to toe, eyes locking as they silently counted down as planned. Giving Jolene time to get untied. One, two, three.

At the same moment, Drago and Riker pulled weapons and turned on the four vampires. In each of Drago's hands, he gripped long, corkscrew-type circular blades designed to destroy a vampire's heart. Drago landed the point in the first vampire's heart before the male ever knew what had hit him, twisting it to destruction.

He whirled around just in time to kick a second vampire solidly in the chest. His attacker stumbled and Drago took advantage of the moment, using his second blade to destroy the vampire's heart.

Poised to attack again, Drago scanned, finding the battle done, at least for now. Riker, too, had been successful, killing his assigned opponents. Relief rushed over him as he found Jolene safe and by Carrie's side, Galen closely guarding her.

Drago started toward her right as Carrie collapsed against Gareth, who picked her up in his arms. Jolene yelped. "Oh, God. Did you take too much blood?"

Gareth gave her a hard look, as if he didn't like being accused of such a thing. "She's fine. I'll take her to the complex for treatment." He eyed Drago. "I called in the location of the third slave camp to team three."

Galen eyed the four bodies. "Perimeters secured. I'll do clean up here."

"Wait," Jolene said. "I need to go with Carrie."

Drago hesitated, hating the idea of letting her out of his direct protection, but knowing he needed to ensure firsthand that Alex was dealt with.

He eyed Galen. "Forget clean up. Take care of my woman."

"And my daughter," Riker chimed in.

Galen looked from one Slayer to the next. "Why do I think I just got handed the most dangerous assignment of my life?"

"Because if anything happens to Jolene," Drago said. "We'll kill you."

"Oh good grief," Jolene said, eying Galen. "Let's go before they get any more out of control."

Drago pulled her close and kissed her soundly on the lips. "I'll never apologize for protecting you."

"I know." Her hand went to his cheek, her eyes tender. "Thank you for saving Carrie." She brushed her lips over his. "Take care of you now. For me." She eyed her father. "And that goes for you, too."

Drago and Riker stood there, side by side, watching her departure, and Drago felt the oddest connection to the other male. A bond born of love for one woman, for Jolene.

And with that realization, Drago whispered the words to her mind, the words he thought he'd never say to another.

I love you, Jolene.

Jolene sat in the chair next to Carrie's bed, her gaze fixed on the machine that showed her vitals, listening to the steady rhythm of the beeping, grateful for her friend's new chance at life. Though she had yet to wake up, the doctors assured Jolene that Carrie would be fine. Likely traumatized and in need of love and support, but fine, nonetheless.

Gareth occupied a chair in a far corner. He had been with the two of them the entire time during the twenty-four hours since their arrival, using duty as an excuse. Jolene got the impression he was here for Carrie, though, not her. Almost as if there had been some kind of bond formed when he'd touched her mind.

Pushing to her feet, Jolene walked to the window, her mind on Drago. Outside, the sun was on the rise, mountains surrounding them in a rainbow of greens and browns. The time apart from Drago, though short, felt like years. She needed the people she loved close and secure.

"He's fine," Gareth said, from behind her. "They both are."

Jolene turned to face him. "I know." She offered a soft, appreciative smile. "Thank you for the support. I just wish they'd get here."

Drago had made contact through their mental path, but not for hours now, and she hesitated to initiate another link, fearful she might distract him in some type of battle.

As if on cue, the door creaked and Drago appeared. Jolene rushed forward and threw her arms around his neck. "Oh, thank God. I was worried."

Drago smiled and kissed her. "You feel so damn good," he said, holding her close and lifting her feet off the ground. "I didn't know I could miss another person as I did you." He settled her to the ground again and gave Gareth a nod.

"I'll stay with Carrie so you two can take some time," Gareth offered.

Jolene thanked him and let Drago lead her to the hall. "My father?"

"He's fine. He's locking Alex up."

"You brought him here?"

His expression turned grim. "I wanted to kill the bastard, but the council wouldn't let me." He offered an apologetic look. "I guess I need to learn to curb my tongue."

"Why?" she asked. "I wanted you to kill the bastard, too."

Drago laughed and tugged her into his arms again. "You really are my mate, aren't you?"

"Was there a question?"

He brushed hair from her eyes with a tenderness that defied the harshness of his prior words. "None whatsoever."

"Why is he here anyway?" She shivered. "I hate the idea of being near that . . . that thing."

"The FBI wants to connect the dots on a string of missing person's cases, all young females without families. The council agreed to help."

"Oh. Well, that's good. That's really good. And the slave camps? Did you save the women?"

"We did. The council sent in a team of doctors who will be evaluating and deciding how to best help each one."

"Maybe I can help?" she asked, feeling deep inside this was a calling for her, a part of her destiny. "I have a unique understanding of what they faced with Alex."

Admiration filled his eyes. "That's an excellent idea. I'm sure there are many things you can do to help. We can talk with the council about it tomorrow." He reached in his pocket and pulled out several keys. "You up for a little tour?"

"Of the complex?"

"No," Drago said. "The council gave us our choice of three houses in a remote section of the complex. They thought we might want some immediate privacy while we decide what our future plans will be."

Excitement filled Jolene. She wanted a life here at the complex. She'd have Drago with her and her father nearby. "Yes. I'd love that."

Drago's eyes twinkled. "I figured we should try out the beds in each. You know, we have to have a good bed."

She laughed. "Why limit ourselves to the beds? I think we should try out all the rooms, too."

Hand in hand, they walked toward the elevator, and for the first time in years, Jolene didn't feel alone. She felt complete.

EPILOGUE

Six months later

With Jolene's unique insight into the ways of both human and vampire, the council had convinced her to serve as a liaison dealing with the two governments. A job she had taken reluctantly fast became the job of her heart.

Jolene sat at the conference table inside the offices of the council, Carrie beside her, reviewing the final details of the menu for the next night's charity event. Jolene had contracted with Carrie's new catering service to handle the event.

Her pet project, a children's hospital for both human and vampire research and treatment, was well underway. This charity event, hosted by the Vampire Council and the New York City Council, should offer the final funding needed to begin construction.

"The headcount is off," Jolene said, pursing her lips. "It's seven hundred and seventy people not six hundred and seventy." She gave Carrie a concerned look. "This is a typo, right?"

Carrie's baby blue eyes went wide. "What? No. This is the number you gave me. I wouldn't make a hundred-person mistake." Her pale face went paler. "Tell me you're joking because I am having a heart attack."

Jolene tried to keep a straight face but she couldn't. She burst out laughing. "I couldn't resist. You are wound so tight I had to tease you."

"That was so not appropriate," Carrie said, glowering at Jolene. "I was seriously freaking out."

A knock sounded on the door and Gareth peeked in through the entrance. "Ready to go?" he asked Carrie. They'd hooked up as soon as Carrie started coming around for the catering event and had been inseparable for weeks.

The instant Carrie looked at Gareth, her expression softened. "Yes," she said, pushing to her feet and straightening her cream-colored dress. "More than ready, actually." She cast Jolene a warning look. "Do that to me again and I might be the one growing fangs."

Jolene laughed and did a playful hiss. "Get some rest tonight. You deserve it." She eyed the blond Adonis, the half vampire waiting at the door, and lowered her voice. "Or maybe it's him you deserve."

Carrie waved off her remark and grabbed her notebook. Jolene watched her depart, happy her friend had recovered fully from her experience in the underground.

The doctors at the complex had wiped Carrie's memory free of Purple Magic, though Jolene hadn't known until after it was done. Despite her mixed feelings about the action, she'd since decided it was a good choice. The doctors had encouraged Jolene to tell Carrie about what had happened. That way, Carrie would own her past, without being tormented by bad memories she couldn't change.

"There you are." Drago appeared in the doorway where Gareth and Carrie had just disappeared. "I went to your office but you weren't there."

She gasped at the effect he had on her, everything inside her warming. Her mate never failed to steal her breath away. In black leather and a matching jacket, his hair wild around his shoulders, he was a fantasy of sex and sin. Even better, the wild warrior, with fiery kisses and talented hands, had also mastered the role of tender, attentive mate.

"And we both know you aren't a patient man," she teased, referring to his comment on the day they'd mated. "You weren't about to sit and wait for my return."

"You know me well," he commented, crossing the room, even as she pushed to her feet, and then pulling her into his arms.

A long, sultry kiss later, she sighed, hands resting on the solid wall of his chest. "You really know how to say hello," she murmured.

A smile touched his lips, something he seemed to offer more and more each day. She loved his smile. "I saw Carrie leaving. Gareth appears quite taken with her."

"I agree," Jolene commented. "And her with him. Any chance they could be mates?"

He shrugged. "There's one thing I learned about shifters, and that's anything is possible."

Shaking her protectiveness of Carrie was hard. "Yes, but—"

Drago kissed her again, easing her back on the conference table, his hand sliding up her leg, and beneath her black pleated skirt. "I was thinking," he whispered, nibbling her lips.

"Someone is going to see us," she complained weakly, moaning as his hand explored the strip of satin along her backside.

"Ask me if I care," he said, but he didn't give her time to respond, his fingers continuing to explore, to tease. "When Carrie finishes this job, I have another one for her."

"You have a catering job?" she asked, her words coming out a bit breathless.

"Hmm." His dark eyes simmered with heat, with admiration, with . . . love. His hands went to her face. "A human wedding. *Our* wedding. You've made your life my world, Jolene. You deserve the chance to be a bride, to have the bond humans recognize. To have the white dress, the cake, the huge list of guests. And the customary ring that's as big and beautiful as you want it to be."

Her hands went to his, and tears welled in her eyes. Six months before, Drago had no understanding of human ways, but for her, he'd tried hard to learn. Each night he asked her questions, prodding her for stories about her youth and her wants and desires.

"I love you, Drago."

"And I love you, my beauty." He brushed his lips over hers. "So you'll marry me?" he asked, as if there was really any question.

She laughed and kissed him, thankful she'd found her Slayer and a real happily ever after.